UNMORROW CURSE

'An epic, action-packed adventure, sizzling with
myth and magic.' SOPHIE ANDERSON

'Richards excels at weaving stories that mesh the real, modern
world and classic mythologies. Readers will clamor for more,
especially those who loved Rick Riordan's Norse-themed
The Sword of Summer.' *BOOKLIST*

'The combination of adventure, appealing characters,
and high stakes should satisfy middle-grade fantasy fans.'
KIRKUS REVIEWS

'A worthy addition to the recent Norse mythology kick,
particularly as it includes some aspects and figures that
have been underrepresented to date.' BULLETIN OF
THE CENTER FOR CHILDREN'S BOOKS

HAVE YOU EVER WONDERED HOW BOOKS ARE MADE?

UCLan Publishing is an award winning independent publisher specialising in Children's and Young Adult books. Based at The University of Central Lancashire, this Preston-based publisher teaches MA Publishing students how to become industry professionals using the content and resources from its business; students are included at every stage of the publishing process and credited for the work that they contribute.

The business doesn't just help publishing students though. UCLan Publishing has supported the employability and real-life work skills for the University's Illustration, Acting, Translation, Animation, Photography, Film & TV students and many more. This is the beauty of books and stories; they fuel many other creative industries! The MA Publishing students are able to get involved from day one with the business and they acquire a behind the scenes experience of what it is like to work for a such a reputable independent.

The MA course was awarded a Times Higher Award (2018) for Innovation in the Arts and the business, UCLan Publishing, was awarded Best Newcomer at the Independent Publishing Guild (2019) for the ethos of teaching publishing using a commercial publishing house. As the business continues to grow, so too does the student experience upon entering this dynamic Masters course.

www.uclanpublishing.com
www.uclanpublishing.com/courses/
uclanpublishing@uclan.ac.uk

Also available by Jasmine Richards

Writing as Lola Morayo
Aziza and the Secret Fairy Door
Aziza and the Ice Cat Mystery
Aziza and the Birthday Present Disaster

Writing as Remi Blackwood
Future Hero: Escape to Fire Mountain

JASMINE RICHARDS

THE UNMORROW CURSE

Cover illustrations by Pypah Santos
With interior illustrations by Jill Tytherleigh

uclanpublishing

The Unmorrow Curse is a uclanpublishing book

First published in Great Britain in 2022 by
uclanpublishing
University of Central Lancashire
Preston, PR1 2HE, UK

978-1-912979-88-2

1 3 5 7 9 10 8 6 4 2

Set in 10/17pt Kingfisher by Becky Chilcott.

A CIP catalogue record for this book is available from the British Library.

Printed and bound in Great Britain by Clays Ltd, Elcograf S.p.A.

To the most magical double-act in the land! Zach and Tamsin.

Keep being each other's biggest champions!

PROLOGUE

Friday, 13th September
4 a.m.

He was behind her. His breath the crackle and spit of sodden wood on a bonfire. Sunna could hear the drag of his leg as it tore through the dead leaves on the ground, and she felt a stab of pride that she had caused that injury.

Yes. He was stronger than her. Her powers had always been feeble when compared to the sheer force of his. Still, the pen she had wielded and plunged into his thigh had worked its own kind of magic.

The flaming branch in her hand lit the path ahead. An orange beacon, cutting through the dark inkiness of the forest. The World Tree wasn't far from here now. She could finally feel it pulling at her – guiding her to its lean silver branches. The tree was hope. Her lifeline to the Runes of Valhalla. But only if she could reac—

A lightning bolt of pain exploded at the base of her skull

leaving the thought unfinished. Sunna's vision went as white as bone as she felt something break at the back of her mind. It was the barrier she had so carefully built to hold Kira in that dark place beyond thought and memory.

No, not now, she thought.

The wall she'd created, so that she could take over the other woman's body, was crumbling.

"For Odin's sake," Sunna cursed, even as a wave of nausea made her sway on her feet. The other woman's desperation to take her body back, to be in control of her own limbs once again, was quickly overwhelming her.

Sunna dropped to her knees and tried to shove the other woman back behind the wall. "I know you did not ask for this, Kira," she hissed with a pained breath. "You did not ask to be a host nor did you know that a goddess slept in your bloodline. But I am awake now and you have to trust me. We are in danger." The fingers of her free hand clenched in the dirt. "We cannot waste time fighting each other."

It was enough.

She felt Kira collapse inwards, her resistance evaporating. Then the other woman disappeared into the internal darkness once more.

For a moment, Sunna was at peace. It reminded her of the dreamless sleep she had enjoyed for centuries. Before the siren that told her Loki was free had sounded in her mind. Before she'd hijacked Kira's body and come to the Tangley Woods. She got to her feet and began to run once more, not sure how long she could go on. Her grip trembled on the branch, and by its flame she could see that Kira's once perfectly manicured nails were bloody and torn from ripping away at the enchanted vines that Loki had set upon them two days ago. Sunna smiled grimly. She had already escaped him once in this forest. *His magic was stronger, but I escaped,* she reminded herself. *And I can do it again.*

"Sunna," a voice thick like smoke snaked out from the darkness behind her. "Why persist in this tedious game of cat and mouse? A game you've already lost now that I am free." The sound of burning wood crackled in the air. "Tell me where the Runes of Valhalla are. I know Odin told you."

Sunna opened her mouth to reply but the words did not materialize. An immense force was pushing at every part of her being. Then it happened. There was a popping sound and she was expelled from her position of control and Kira took charge of her body once more.

That sneaky mortal tricked me, Sunna realized as she entered the darkness, becoming a jumble of thoughts and fears without an anchor. Kira had never gone back behind the barrier, she'd just been waiting to pounce.

"The name is Kira Bright, not Sunna," the other woman told her pursuer, her steps slowing. "And we need to have a little chat."

Sunna heard the words as if from underwater. She was spinning in the gloom, looking for a way back before it was too late. Before he caught them.

3

The smoky voice gave a hiss of annoyance. "You may be Kira now, but that was not your name when you put me in the ground. When you stole my daughter's kingdom to keep me prisoner." There was silence as even the drag of his leg through the leaves stilled. "What had I ever done to you, Sunna?"

Kira heard genuine bewilderment in his voice, and a pang of guilt lanced her even though the crime was not hers. She stopped.

"This Sunna person has been dealt with." Kira turned towards the darkness of the forest. "I'm in the driver's seat now. I don't understand what is going on here but I'm sure we can sort out this whole mess and—"

The unseen figure's laughter interrupted her and the dry, desolate sound filled up the forest.

Listen. Kira felt rather than heard Sunna's voice. *You need to stop arguing and start running. He has not forgotten and he will not forgive.*

But why did you imprison him? Kira asked the intruder in her head. *What had he done?*

It is a long story. Sunna had managed to stop spinning in the dark abyss and was now condensing herself into a hot ball of concentration. *But here is the short version – it was not my idea.*

But you didn't stop it, Kira pressed.

No, I did not. Sunna felt a flare of annoyance at Kira's accusing tone. In her day, mortals did not question gods, let alone rebuke them. But then, a lot had changed in the last millennium.

Enough was enough.

Sunna's fiery ball of intent was now white hot, and she hurled herself forwards, pushing Kira out. Retaking control. "You left us no choice, Loki," Sunna said, glad to have a voice once more. The gold, lightning-shaped pendant around her neck slapped against her skin as she scurried ahead, and despite everything, Sunna could feel its memories. Kira had bought the pendant, never knowing that the lightning bolt was the symbol on Sunna's rune. The link between host and god had been there even when Sunna had been in a deep sleep.

"There is always a choice." Loki's voice was quiet. It was close.

The goddess felt a surge of relief as she glimpsed a flash of silver bark through the forest of thick trunks. "You wanted to destroy us – all of the day guardians. We couldn't let you."

"Destroy?" Loki echoed. "All I wanted was honesty. Balance."

"We had balance." Sunna shouted the words over her shoulder but didn't stop running.

"We had tyranny," Loki replied. "And because of what you, Odin, and the rest of the day guardians did, my family was torn apart. My son Vali was driven mad. Fenris was banished, Jörmungandr was thrown into the sea, and my daughter, Hel—" He broke off, unable to finish.

Sunna felt the forest fill up with the ancient, awful truth of his words. It filled every nook and crevice. "Odin could have killed you but he didn't, remember that." Her words sounded pathetic. Uncertain. And even though Kira had been pushed right back into the darkness, Sunna could feel the strength of the other woman's disapproval.

"I remember everything, I assure you," Loki breathed. "But you remember this: sparing me was Odin's greatest mistake." The crackling voice was right behind her now, a tickle in her ear, and Sunna knew she was caught even though she hadn't heard any movement.

"The Runes of Valhalla will be found," Loki promised. "I will take their power, and I will find the rest of the day guardians who wronged me. This realm that you call home will be mine. It will belong to the chaos."

Sunna could feel Kira's terror pinching at the back of her mind, and all she could think to say was *sorry*.

Then she was engulfed by the smoke.

PART I

TIME LOCKED

CHAPTER ONE

THE GIRL IN THE COBWEB LEGGINGS

Friday, 13th September
12:15 p.m.

The Internet lied. Red pants aren't lucky. Fact.

Buzz trudged into the dining hall, scanning the sea of faces for Samraj. His best friend was nowhere to be seen. With a little sigh, he grabbed a tray, a plate, some macaroni cheese, and then the empty table in the corner. It only had two seats, but then he and Sam would need privacy if they were going to come up with a plan to fix the mess he'd created.

And it was a mess:

Late for school this morning = detention.

Detention = no football practice this afternoon.

9

No football practice = being a sub for the semi-finals of the Crowmarsh youth cup tomorrow.

"Why'd I think today would be any different?" Buzz muttered to himself, annoyed that he'd believed he could make this Friday the thirteenth any less unlucky than usual.

Obviously he hadn't meant to be late for school. But how was he supposed to know that colouring underwear with your sister's hair dye (Ruby Kiss) and blasting it with a hair-dryer (a Sonic 500) would be so time-consuming?

Buzz scanned the dining hall again. Sam was still nowhere to be seen, but he spotted his sister (and her bright red mass of tight curls) talking to a tall, Black girl with hundreds of long, thin braids twisted up in a bun. She was definitely a new kid. There weren't many Black kids in their Cotswold school and Buzz knew all of them. Tia was pointing over at him and the girl was nodding enthusiastically.

What's Tia up to now? Buzz wondered, peering at his sister. Then he understood.

The girl with the braids was striding over to him, lunch tray gripped tightly in her hands.

She was dressed like no one he'd ever seen. Her top half was swathed in a brightly coloured patchwork shirt that was miles too big for her, and she wore leggings with a purple cobweb print. Students fell quiet as she walked by. It was as if they needed all their concentration to take in her outfit. The braids piled high on top of the girl's head were held in place by a fluorescent purple pencil with a fuzzy star at its end, and she wore an enormous watch on her wrist.

Buzz groaned inwardly. His sister had a thing for collecting and protecting misfits, and now she was sending one his way. He dived into his backpack to find his mobile. *Where R U?* he'd text Sam. *You need to find me in the dining hall. NOW!* But his phone wasn't there.

Strange. He was sure he'd had it this morning.

"Hi. Do you mind if I join you?" a voice with a warm American twang said.

Buzz lifted his head to see the girl in the cobweb leggings gazing down at him. Her brown eyes looked hopeful behind her wing-tipped tortoiseshell glasses.

"Um—" he replied.

"It's just that I'm here for a test-run day. I might be starting at this school next term." The purple star in the girl's hair bobbed about violently as she spoke. "And your sister, Tia, saw that I didn't have anyone to eat lunch with, so she said I should come over here because we'll be in the same year and—"

"But why can't she have lunch with you?" Buzz interrupted. He knew it sounded rude, but his sister wasn't exactly being fair here.

"She had to go to Chess Club." The brown eyes behind the glasses were looking less hopeful now. "And I've kinda lost track of the person who was supposed to be showing me around, so . . . so can I sit with you?"

"Oh, right," Buzz began. "The thing is, I'm sort of waiting for some—"

"Mate, we've got a problem." Sam collapsed into the seat opposite Buzz, taking the free chair. "A big problem."

"You heard about my detention, then?" Buzz asked. "We've got to think of something, and quick. Coach is going to be *so* mad that I'm missing practice after school. What if he doesn't let me play tomorrow?" Buzz suddenly remembered the girl and looked up. But she'd gone. Buzz felt a flash of guilt. Mum always said that being kind didn't cost a thing. He could have been a bit nicer. Mum would have wanted him to be a bit nicer.

If she was here.

"Coach Saunders is the least of your worries right now," Sam said, distracting him. His friend whipped out his phone. "Look at this text you sent me. About twenty minutes ago." Buzz stared at the screen. His stomach twisted into knots as he read the words:

I, Zach *"Buzzkill"* Buzzard do solemnly declare that I am a total epic loser and I miss my mummy ☹.

"I didn't send that," he spluttered.

"Well, obviously you didn't." Sam rolled his eyes. "But someone sent this message from your phone and not just to me. I did some asking around, and pretty much everyone in your phonebook got the text."

"Theo," Buzz growled. He scanned the hall and spotted him.

The other boy was holding court at a table in the middle of the lunchroom, as usual.

Sam nodded. "He'll be trying to mess with your head before the match tomorrow. Everyone knows you're a better player than him."

"Right, come on. We're getting my phone back."

"Hold up, Buzz. You're a better player, but Theo's bigger." Sam made a steeple of his fingers. "Just leave this to Tia. When she finds out what happened she's going to *end* him. It's well out of order that he's brought your mum into this."

A prickle of heat crept up Buzz's neck. Theo's text message was embarrassing enough, but having his sister fight his battles would be far worse.

"I don't need Tia's help." Buzz pushed his chair back with a harsh scrape of metal.

"Of course you don't." Sam held up his hands. "I'm just saying that Tia is really good at getting stuff sorted."

"SAM! This is my stuff to sort." Buzz stalked across the dining hall, with Sam trailing reluctantly behind him. "How'd you get my phone?" he demanded, as he reached Theo's table.

A smirk crossed the other boy's annoyingly zit-free face. "Maybe you lost it. Just like you lost the plot with that English essay you read this morning," Theo replied. "Mrs Robertson looked like she was in actual pain."

"Yeah, right, because you're a master of the English language?" Sam shot back, slipping just a little bit further behind Buzz as he did so. "I mean, when's the last time you even finished an essay?"

Theo shrugged. "Nobody expects me to be good at essays. I've got other talents." He nodded his head over to Buzz. "But Buzzkill here is the son of a famous professor – his dad is always on TV." Theo shook his head mournfully. "If I was Buzzkill's dad, I'd be majorly embarrassed by his performance today."

Buzz could hear and feel the grind of his teeth. Theo was right. The Prof would have been embarrassed by his son's presentation, especially because the topic for the essay had been his specialty, mythology.

Looking back, Buzz probably should have just owned up to the fact that he hadn't written the blasted thing. Couldn't be bothered to write it, because mythology was such a momentous waste of time – or "Buzz kryptonite," as his mum used to call it. Instead, he'd tried to make up the essay as he went along, his main argument being that if the ancient Greeks were clever enough to invent the catapult, they could have just given Theseus a map and saved everyone – including that Minotaur – a lot of inconvenience.

His English teacher hadn't been impressed, and Buzz had made sure he was the first one out of the classroom so he didn't get the *lecture*.

Buzz shook the memory off and slammed his hand down on the table, making the lunch trays rattle. "I want my phone back."

"Manners, manners," Theo reprimanded. "Just because

your mum isn't around doesn't mean you shouldn't say please."

"DON'T." The command reverberated around the dining hall. "Don't talk about my mum." His voice cracked on the last word and Buzz hated himself for it.

Everyone was completely quiet now. Watching.

Theo leaned back in his chair. "Or what?" He held Buzz's gaze, his mouth a thin, pink line.

"There's no or what." Sam put a hand on Buzz's shoulder. His voice became a bit louder. "You really shouldn't have sent that message about his mum. Now, just give the phone back,"

Buzz could feel Sam's hand trembling. It had taken a lot of bravery for his friend to say that.

There were some murmurs of agreement from others in dining hall.

"Yeah Theo. Don't bring his mum into it," a girl named Ava said.

"Seriously, that ain't right," a boy called Ezra from Year 8 added. Theo frowned, his eyes flashing with annoyance. Then he shrugged.

"Fine. You can have your phone back, Buzzkill."

Buzz held out his hand.

"But you'll have to go on a little quest to get it," Theo continued. "Just like they do in those make-believe myths your dad loves so much." He rubbed his hands together. "I'll even draw you a map if you like. You'll need it to guide you to the . . ." He paused for effect. "The Toilet of Doom."

"Oh, gross," Sam whispered. "He means the one that doesn't flush on the second floor."

"Theo Eddows! A map will not be necessary," a dangerously quiet voice said from beside them. Mrs Robertson stood there, having appeared like some kind of ninja English teacher. Her face was granite. "It sounds like you know exactly where Buzz's phone is, so please go there and retrieve it." She pursed her lips. "After you bring it to my classroom, you can make your way to the headteacher's office."

A few snickers of laughter erupted in the dining hall.

All eyes were on Theo.

"But Miss," he protested. "It wasn't me."

The English teacher gave a hoot of laughter. "Now *that* really is make-believe. Go. I won't tell you again."

Theo shoved back his chair and stomped out of the dining hall, but not before throwing Buzz a look that said he'd make him pay.

Mrs Robertson turned to Buzz. "And you follow me. I didn't get a chance to have a word with you earlier."

Sam patted Buzz's shoulder. "I'll catch you later."

Buzz slinked out of the lunch hall, head down so he didn't have to meet anyone's eyes. They were probably all feeling sorry for him.

He could feel the weight of someone's gaze on him and he forced himself to glance up. It was the girl in the cobweb leggings. She was sitting alone, her lunch untouched, and she was close enough that she must have overheard the whole argument with Theo. The girl was staring right at him, but her eyes seemed dark and cloudy, as if she was deep in thought.

Buzz looked away, but the image of the girl remained stubbornly in his head as he walked into Mrs Robertson's classroom. The English teacher urged Buzz to take a seat and then sat behind her desk. Now that they were out of the dining hall, the granite in her face had softened.

"Listen, I know things are tough for you at the moment, Buzz," she began, "and Theo's prank was very cruel." She gazed at him steadily. "But don't judge him too harshly. You both have missing people in your lives. It's a lot to deal with. And then there's all that coverage about the mysterious disappearance of that weatherwoman. And all that fog that was following her. Such a strange story."

Buzz frowned. Theo's brother had gone missing more than a year ago now. People said he'd got mixed up in the wrong crowd. *But that's nothing like what's happened to Mum,* he thought. And the whole thing with that weatherwoman, Kira Bright, was different again. A case that had left everyone puzzled. *Why was Mrs Robertson even trying to compare them?* He realized that his English teacher's lips were still moving and he forced himself to concentrate on what she was saying.

"You're a smart kid Buzz," his teacher said. "And that's why I'm giving you this second chance." She wagged a finger at him. "You're too quick to give up on things you don't understand,

and you don't like asking for help. I want you to work on that."
Mrs Robertson drummed her slender fingers on the surface of
her desk. "So, do we have a deal?"

"Not sure, Miss," Buzz replied honestly, wondering what
he'd missed.

His teacher's blue eyes filled with disappointment. It was
an expression so similar to the one his father wore whenever
they spent time together that it made Buzz's throat close up.
Mrs Robertson's fingers stilled on the desk. "You've got the
weekend to write the essay on Theseus and the Minotaur again.
You're far better than what you produced today and I want you
to prove it."

Buzz crossed his arms, wondering when Mrs Robertson
and his father had become the same person with the same
speech. *Maybe they get their material off the same website: www.
areallylonglecture.com.*

"If you get stuck, just ask your father," Mrs Robertson
continued, and Buzz noticed that she had a star-struck
expression on her face. "He's an expert in this area, after all.
You're really very lucky to have access to such a famous and
well-respected professor of mythology."

Buzz snorted to himself. *If by "access" you mean never at
home, then yeah, my father is just awesome.* He felt a nerve twitch
along his jaw. There was no way, never in a month of Sundays,
that Buzz would ask for or accept the Prof's help.

CHAPTER TWO

FRIGGATRISKAIDEKAPHOBIA

Buzz kicked the empty drink can and watched it skitter across the deserted lane, its crushed sides scraping against the ground. It was probably the only kicking he'd get to do for days. He still had no idea if Coach Saunders would let him play tomorrow – Sam said he'd do his best to convince him, but they both knew Coach could be stubborn.

He kicked the can again, enjoying the loud crunch as his foot connected with the aluminium. Unfortunately, the sound of his soggy phone sloshing in his pocket was louder.

Yep, just another Friday the thirteenth, Buzz thought. *Full of ritual humiliation, pain, and disappointment.*

"Friggatriskaidekaphobia," a familiar American accent said from up above him. "That's what you've got."

Buzz stopped and looked up. He had no idea where the girl from the dining hall was hiding, and for a moment he wondered if she was actually invisible.

He narrowed his eyes as he spotted a pair of battered purple Converse poking through the foliage of the tall oak that hung over the lane.

"Friggatriksa—" Buzz gave up. He wasn't even going to try and get his mouth around that word. "What?"

"Friggatriskaidekaphobia," the voice repeated. "It's a phobia of Friday the thirteenth."

"Listen, I don't have a phobia of Friday the—" Buzz broke off. "Hey, how'd you know what I was thinking about?"

The oak leaves rustled, and then the girl in the cobweb leggings suddenly dropped onto a lower branch of the tree.

She grinned. "That's not important. Surely, what's far more interesting is how Friggatriskaidekaphobia got its name." She began to shimmy along the branch. "Although that Theo boy said your dad is a professor of mythology, so I'm guessing you probably know already."

"You guessed wrong," Buzz replied. The girl's smile became even wider, and he could tell that she was bursting at the seams to tell him. "Okay, how'd it get its name?"

"Well, the first part of the word *Friggatriskaidekaphobia* is derived from the name Frigga." The girl slid a bit further along the branch until she was directly above his head. It bent alarmingly. "You know who Frigga was, of course."

Buzz was distracted. *That branch really doesn't look very safe,* he thought, although he'd be the first to admit that heights weren't his thing and so he wasn't great at climbing trees. "Don't you think you should come down?" he asked. "What are you doing up there?"

"I was waiting for you," the girl replied. "Plus, I'm really good at climbing trees, so I thought I'd give this one a go."

"You were waiting for me?" Buzz repeated, wondering why he wasn't more creeped out. "Why? And how'd you know I'd even come this way?"

The girl wrinkled her nose, pushing up the glasses that perched precariously at the end of it. "You seemed nice, and your sister told me what route you'd walk home."

"How very helpful of her." Buzz shook his head, wondering why Tia was so determined for him to be friends with this girl.

"So, where were we?" the girl asked. "Ah, yes, Frigga. So obviously you know who she is."

Buzz scratched his head, curly tendrils snagging his fingers. The name did actually sound kind of familiar. The Prof must have mentioned the name to Tia at some point. But, as Buzz usually tuned out when his father was talking about mythology, he had nothing. Buzz shook his head.

"Frigga was the Norse goddess of the harvest and the family, and wife of the chief of the gods, Odin," the girl explained. "In English, the day Friday is named after her. Frigga's day."

"Oh, yeah, that's right," Buzz said. "All the days of the week are named after Norse gods, right?"

"Wrong." The girl sniffed. "All but one – Saturday. That one

21

is named after the Roman god Saturn, but some say that Saturday once belonged to the Norse god Loki." She edged a bit further along the branch, and it bent even more alarmingly. "Saturday was Loki's day. A day of mischief."

Despite himself, despite the fact that it had something to do with mythology, which was all a load of made-up rubbish, Buzz felt his interest spark. "Really? What happened? Why'd this Loki guy lose his day?" He heard the branch give a protesting creak. "Hey, get down, will you?"

"Okay, okay." The girl dropped down from the tree in a swift, graceful movement and gave a little bow. "Happier, now that I'm on the ground?"

Buzz nodded. "Much happier. Tell me more about Loki, then."

"Actually, Loki brings us to the second part of the name for your phobia."

"I don't have a phobi—"

"*Triskaideka* means the number thirteen." The girl leaned back against the trunk of the tree. "And it's thanks to Loki that many think the number thirteen is unlucky."

"Go on." The Prof didn't speak much about the legends of the Norse gods – his specialty was in the mythology of lost civilizations – but this Loki guy sounded interesting.

"There was a feast," said the girl, her voice low, "where all the Norse gods were gathered. It was at this feast that Frigga and Odin's beloved son, Balder, was killed. His death was caused by the thirteenth guest at the feast. It was caused by Loki."

"Why did Loki want Frigga's son dead?"

"Why did Loki do anything?" The girl sat down under the tree and beckoned for Buzz to do the same. "Loki did it because he could. Because he was a trickster and mischief was what he was best at. This time, he did not go unpunished. Loki was chained to a rock deep underground. A snake was created to guard him, to drip *burning* venom on his head until the Ragnarok."

"Ragnarok?" Buzz echoed. *It sounds like a kind of disease.*

"It means the end of the world," the girl explained. "It was prophesized that Loki would one day escape his bonds and try and destroy the earth. But the Norse gods would be waiting for him to have their final battle."

Buzz let out a low whistle. "That sounds totally epic."

"It does, doesn't it?" The girl adjusted her glasses which had slipped down her nose again.

"How do you know so much about this kind of stuff?" he asked.

"I know a lot about a lot of things. I'm pretty smart." She stuck out her legs and crossed them at the ankles. "But I don't know why Friday the thirteenth is making you so miserable. It's only a day."

"The worst of days," Buzz said. "The Friday the thirteenth before last, I lost the 100 metre race at our town's annual swimming competition because I . . . I . . ." He faltered. "I had some technical difficulties."

The memory rose to the surface just like his swimming trunks had.

The girl shrugged. "So you lost your swimming trunks. I bet it made you more aerodynamic in the long run."

Buzz felt his cheeks get hot. "Hey, I didn't say that."

"You didn't need to. I guessed. I told you, I'm really smart."

"And modest," Buzz replied, surprised at how much he liked talking to this girl. He just felt bad that he hadn't worked that out in the dining hall. "The Friday the thirteenth before that, I broke my ankle after trying to surf in a shopping trolley," he continued. "That was just dumb," the girl replied. "It has nothing to do with the date. You're going to have to do better."

"Fine. Last Friday the thirteenth, my mum went missing, and I don't think she's ever coming home."

CHAPTER THREE

THE WOODS

At least, those were the words Buzz formed in his head. They sat on the tip of his tongue, fully formed, but he couldn't say them out loud.

He took a steadying breath. "I guess Friday the thirteenth has just always been kind of unlucky for me," he said instead. "You saw what happened in the dining hall today." He frowned. "I just wish this day was over and it was Saturday already."

"I don't know about that." The girl leaned back against the tree and crossed her arms, as if to keep herself warm. "Saturdays are totally overrated in my opinion."

"Overrated!" Buzz shook his head in disbelief. "Saturdays are totally epic. You get to sleep in. You don't have to go to school. You get to hang out with friends all day long. Watch sports, play sports, and get takeaway. What's not to love?"

"That type of Saturday does sound pretty epic," the girl

conceded. "But back home, Saturday is always the day my parents argue the most. They argue about who should do the shopping. Who should do the gardening, who should do the—" She whacked a hand over her mouth. "Oh, man," she mumbled. "I do that. My therapist says my filters work differently to other people." She dropped her hand. "Forget what I just said? I'm staying with my grandmother for a little while and she likes to plan enriching activities for Saturdays. She doesn't have a TV, let alone Wi-Fi, and certainly doesn't believe in getting takeout. We're talking braised liver with dumplings for dinner on all days ending with a Y. She says it's nutritionally dense."

Buzz winced. "Holey pyjamas. That is all kinds of miserable."

She gave him a quizzical look. "Holey pyjamas? Is that a well-known phrase around here?"

"It's one of my mum's sayings." Buzz felt heat creep into his cheeks. He had no idea why he'd said it out loud. "Where's your home normally, then?" he asked quickly.

"We've lived in lots of places but right now it's New York. The Big Apple. The Melting Pot. New Amsterdam until 1664," she replied. "Ever been?"

Buzz shook his head. His dad hated leaving Crowmarsh, which meant most holidays were spent camping in Tangley Woods. "I'd love to go, though. So many people. So much to do. I bet you never get bored there."

The girl leaned forwards and played with the frayed laces of her Converse sneakers "No, but you do get lonely. At least I do.

I always kind of wished that I had a sibling. Your sister seems nice."

Buzz thought about Tia and how she loved to interfere in his life. "Trust me. It's not all it's cracked up to be."

"But at least you have someone to talk to – when things aren't great at home. Someone who'll understand."

"I guess," Buzz responded. He and Tia tended to avoid those types of conversations. They definitely never spoke about the frostiness that existed between their parents or how that had become glacial in the months before Mum's trip. "You're a guy of few words, aren't you?" the girl said. "My parents say you have to talk the talk if you are going to walk the walk." Her brow creased. "That's what they're doing right now. Talking about whether they're going to walk out on each other. Talking about whether Dad is actually going to move to the UK with me. But I'm not supposed to know that." She whacked a hand over her mouth again. "I'm doing it again, aren't I?" she said through her fingers. "Oversharing? Grandma says it's not dignified to air one's dirty laundry. But I think sometimes your washing machine may be broken and you just have to make the best of a bad situation, right?" She pinned him with her an intense gaze. "What do you think?"

"Um," Buzz began. He really wasn't sure how to answer.

"Not um – the name is Amaryllis, but you can call me Mari." The girl arched a dark, slightly messy eyebrow. "But never Scary Mari, just Mari, okay?"

"Okay," he promised. "I'm Buzz."

"Buzz, as in the sound a bee makes," the girl mused. "Interesting. Did you know that bees are the only insects that make food that humans can eat?"

Buzz shook his head.

"Or that eating honey makes you smarter?"

Buzz shook his head again. *I bet she eats a lot of honey.*

"Why are you named after the sound a bee makes, then?" Mari asked, hardly pausing for breath. "Is your mom an apiologist?"

"No. At least I don't think so. She's a botanist," he said. "What's an apiologist?"

"It's a person who studies honeybees," the girl replied. "While a person who keeps bees is called an apiarist."

"Right." Buzz could feel all the girl's facts raining down on him like hail. It wasn't wholly unpleasant – it just stung a bit. "Buzz is actually short for Buzzard. My name is Zach Buzzard."

"So you're named after a bird, not a bee. In fact, you've got a whole animal kingdom thing going on. That's awesome!"

"Awesome?"

"Yeah, you could have been named after a flower. Imagine how annoying that would be."

"Er, I guess," Buzz conceded, not that he could think of any boys' names that were flowers.

"Yeah, your name is definitely not on the annoying spectrum."

"It's my father's name, really," he found himself explaining.

"I'm Zach Buzzard the second, but strictly speaking I should be Zach Buzzard the third because my father was named after the founder of the children's home he was brought up in—"

Mari began to chuckle.

"What?" Buzz questioned. "What's so funny?"

"I don't know," she said. "There I was thinking you were the silent type when actually you're quite verbose."

Buzz was pretty sure verbose meant talkative, which seemed rich coming from Mari. "You're pretty chatty yourself, you know," he pointed out.

"No filters, remember?" She looked at her watch, with its enormous, digital face. "I'd better get home. It's getting dark, and Grandma will worry." Mari jumped to her feet, held up her watch, and turned in a slow circle.

The watch gave a little beep as she faced one of the lanes that curved off to the left. A robotic voice reeled off a list of directions: "Fifteen Glover Drive. One-point-five miles away. Stay on the path ahead."

"Whoa!" Buzz scrambled to his feet. "Did your watch just tell you the way home in the voice of Darth Vader?"

Mari's expression was smug. "I made it using parts from my dad's GPS and my cell phone a couple of weeks ago. Dad was delighted, obviously." She polished the face of the watch on the material of her leggings. "It's still got a couple glitches, but it's pretty darn impressive."

"Your humbleness is astounding," Buzz replied. "Come on,

you don't live that far from me. I'll show you a shortcut through Tangley Woods." He bent down, shoved the fizzy drink can he'd been kicking into his rucksack, and slung the bag over his shoulder. "I live in there, so we won't get lost."

"Ahem!" Mari gave a theatrical cough. "I'll draw your attention to exhibit A." She tapped her watch. "I can't get lost with this innovation strapped to my wrist. But walk me home if you like. You can tell me what else there is to do in Crowmarsh."

"Sure." He turned to her as they began to walk. "So, the first thing you to need to know is that there's absolutely nothing to do in Crowmarsh. The second thing you need to know is that absolutely nothing ever happens in Crowmarsh."

Mari laughed. "I'm sure it isn't that bad! I was born here, you know, but then my parents moved for work."

"Lucky escape," Buzz said.

"Maybe. But you get to live in the middle of a forest. That's pretty lucky if you ask me."

"Prof built our house in Tangley Woods when my sister was just a baby and before I was even born," Buzz explained as they entered the line of trees that made up the border of the forest.

"Prof?"

"It's what I call my father."

"I see," Mari said, and Buzz had the feeling that she did see a whole lot. He knew it was odd that he called his father Prof, but Dad just didn't sit right with him.

"Prof's kind of obsessed with this place." He talked fast to cover the awkwardness. His gaze took in the familiar play of light that slanted through the trees. "He thinks this wood is the epicentre of many key mythologies. A place where people's beliefs have all converged through the centuries. The Tangley Woods theory is what he's famous for, why he's on TV. He just hasn't proven it."

"Oh?" Mari said. "How long has he been trying to prove it?"

"Twenty years, give or take."

"That's a long time."

"It sure is." What he didn't say was that by now, most people at The University thought that the Prof was a joke, which is why he didn't get invited to the annual garden party anymore.

They were deep in the forest now, the trees silent witnesses to their conversation. The light was gradually fading – the shadows converging – but Buzz wasn't worried. He knew the woods' paths better than anyone.

"Wow, your mom has got to be the most laid-back person in the world," Mari said after a moment. "If my dad tried to build a house in a forest so that he could be closer to his work, my mom would go nuclear."

"That's not her way," Buzz explained. His mum never got angry. She just got very, very still and that was worse. Besides, she loved this place as well. She'd crawl around on the mossy ground of Tangley Woods for hours at a time, mud streaking her deep brown skin. She'd hum that song, "1 Thing" by Amerie whenever she unearthed a spongy spore of fungi. No wonder

Theo Eddows thought Buzz was odd – his family was pretty strange. *How many mothers dried poisonous plants in the airing cupboard instead of tea towels? How many fathers wrote books on the importance of caves, root systems, and forgotten gods?*

He could almost hear his mother's voice in his ear. *"Stuff Theo Eddows and stuff being normal. I had plenty of people tell me I would never be a botanist. Good thing I never listened. Right? We are who we are and we live where we live."* He could feel her hands on his shoulders now. *"Do you feel how old this place is, Buzz? These trees were here long before Theo Eddows, and they will be here long after him."* Buzz's chest suddenly felt very tight, and for a moment he couldn't breathe as sadness pushed all the air from his body. She'd left home six months ago now. Deep in the Amazon rainforest, she'd been looking for a rare plant that would change the face of medicine forever. And then she was gone. Now, no one could tell them where Natasha Buzzard and her team of botanists were. And as much as Buzz tried to tell himself that Mum would be home soon, it was getting harder.

"Hey, Buzz, you okay?" Mari asked. "You don't look too great."

Buzz took a gulping breath. "I'm fine – rea—"

"Help!" The hoarse cry shattered the quiet of the woods. "Is someone there? Help me, for the love of the gods, help me!"

CHAPTER FOUR

THE DISCOVERY

Mari gripped his arm, cold fingers sinking into his skin. "Did you hear that?" Her brown eyes were wide behind her glasses in the gloom of the forest.

Buzz put a finger to his lips and nodded.

"HELP ME!"

The words ripped at the silence again and Buzz listened hard, trying to figure out which direction the cry had come from. It wasn't easy. The words seemed to bounce off the trees like pebbles from a slingshot, and his own heartbeat whooshed and ebbed in his ears. He concentrated on the voice, using the map in his head to try to locate its origin.

"I think she might be near the lake." He turned to Mari. "You'd better stay here. It'll be safer for you." He was proud that he sounded braver than he felt.

"This is not a nineteenth-century novel," Mari shot back.

"And I'm not some helpless heroine who is going to stand around wringing her hands. I'm coming with you."

Buzz hadn't read many nineteenth-century novels (none, in fact), but he got the message. Mari cupped her hands around her mouth. "Hold on, we're coming," she yelled. "Keep talking and we'll find you."

"Quick! You must be quick." The terrified voice replied. "Before the dragon comes."

Dragon? Buzz thought. *I can't have heard that right.*

Buzz pointed deep into the woods and tried not to notice that his hand was shaking. "This way."

They tore through the trees, the woman's voice punctuating their journey through the quiet of the forest.

Buzz was the fastest player on his football team, so he expected that Mari might struggle to keep up. She didn't.

They came to a clearing just left of Mornings Lake, where a tree with deeply ridged bark stood in regal isolation. It looked a bit like an ash tree, but Buzz had never seen an ash with bark this colouring before – charcoal grey with slivers of silver crisscrossing the entire surface.

It's tall, he thought. *Really tall.* Even tipping his head way back, Buzz couldn't see the top of it. The ground surrounding the base of the tree pulsed with energy, and stones danced on top of the soil like popping corn in a hot pan. The tree's trunk was the thickest Buzz had ever seen and it would easily need twenty people holding hands to get around its circumference.

"Who's there?" The broken voice seemed to come from the tree itself, but then Buzz saw her – a woman strapped to the massive trunk by a thick rope that looped around her waist. He hadn't noticed her at first because her grey suit, tattered and smeared with mud, blended so perfectly with the bark of the tree.

The woman's dark hair hung in rat tails around her face, but Buzz caught a flash of amber eyes as she turned her head at their approach. "Thank the gods," she gasped. "You must help me. And quickly, before Nidhogg comes. He has been summoned."

Her voice was hoarse from screaming, but Buzz was sure he recognized it. "Wait a second, I know you!" he said. "You're Kira Bright, the weatherwoman." Kira's unusual amber eyes held his gaze. "Yes. That is true. Well, at least partly true."

"I can't believe it's really you!" Buzz exclaimed.

"Buzz, now's not the time to get star-struck." Mari bent down and began to scan the rope that strapped Kira to the tree. "You can get her autograph another time."

"No, you don't understand," Buzz said, even as his eyes searched the rope for the knot that must be securing it to the tree. "Kira Bright has been missing for almost a whole week now. It's been all over the news." Kira blinked rapidly for a moment, her whole face seeming to shift in and out of focus. Then she flashed an impossibly white smile. "Really? Did I make national news?" Kira's voice sounded different. Younger somehow.

"You did, actually," Buzz said. "People have been calling it the most baffling case of the decade. Especially because of the fog seen around your car just before you disappeared."

"Hey you two, none of that matters," Mari said impatiently. "I can't see a knot here."

Buzz sprinted around the whole tree and shook his head. "I can't see one, either."

"Strange. It's got to be somewhere." Mari planted her knees in the earth and reached out for the rope. "Perhaps if we give it a really good tu—" She broke off with a howl of pain and fell backwards.

"Mari, are you okay?" Buzz knelt beside her and gently sat her up.

Mari stared at the rope even as she cradled her right hand, where blisters bloomed on her palm. "It's not a normal rope, Buzz. Look!"

A neon blue flame was now racing along the length of the rope, swiftly turning it into a thick lasso of fire, which encircled the weatherwoman.

It flared brightly, illuminating the reddish strands in Kira's dark hair and the fear on her face. The weather woman opened her mouth to scream, but then her features blurred again, and her expression changed to one of absolute calmness. It was as if someone had turned the page of a book and Buzz was now seeing a new chapter. He realized that the blaze was not even touching Kira, and almost idly the woman brought her lips together and blew on the flames.

The blue fire instantly dulled, solidified, and then split itself into three threads that plaited themselves into rope once more. "What. Exactly. Is going on here?" Buzz's voice was a croak. "There's no time for that now." The voice was different again, deeper and more authoritative. *Kira Bright but not Kira Bright,* Buzz thought. *But how is that even possible?*

"We need to think of another way to free me." She pointed upwards. "I need to climb this tree and gather the Runes of Valhalla. It's the only way to stop him."

Mari's face was tight with pain, but she didn't once take her gaze off the weatherwoman. "We're not helping until you tell us what's going on. All of it."

Kira inclined her head. "This rope that binds me is enchanted. If I try to break it, it turns to fire. A fire I cannot cross," she explained. "I thought the enchantment might not initiate if a normal mortal touched it. I was wrong. I'm sorry that you got hurt, but you've got to find a way to free me."

"Come on, that's not the full story," Mari said. "Why have you been brought here?"

"There's no time—" the woman began, but something in Mari's stony expression stopped her. "I have been left here for the dragon Nidhogg," she said as calmly as if she was reading a weather report. "The dragon lives in one of the underworld realms, deep in the earth, and Loki has summoned it to take me prisoner and guard me until he has found all of the runes." Kira began to shake, her composure cracking. "The trickster god has escaped his prison and is searching for the Runes of Valhalla right now. If Loki manages to activate them and absorb their power, we are all lost."

"Loki?" Buzz's voice had graduated from a croak to a squeak as he cast a quick look at Mari. They'd just been talking about that guy. "Enchanted rope? Dragon?" he continued. "You're not serious." Kira began to honk with laughter, and for a moment Buzz was reminded of his mother. She had a completely unexpected laugh as well.

"I do not think I have ever been more serious, young man," the weatherwoman said.

"But dragons don't exist!" Buzz's voice echoed around the forest, taunting him with its shrillness.

"Actually," Mari interjected. "There is the Komodo dragon, which has been known to grow as large as nine feet."

"Not now, Mari." Buzz pinched the bridge of his nose.

"Sorry."

"Loki doesn't exist, and enchantments definitely don't exist." Buzz made sure his voice was a bit quieter this time. "Because magic doesn't exist." Kira's jaw clenched, impatience radiating from her like sunbeams "And so how do you explain what you just saw?" she asked. "This rope turned to fire and back again. You saw it. This is Loki's magic."

"It's got to be some kind of trick." Buzz jumped to his feet and started peering into the dense foliage of the forest. "I get it – I'm on a reality show, right? One of those prank ones."

He started waving his hands wildly. "Hey, camera people, you can come out now. They don't pay you enough to sit out there in the cold."

"Stop waving your arms about, Buzz, and look at my hand." Mari stood and held out her palm. "That's no trick."

"And I'm no trickster." Kira's voice was soft. "That title belongs to Loki, and he has left me here for Nidhogg." The last words were thick with painful defeat. "I will tell you my story if only so it is not forgotten. My real name is Sunna, and I have taken control of Kira's body. An eternity ago, my kind were worshipped as gods and goddesses. We were the day guardians, tasked with keeping the natural order of time." She laughed bitterly. "Then, it came to pass that I and five of the other day guardians battled Loki – Saturday's guardian – and imprisoned him. The battle left us weak." Her fingers clenched, then unclenched slowly. "Odin, the head of our council, issued a prophecy. He said we would face Loki again in the Ragnarok and that we must be ready." She nodded to herself. "So we placed what little was left of our magic into stone runes, hoping a long rest would help to rejuvenate our powers. We then put our god selves into a deep sleep, dormant within the minds of our most faithful followers. Since then, the other day guardians and I have travelled down the bloodlines of their descendants."

She touched her neck, and for the first time Buzz noticed the lightning-shaped pendant that sat at the hollow of her throat. Sunna seemed to come back to herself, and she stared at them, her amber eyes almost seeming to glow. "Loki will soon discover that I lied to him." Her voice was urgent. "I told him that the runes were in the Realm of Valhalla. They are not." She grabbed Buzz's hand with surprising strength for someone so slight. "He plans to make the day guardians pay for what we did to him and his family. But trust me when I tell you that the whole world will suffer a curse of unmorrows."

A curse of unmorrows? Buzz knew he wasn't the smartest – not like his parents, Tia, or even Mari. And right now, he was treading water in a sea of questions that threatened to drown him. But one thing was clear: *Kira – no, Sunna needs our help.*

"Okay," he said. "Let's say for one moment that this rope is enchanted, and that you are a goddess who needs to find some stone rune thingies to stop Loki – and I'm not saying I really believe that. But if I did . . . How do we free you?"

Sunna sat up a bit straighter. "You will need to find something that will break the flame's circle once it has been called forth."

Mari leapt to her feet. "Buzz, you still got that soda can you were kicking about?"

He nodded and reached into his backpack to retrieve it. "What're you gonna do with it, play football?"

"You mean soccer." Mari took the can, and pointed at a symbol on the side. "Aluminium. It has a decent heat-resistance threshold. We'll get the rope to turn to fire and then break the line of flame with the can."

"Oh, right," Buzz said, nodding. "Good idea."

Sunna nodded. "It's an excellent idea. It might just give me enough time to—"

She broke off as the ground just to their left made a terrible yawning sound. The earth was opening up.

"Nidhogg," Sunna cried, staring at the widening chasm. "Quick, he's coming. Throw me the can."

Mari launched the precious missile and Sunna caught it. In one swift movement, she touched the rope with a finger, and it burst into flame. She held the can in the path of the fire, and for a second, the scorching flare of the enchanted rope was broken. The goddess launched herself forwards, and Buzz and Mari each grabbed a hand and pulled her to her feet. She was free.

Buzz noticed straightaway that Sunna's hands were hot – much hotter than could ever be considered normal – but the thought was chased away by the goddess's dazzling smile. "Thank you," she gasped. "But I must go. I must ascend the tree and find the runes—"

An awful screech tore at Buzz's eardrums as something red, fast, and huge shot out of the torn earth near the tree. It was an enormous beast. Buzz could only take it in as fragments: a tail that flashed with blue sparks and carried the acrid scent of sulphur, a yellow bloodshot eye, a mouth that stretched open to reveal glistening, needle thin teeth.

"No, no," Sunna cried as the muscled tail, rippling with iridescent scales, whipped towards her and wound itself around her midriff.

"Hold on to us," Buzz cried as he and Mari gripped Sunna's hands even more tightly. "We won't let go." The dragon's tail pulled again, and Buzz felt like his arms might pop from their sockets. But still he held on.

The tail snapped up into the air, taking all three of them with it, and the force of it pushed Buzz's cheeks back into a mockery of a smile. He broke through the canopy of the trees, catching a dizzy blur of blue and clouds, and then the tail slammed down again. A shooting pain sliced through his temple as he hit the ground. His fingers released just for a second, but it was enough, and he went tumbling across the forest floor.

His cheek rested against the roughness of the leaves, his world muffled and in soft focus. He had a skull-cracking headache, and the urge to be sick was too strong. He retched. *Get up,* he told himself, but his body wouldn't listen.

"Yer need to move," he heard a gruff voice cry, and then he saw a flash of red fur dart to his side. It pushed at him, jabbing at his ribs. It hurt, but Buzz rolled over.

The tip of the dragon's tail landed with a crack, leaving a fissure in the ground where, moments before, Buzz's head had been.

He forced himself to stand. The world was screamingly loud and moved in slow motion. The flash of fur was gone, but he could see that Mari had also been thrown across the clearing by the dragon. She was only now staggering to her feet.

The dragon was pushing its way back underground but still

held Sunna in a crushing embrace just a few metres from the forest floor. "Take this," the goddess cried. "It will help you remember what happened here when the unmorrow curse takes hold." The goddess ripped the lightning pendant from her neck, and it fell to the ground. "Find the Runes of Valhalla. Use them to seek out the sleeping day guardians. It's the only way to stop Loki. The only way to save your realm."

Mari stood on her tiptoes and reached for Sunna. "Take my hand," she yelled.

Buzz reached up as well.

The goddess shook her head and then the dragon's tail slammed to the ground and dragged Sunna along the ground.

"The World Tree will help you." Sunna's voice echoed around them even as she disappeared into the chasm. "Remember . . . Remember . . ."

CHAPTER FIVE

THE MYTHOLOGIST'S SON

The forest was quiet.

The ground had closed up.

Sunna was gone.

Buzz dropped to his knees and clawed at the dirt. Mari joined him, digging furiously. But the churned-up ground revealed nothing. The earth's gaping wound that had spewed out the dragon hadn't even left a scar.

"Sunna!" Buzz cried. "Sunna, can you hear me?" His voice sounded thin and wobbly.

"It's too late, Buzz. She's gone." Mari sat back on her heels, two golden fragments in her hand. It was Kira's lightning-shaped pendant, snapped in half.

"But she was right here," Buzz said. "Why didn't she take your hand? Or mine?"

"Because she wanted us to stay safe. So that we can find

the runes and these day guardians."

Buzz stood up. "We've got to get help." He nodded to himself. "We'll call the police or something."

Mari rose to her feet, cradling her injured hand close to her body. "What are the police going to do?"

"They can get diggers. They'll dig down until they find her."

"But Sunna said Nidhogg lived in one of underworld realms. Somehow, I don't think diggers are going to be able to reach her. We're talking about a magical world here." Mari dropped one half of the pendant into her pocket and gave the other half to Buzz, who put it in his bag. "Besides, who's going to believe us? They'll think we're lying, or worse . . . c-c-crazy." She just about managed to force out the last word.

"But we've got to do something." Buzz reached into his pocket and took out his mobile. It squelched in his hand, and immediately he remembered the little swim his phone had taken earlier today thanks to Theo Eddows.

"Mari, pass your phone."

Mari held up her watch. "I used it for parts, remember?"

"Okay, we're not far from my house. We'll call the police from there," Buzz reasoned.

"There's no point." Mari crossed her arms. "The police aren't the answer. We need to stop Loki, just like Sunna said, and get the runes ourselves. Sunna said the tree would help us. The World Tree, she called it." Mari looked up at the tree as if the answer might lie right there in the branches.

Buzz raked a hand through his hair. Neither he nor Mari were gods. How on earth did she think they could go up against Loki? They needed help. "I'll ask my Uncle Mark," Buzz said, hardly believing he hadn't thought of him straightaway. "He'll know what to do. He's an inspector in the police force."

Mari shook her head. "Sunna said the tree would help. I'm staying here."

"You can't." Buzz's head felt like it was caught in a vice, and the feeling of nausea would not pass. "Loki could be back any minute."

Mari's face fell. "Good point," she said. "Okay, I'll go home and see what I can find out about the tree when it comes to Norse mythology. It might give us a lead."

"Fine," Buzz said. "Let's get out of here."

They ran through the woods in silence. Buzz guessed that seeing a woman kidnapped by a dragon was enough to make even Mari quiet.

Her watch began to beep. "Turn left for Glover Drive," it said in its robotic voice.

"This is me," Mari said. "I'll see you later this evening, right? I live at number fifteen. We'll think of a way to save Sunna, I promise."

Mari tore off into the trees before Buzz could say a word.

I need to get help. I need to get help. Buzz repeated the words in his head until they became a chant. He raced up the long path that led to his house. The red of his front door was almost maroon in the light of dusk. Seeing his dad's car outside, Buzz felt a surprising wave of relief.

He was the son of a mythologist. If anyone was going to believe him, help him get Sunna back, the Prof would.

Buzz threw open the door, and his father immediately strode out of the office, a stack of essays clutched in his hand. "You know you should call if you're going to be late," the Prof began, but he stopped as he had a proper look at Buzz. "What on earth has happened to you? You're bleeding."

"In the woods. We found her."

"Who? Your mother?" The essays slipped from the Prof's grip and fluttered to the floor. "How . . . how can that be? Where?"

"No," Buzz said, his rib cage suddenly too tight around his lungs. "We found Kira Bright."

"The weatherwoman?" The frown lines in his father's forehead were deep ravines.

Buzz nodded, the action causing the pain in his head to pound even more violently. "But she wasn't really Kira, she was a goddess. Her name was Sunna and she was tied to a tree with an enchanted rope. We tried to free her but now a dragon has taken her prisoner. Taken her to another realm deep underground." He took a gulping breath. "Prof. We've got to help her."

His father stared at him hard before lifting a hand to gently sweep aside the curls on Buzz's forehead.

Buzz felt his breath catch – it was not like the Prof to smooth his hair away like this. It was something that his mum always did, especially when Buzz was upset.

"Enough of this nonsense, Buzz. How did you get this cut on your head?" his father demanded.

"It must have happened when the dragon dropped me." Buzz swallowed his disappointment. His father hadn't believed a word he said. Why had he thought, even for a moment, that he would?

The Prof reached for his coat from where it hung in the hall. "We're going to the hospital." He put a hand on Buzz's shoulder to steer him through the door.

Buzz jerked away, the sudden movement making the dull thumping behind his eyes become a pounding hammer. "I know it sounds crazy, but it's all true, Prof. I promise. A dragon came – it was called Nidhogg." Buzz could still smell the acrid smoke that had come with the dragon, and it made his eyes water. "Loki summoned it." The Prof shook his head. "Loki and Nidhogg are just stories, myths. You've hurt yourself, you're not making sense, and it is my duty to make sure you are taken care of."

Duty. The word sounded so cold, but Buzz knew that now was not the time for hurt feelings. "Prof, just listen to me, please."

"Fine." Buzz's father pulled on his coat. "Tell me from the beginning and then we're going to the hospital." So Buzz did. He told his father about Mari and the tree, the enchanted rope, and how Sunna and Kira were the same person. He told him about the Runes of Valhalla and the day guardians and how the ground opened up and spat out a dragon. "Then he took her and they were swallowed up by the earth." Buzz rubbed at his arms, feeling cold and shaky. "Don't you see? We need to do something. *Right now*."

His father stooped down to pick up the fallen essays from the floor, his face hidden from sight. "Buzz, you're right. We do need to get some help."

Buzz heaved a sigh of relief. "So what d'you think we should do? Call the police, right? I thought Uncle Mark might be the best perso—"

"Hang on." Buzz's father was on his feet. "I've listened to you, and now you need to listen to me. You've hit your head. You've been under a lot of pressure with your mother gone. You're hardly sleeping."

"How'd you know about that?" Buzz felt a flash of rage. "You spying on me now?"

"I hear you at night – so does your sister. I should have said something sooner. It's clear you need help. I was wrong for not recognizing that you were at the breaking point."

"Breaking point?" Buzz felt heat climbing up his chest and his neck. "You don't know anything about me. What would you know about my breaking point?"

"Buzz, I'm not your enemy. I'm simply saying that maybe we need some professional guidance about how to deal with the vividness of your imagination and—"

"I'm going to call Uncle Mark," Buzz said, cutting his father off. He suddenly felt incredibly tired. "He'll believe me, and he'll know what to do."

"Wait—"

But Buzz already had the house phone and was hitting number six on the speed dial.

"Hello, Crowmarsh Police Station," a kindly voice said at the other end of the line.

"Hello, can I speak to Inspector Mark Tyler?"

"And who should I say is calling?"

"Buzz, I mean Zach Buzzard – his godson."

CHAPTER SIX

THE VISIT

"So, let me make sure I understand you correctly," Uncle Mark said. "You saw Kira Bright?"

Buzz nodded, trying to ignore his father, who was glaring at him from his chair in the corner. "Yes, I told you. She was tied to a tree in the middle of the woods."

Uncle Mark jotted down something in the small notepad in his hand. "And then a dragon came, took her away, and is now keeping her prisoner in another realm, deep underground?"

"Yes," Buzz insisted.

"Anything else?" he asked. "You mentioned these rune things a couple of times. They sound important."

"I think they are, but finding Kira and Sunna is even more urgent."

Uncle Mark folded his hands over the notebook and gazed at Buzz. "So, what do you think our next steps should be?"

Buzz stared straight back at him. "I don't know, you're the policeman, Uncle Mark." He tried to keep his voice level, but it trembled. "You find missing people. Find her."

"Hey, buddy, it's going to be all right." His godfather's voice was gruff, a little deeper than usual. "We're going to get this sorted. If you say you saw Kira Bright, then I believe you. I will get my team to do a sweep of the woods. First things first, we need to find that tree you were talking about."

"This is a farce." Buzz's father exploded from his chair. "I let him call you because I thought you might be able to talk some sense into him, but you're just encouraging this fantasy."

"It's not fantasy," Buzz cried.

"You're injured and sleep deprived," the Prof growled. "The facts are plain. You are not in possession of your faculties."

"Hey, go easy on him, Zachary." Uncle Mark held up a calming hand. "Buzz is a good kid. If he says he saw Kira, then he saw Kira."

The Prof began to pace. "He also says he saw a dragon."

Mark's brow wrinkled. "Yes, there is that, but as strange as it might sound, I will investigate it." He pursed his lips. "Natasha would ask me to do the same if she was here."

The Prof whirled on Uncle Mark. "Don't you dare tell me what my wife would say about my son." His normally calm voice was ragged, but he took a deep breath before facing Buzz. "I know you don't want to hear it, Buzz, but this whole episode with Kira and that dragon is in your head." He took a step forwards. "Think about it. Your mother is missing. So is Kira

Bright. If Kira is found, then maybe Mum will be as well. You don't think I want that?"

Buzz couldn't look at him. "You don't talk about it. You don't talk about her."

"Buzz, I'm doing the best that I can." The Prof's voice was low. "But this make-believe needs to stop here before you get yourself into trouble. I'm your father and it's—"

"It's your duty to look after me." Buzz finished the sentence for him.

"Yes, you keep saying." The Prof frowned.

"It is a duty that I take very seriously, Buzz. I'm going to keep you safe."

"As will I." Uncle Mark crossed his arms "I am your best friend, Zachary. Have been ever since that day in Buzzard House when you translated that Latin motto for me so I wouldn't get in trouble." He gazed at the Prof. "Remember that? *Faber est quisque fortunae suae*: Every man is architect of his own fortune." He nodded his head at the memory. "Then you shared your sandwich with me because you'd got the last cheese one." Uncle Mark's open and honest face was filled with concern. "You're the only family I've got, and I won't let Buzz come to any harm. I'll sort this all out." He smiled in encouragement at Buzz. "Where does this Mari girl live? I need to hear her side of things. Get a full picture of events."

Buzz's fingers tunnelled a path through his hair. "Fifteen Glover Drive," he said. "She's there with her grandmother."

"Let's go, then," Uncle Mark said.

The Prof nodded. "I'm ready."

"We don't need you." Buzz didn't even bother to look at the Prof. "It's not like you believe me anyway."

"Buzz, that's not fair."

"Stay here, Zachary." Uncle Mark's voice was soothing. "I'll bring Buzz back safe and sound. I promise."

* * *

"No, Inspector, I didn't see a dragon," Mari said. "And I didn't see Kira Bright."

"Are you sure?" Uncle Mark pressed.

Mari stared at the flames in the ancient wood burner that sat on the flagstone hearth. "I'm sure."

"Mari?" Buzz whispered. Her name was a question, just loud enough to be heard over the spit and crackle of the fiery logs in the burner. Buzz tried to catch her gaze but it remained fixed on the flames in front of her.

"Just to clarify: You were in the woods today with Buzz?" Uncle Mark asked.

"Yes," Mari replied. "But this thing with the dragon and Kira Bright? It just didn't happen. I'm sorry." Mari met Buzz's eyes for a moment, but then she crossed her arms and looked away.

"I think, Inspector, that this young man has wasted enough of our time," Mari's grandmother declared, standing up from the faded couch. Her silver afro hair was tucked up in a severe looking bun. "I imagine that concludes the questioning?"

Uncle Mark nodded and placed a hand on Buzz's shoulder. "Thank you for your time. Come on, buddy. Let's get you home."

Buzz threw off the hand and took a step towards Mari. "Why are you lying?"

Mari hung her head. "Buzz, whatever you think to be true – it isn't. I'm sorry."

Whatever you think to be true – it isn't. He repeated the words to himself and he felt the fabric of his memories rip. Buzz put a hand to his injured temple and found the spot of waxy soreness. *Had he really imagined the whole thing with Kira Bright? Was that really possible?* His eyes raked over Mari and rested on her right hand, which was wrapped in a bandage.

"How'd you hurt your hand?"

Mari gave a start but paused for only a second. "We were trying to build a fire, remember?"

Buzz shook his head. "That's how you hurt yourself," Mari continued. "A fragment chipped off the rock we were using as a flint and you were knocked out cold. I was trying to wake you up and that's when the fire got out of control." She studied her bandage. "I hurt my hand trying to put the blaze out."

"And how about the lightning bolt pendant?"

"Pendant?" Mari repeated.

Buzz reached into his bag and pulled out his half of the lightning bolt. "You have the other half of this."

Mari shook her head. "No, I don't, but I was there when you found that. It's just a bit of scrap metal. I told you that at the time."

"I see." But in truth, he didn't. He just wanted to get home. He turned to Uncle Mark. "I'm ready to go now."

"Then let's go, buddy."

"Inspector, don't you think you should get the boy to the hospital?" Mari's grandmother peered down her nose at him. "He's clearly not . . . well." She gave a strained laugh. "He thought he saw a dragon."

"Buzz is going to be just fine." Uncle Mark tucked his notepad away. "But I will pass on your concern to his father." He nodded his head. "Thanks again for your time."

With a gentle pressure at his back, Buzz was steered to the front door by his godfather. He focused on his steps. A pattern of movement that made sense when nothing else did.

He heard the slap of hasty footsteps behind him, and then Mari was at his side. Uncle Mark had reached to open the door, but Mari placed her hand on the wood to keep it closed. "Buzz," she said softly. "Come and find me, okay? We're still friends."

Buzz stared straight ahead at the door and did not respond. Either he was losing his mind or she was lying about what had happened in the woods. Both scenarios meant that he should stay well away from her. "I only met you today," he said. "And you're telling me I imagined half of it. That doesn't make us friends, does it?"

"Buzz." Her voice was urgent. "Please, I—"

A tutting sound came from behind them. "I don't think you'll be seeing this young man again, child," Mari's grandmother said. "I fear he has a rather overactive imagination, and we don't want that rubbing off on you, do we? You've been doing so well lately, Amaryllis, and we wouldn't want to do anything to jeopardize that."

"No, Grandma."

"So best for this to be a final and proper goodbye."

"Yes, Grandma." Buzz heard Mari swallow hard. "Bye, Buzz."

Buzz took his eyes off the door and looked at Mari. Her eyes glittered with anger or tears, he couldn't tell which, but he felt too numb to care. "Goodbye."

Uncle Mark opened the front door, and they stepped into the chill of the evening air. His godfather quickly checked his phone, his face impassive as he looked at the screen.

The drive back to Buzz's house was quiet except for the low hum of the engine, which itself faded away as they pulled up in front of the red door.

Red, just like my lucky underpants, Buzz thought. *The luckiest colour there is. What a joke.*

"Buzz, you should know that I've had an expert squad combing Tangley Woods for the last hour or so." Uncle Mark's brown skin looked yellow and mottled under the harsh street lamps. "All off the record, of course." He frowned, deep lines wrinkling his forehead. "My squad members do not feel the need to ask questions. They are looking as a favour to me. But they texted me to say there is no sign of this tree you were talking about." His fingers splayed across the steering wheel. "It doesn't exist."

Buzz opened his mouth, ready to say that there must be some mistake, but all words seemed to have emptied from his brain. He just nodded instead.

"Buddy, you need to get yourself some rest." The furrows in Uncle Mark's brow got deeper. "It's Saturday tomorrow. Have yourself a lie-in. And go easy on your dad, okay? He's doing the best he can." Uncle Mark squeezed Buzz's shoulder reassuringly. His hand was warm.

Buzz's only reply was to open the car door and walk back towards the house, the whole time wishing he was about to face a dragon instead of his father.

CHAPTER SEVEN

SATURDAY PANCAKES

Buzz yawned and rubbed at his eyes, which felt like they were full of grit. He reached for his phone to check the time but cursed as he noticed the bubble that blobbed wetly behind the dead screen. "Thanks a bunch, Theo," Buzz said to the quiet room.

He rolled onto his back and looked at the ceiling. His tired, sore eyes traced the painted constellations of stars that stretched above him.

His gaze lingered on the big dipper.

Some called it Odin's Wagon.

The fact dropped like a pebble into a still pond, sending powerful ripples out.

He focused on the ceiling again, remembering when he'd painted it with Mum and Tia the day he turned eight. They'd waited for the Prof to join them all day before starting, but he hadn't come home from Tangley Woods. It was the day Buzz had started to hate mythology. The day he realized that his father's obsession left no room for family.

Some called it Odin's Wagon.

Images of the dragon, Sunna, and Kira Bright slammed into Buzz, chasing away the sad memories. Fantasy. His father called it fantasy.

"Okay," Buzz said out loud. "Last night I saw a woman being kidnapped by a dragon. True or false?"

True, the voice in his head responded straight away. *You can even smell the dragon still – brimstone and mulch. It's true. You just need to believe it.*

"But what's the real evidence?" Buzz shot back, and the voice in his head did not answer because it knew there were no witnesses other than him and Mari.

He swung his legs out of bed and rested his feet on the wooden floor, welcoming the coolness of the creaky planks. He held on to the sensation and forced himself to think logically. *I hit my head yesterday. Hard. And I haven't slept properly for weeks.* His toes dug into the wood. "So maybe I made the whole thing up." He nodded. "Maybe I did hallucinate about a dragon, a missing weatherwoman, and a Norse god with a grudge." He dug his toes even deeper into the wood, his nails scratching the varnish. Mari had been talking about Loki just before they went into the woods. *That's why the name Loki was even in my head.* Buzz touched the gash at his temple, feeling the roughness of gauze and underneath it the contours of the scab that had formed overnight. The doctor who had dressed the wound last night had told Buzz and the Prof not to worry. "It was quite a whack," she said. "But I don't think you need an overnight stay in the hospital. Just make sure you get rest and drink lots of water."

Buzz snorted at the memory. The doctor might have kept him in if he'd told her about the dragon. *But I didn't, and neither did the Prof. After all, he doesn't want it getting out that his son has completely lost it.*

Buzz's stomach began to growl, and he realized he hadn't eaten since lunch yesterday. He sniffed the air and was greeted with the vanilla scent of pancakes. Mum always made pancakes on Saturdays, and Tia had demanded that their father keep up the tradition. No one argued with Tia, not even the Prof. And besides, one thing that Buzz and the Prof could agree on was the fact that no one wanted to eat Tia's cooking, and if the Prof didn't make pancakes, she would.

Buzz padded down the stairs and found his sister sitting at the breakfast bar tucking into a short stack of pancakes covered in maple syrup and strawberries. She looked up at him briefly, her fire-engine red hair a pop of colour in the muted light of the autumn morning, and the sequins of her Stranger Things T-shirt twinkling cheekily. "You look horrendous, little bro. Was your Friday the thirteenth really that bad?"

Buzz's eyes widened. "You don't know what happened?"

Tia shook her head. "I was over at Clarissa's."

With a clatter, the Prof placed a plate of pancakes on the counter. "Your brother got lost in Tangley Woods yesterday and tripped and hit his head." His voice seemed too loud for the kitchen somehow. "Eat up while they're still hot." The Prof shot Buzz a look that was pretty easy to read. *Do not tell Tia about yesterday.*

His father strode back over to the stove and poured more batter into the pan from Mum's favourite jug. The one with the tiny hibiscus flowers that had belonged to her grandmother in Jamaica. Buzz slid onto the barstool.

Tia leaned towards him, stripes of angry colour shading her cheekbones. "That bandage on your head doesn't have anything to do with Theo Eddows, does it?" she hissed.

Buzz shook his head.

"Do you promise? Because if that cretin touched you, he is in more trouble than he can ever possibly imagine, and I'll—"

"Tia, Theo Eddows has nothing to do with it," he hissed back. "And I really don't need you to fight my battles."

Tia crossed her arms her caramel skin flushed with anger. "From the state of you, I beg to differ."

Buzz reached for the chocolate sauce on the table. "Prof told you, I got a bit lost and then I tripped. End of story."

Tia frowned as if she wasn't sure whether to believe him. Buzz saw that furrowed brow a lot more than he used to. Tia was good at hiding her feelings, but he knew that she was missing Mum just as much as he was, and finding out that her little brother was quite possibly hallucinating about dragons and missing weatherwomen wouldn't make her feel any better.

His sister's lips became a thin line. "Where's your head at, Buzz? You know those woods better than anyone – even him." She jerked her head in the direction of their father. He was flipping pancakes with a measured and methodical movement, with none of the will-she-or-won't-she drama that came from Mum's attempts.

"I guess I wasn't concentrating." Tia was right: he did know the woods better than anyone. He'd grown up in those woods, knew every hiding place, and yet he had never seen that giant tree with its shimmering silver bark until yesterday.

His fingers tightened on the bottle of chocolate syrup as he realized that he must have imagined the tree as well. The whole thing – Kira, Sunna, the dragon, and the enchanted rope – was just a fantasy, like his father had said.

"Bro! It's meant to be pancakes with chocolate, not chocolate with pancakes."

Buzz gave a jolt and flipped the bottle up, chocolate sauce running over his fingers. "I got a bit carried away." *And in more ways than one.* He cut into the pancakes and scooped up the pieces, enjoying the gooey mess in his mouth. Pancakes at least made complete sense to him.

Tia shook her head. "You're funny, you know that, Buzz?"

Her eyes lit up. "Hey, did that girl Mari come and find you yesterday after school? She seems really nice." Buzz shook his head. Mari was the last person he wanted to talk about. His gaze travelled along the breakfast bar and rested on a newspaper that lay folded on the wooden surface. It was dated September 14, and although the face was folded in half, with just a pair of eyes visible, Buzz recognized Kira Bright instantly. Above her half face, the stark headline read, Weather Woman Mystery Deepens. Fog Over Disappearance Refuses to Lift.

Buzz unfolded the newspaper, leaving a smear of chocolate sauce over Kira Bright's smiling face.

"It's all so strange. People say they saw fog following her car before she disappeared. I wonder what happened to her?" Tia said, even as Buzz skimmed the newspaper for any new information.

The shrill ring of the telephone made them both jump.

"I'll get it." Tia slipped down from her stool and bounded over to the phone.

"Hello, the Buzzard residence," she said in her best telephone voice.

Tia was silent for a moment but then took in a sharp intake of breath. "Mum? Is that really you?"

Buzz and the Prof were by the phone in two strides.

"Mum, I can't believe it." Tears crested at the corner of Tia's eyes, and she took a gulping breath. "I've missed you, too." She listened for a moment, a tear now tracking down her cheek.

"Okay, I'll pass you over." Tia handed the phone to the Prof, and Buzz felt a sting of annoyance that she hadn't given the phone to him. He pushed the thought away. *Mum's alive! She's alive!*

"Natasha, are you all right? Where have you been? We thought . . . well, you can imagine what we thought." The Prof swallowed and Buzz could see that his hand was shaking on the receiver.

Buzz could hear his mother's voice but not her words as the Prof listened intently.

"Natasha, the line is breaking up. Yes, of course, I'll tell him. I lo—" He broke off and looked at the phone in frustration. "She's gone."

"Gone," Buzz repeated. "But I didn't get to speak to her." He hated the desperate quality to his voice, but he couldn't help it.

"I'm sorry," the Prof said. "I am. But it sounds like she had to move heaven and earth to make the call and the line was temperamental."

Buzz's throat felt tight, but he nodded.

"Where's she been?" Tia asked.

"There was an electrical storm," the Prof explained. "They were deep in the Amazon and their equipment got completely fried. She said they lived there alone for months until they came across a settlement who helped them find an outpost where they could make a call." Dad put the phone back in the stand with a click. "The good news is she's flying out of the forest tomorrow. There's a light aircraft that leaves every

Sunday and she has a seat." The Prof's lips curved upwards. Buzz couldn't remember the last time he'd seen his father smile. "Your mother is coming home."

CHAPTER EIGHT

DRAGON BOY

Buzz ran to the sports club for the semi-finals of the Crowmarsh youth cup, the autumn sun making everything crackly with orange fire.

Tia had left for her Saturday job at the library, and Buzz had decided he needed to get out of the house as well. With a football match, at least, he knew what he was meant to do, and wouldn't have to deal with the memories, imagined or not, of dragons and magic.

His head still throbbed a bit, but since the phone call from his mum he'd been feeling much better. He must have looked better as well because he'd somehow managed to convince the Prof that he was okay to play in the match. To be fair, his father had been distracted, as Tia had left him a really long list of chores to get the house looking good for Mum's return. Coach Saunders raised an eyebrow. "Good of you to turn up, Buzz.

More than you managed yesterday."

"Sorry about that, Coach," Buzz said, remembering how worried he'd been that Coach wouldn't play him in the match today. That all felt like a really long time ago now.

Coach tried to look stern, but a smile spread across his moonlike face, and he pulled out a piece of paper folded into four. "Luckily for you, I've got my game plan all set and you're pretty integral." He peered at the bandage on Buzz's head. "You sure you're okay to play?"

Buzz nodded. "I feel great, and we got some news." He grinned. "My mum's coming home tomorrow."

"That's amazing!" Coach Saunders clapped a hand on Buzz's shoulder. "Go and get your shoes laced up and let's see if this day can get even better."

* * *

It didn't. Buzz's team lost 4–1. They wouldn't be going through to the Crowmarsh youth cup final.

Buzz muttered a word that he'd never say in front of an adult as Theo Eddows's tall and solid figure walked over to him, achingly new trainers flashing white on his feet. Theo's swagger was even more pronounced than usual. *But then he did score three of the four goals for his team. And I spent most of the match hemmed in and shut down.* Buzz hated to admit it, but Theo's team had done a great job of neutralizing them – so much for the coach's grand game plan.

"How's your head?" Theo asked. The football was balanced on his finger, a spinning blur of black and white.

Buzz frowned. Since when did Theo show any interest in anyone other than himself? "It's fine, thanks."

"How'd it happen?" Theo was watching him with a lazy smile.

"It doesn't matter."

"Don't be shy. Go on, tell me."

Buzz felt a prickle of annoyance. "I must have tripped over your massive ego and hit my head."

"Hey, I was just making conversation." The ball stopped spinning and Theo began to bounce it, the ball edging closer and closer to Buzz's feet.

"Whatever." Buzz slung his bag over his shoulder. "I get it. You're mad that you had to go and get my phone from the Toilet of Doom. Maybe you shouldn't have put it there in the first place." He stepped forwards but Theo blocked his way. Buzz curled his lip. "Or is it that you're worried about Tia?" He snorted. "I guess you want me to call her off."

The beat of the ball lost its steady rhythm for a moment, but Theo quickly got the ball under control. "I'm not scared of a girl." His grey eyes said different.

"Sure you're not," Buzz replied. "But just in case, I've already told her I can fight my own battles." He gave a little wave. "There you go, we've had a conversation and now it's over." Buzz went to move again but Theo kept blocking his way, step for step.

"No, Buzzkill, we've still got plenty to say." Theo's ball sped up, the sound ricocheting around them until the thump of Buzz's headache was back.

Buzz tipped his head to one side. "You want to gloat, is that it? I'll save you the trouble. We got thrashed – well done. Have a great weekend, now. This conversation is over."

Theo's lazy smile came back to play around his lips. "Thing is, it's easy to win when you have all the information, Buzz." He gave a low chuckle as he stared over at Coach Saunders, who was slinging a bag into his beat-up Ford Focus. Theo's smile became a full-on smirk.

It's easy to win when you have all the information. The words hung between them.

"You stole his game plan." Buzz's words were a whisper. "That's how you knew. That's how your whole team knew our moves before we even made them."

"I don't know what you're talking about." Theo couldn't even be bothered to keep the lie from his voice.

Buzz shook his head in disgust. "You're pathetic, you know that? How do you even stand yourself?"

Theo's nostrils flared, and he stopped the ball dead. "You've got some cheek, Buzzkill. To my thinking, pathetic is saying you saw a dragon in Tangley Woods. Pathetic is claiming that you found Kira Bright. But maybe that's just me. We can ask everyone at school on Monday and see what they think."

Ice crept up Buzz's spine. "What'd you say?"

Theo gave a shark-like grin. "You heard."

"Who told you that?" But even as he asked the question, Mari's betrayal cut at him.

"Let's just say neighbours are full of useful information. Especially the older ones. They love to chat to my mum."

Mari's grandmother, Buzz realized, and for a moment all he felt was relief that it hadn't been Mari who'd told Theo about his delusions.

But the relief was fleeting. Theo was a threat that needed neutralizing. "Listen, Theo, your mum must have misunderstood, or your neighbour did. It was just something stupid I said." He spread his arms wide. "A joke that's gone too far."

Theo barked with laughter. "You're the joke, Buzzkill. I'm just thinking of the best way to let everyone know it." He winked at him. "Guess what? Now the conversation is over. Have a good weekend, Dragon Boy." Theo walked off, ball tucked under his arm.

Buzz watched him go, his stomach churning like laundry on a fast cycle.

"Hey, mate." Samraj arrived at his side and raised an eyebrow. "You okay? You look a bit green."

"Yeah." Buzz swallowed. "I'm fine."

"And I'm good at football." Sam smiled ruefully. "There you go, now we're both lying!"

Buzz smiled despite himself. Sam was good at lots of things, including athletics and researching vintage action figures, but not football. For a moment, Buzz thought about telling his best friend about what had happened in the woods. But Sam wouldn't believe it. And why should he? Buzz was pretty sure he didn't believe it anymore himself. Besides, on Monday morning, Theo would be telling everyone about the adventures of Dragon Boy. *I might as well enjoy my last weekend of being normal.*

"It's nothing," he said.

"All right, mate, but whatever it is – it'll sort itself out." Sam clicked his fingers. "Hey, why don't we take your phone to the repair shop? And then you can come over to my house to watch the match on TV. That'll cheer you up."

Buzz visualized his soggy phone still lying on his bedside table. He could really do with getting it fixed, and hanging out watching the Saturday match was exactly the kind of normal he needed right now. But the woods were calling to him. He wanted to see if he could find that strange silver tree. See if there were any signs of Kira or the dragon. He needed to know for sure whether he had imagined the whole thing or not. "I don't know, Sam. I was kind of thinking I might have a walk round Tangley Woods."

His friend frowned. "Listen, your head is all messed up because of that place – you blatantly need to give it a rest for a while."

"What d'you mean, my head's all messed up?" Buzz's heart began to jackhammer in his chest. Had Theo already started telling people about what Buzz thought he had seen in Tangley Woods?

Sam pointed to his friend's temple. "You tripped and fell in the woods, right? That's what you told me earlier." He raised an eyebrow. "I know you love the place, but if I were you, I wouldn't be going for a ramble."

Buzz's hand went to his head. "Right, yeah, I see what you mean."

"So, let's get your phone fixed."

Buzz nodded slowly. "Cool. We'll need to swing by my house first to get it. Don't say anything to the Prof about the phone if we see him, okay? He'll just ask more questions."

Sam laughed. "When do I even say more than two words to your dad, anyway? He's so clever, it's kind of terrifying."

They headed towards Buzz's house, deliberately taking the route that didn't go through the heart of the forest. Sam was right. Tangley Woods could wait. That place had messed with his head enough, and searching for a tree or a dragon that didn't exist wasn't going to get his head straight anytime soon.

CHAPTER NINE

THE PHONE CALL

Buzz opened his eyes and stretched his arms above his head, his fingers pushing against the headboard. He rolled over to check his phone and frowned as he was greeted by a dead screen and a bubble of water that blobbed behind the plastic. He and Sam had gone and got the phone fixed yesterday, and it had worked when they'd left the shop. *So why isn't it working now?*

He sat up in bed and swung his legs out from under the duvet, his feet hitting the wooden floorboards, making them creak. For the first time in a very long time he felt rested. The familiar tired feeling that filled his eyes with grit and made his stomach feel hollow was gone, and he realized that it was because he had slept – properly slept. *Mum is coming home.* Nothing could ruin that feeling. Not even a broken phone or Theo Eddows and his stupid threat to tell everyone about Buzz's dragon delusions.

He sniffed the air. He could smell pancakes.

Strange.

Tia may have convinced the Prof to make them pancakes on Saturdays, but there was no way he'd do it on a Sunday as well – he'd be far too busy with his research.

So if it wasn't the Prof cooking, who was it?

Mum.

The word exploded in his head like a firework and rocketed him out of bed.

Mum.

Yanking open his bedroom door, he charged down the stairs, all but tumbling down the last few steps.

Tia looked up from the breakfast bar where she was tucking into a short stack of pancakes.

"Whoa! Where's the fire, Buzz?" she asked, a little crease forming between her eyebrows.

"Mum!" Buzz exclaimed. "Where is she?" His gaze eagerly swept over the kitchen, and he expected to see his mum's willowy frame at any point, her thick black hair in twists and piled atop of her head. But instead he saw only his father. The Prof stood at the stove, very still, a jug of batter in his hand. The purple hibiscus flowers on the porcelain looked smudged, and the jug somehow looked wrong and fragile in his large hand.

"Buzz, your mother is in the Amazon rainforest." The Prof gently set the jug down and turned off the gas under the frying pan. He turned to face him. "It's where she's been for the last six months." He said the words carefully, as if they were sticks of dynamite that might go off.

Rapid heat flooded Buzz's cheeks. "I know where she's been, but I smelt the pancakes – I just thought that she must have come home earlier than expected."

His father frowned deeply. It was the same expression he'd worn on Friday evening when Buzz had told him about seeing Kira Bright and the dragon in Tangley Woods.

"Earlier than expected?" he repeated.

"Yeah, her plane's supposed to leave today, right? I just thought she might have got an earlier one."

His father took a breath. "Why don't you sit down, Buzz? I'll bring you over some pancakes and get you some water."

"Thanks." Buzz slipped onto his stool, watching his father's movements as he went over to the fridge. They seemed tense and wooden. He felt the pinprick of Tia's gaze on him and he turned to face her.

"What's up with you, Buzz?" his sister asked.

"Good morning to you as well."

"That's not an answer." Tia looked upset.

Buzz stared at his sister, noticing that she was wearing her sequin-encrusted *Stranger Things* T-shirt again. *Since when does Tia ever wear an outfit two days in a row?*

"I'm fine, Tia. I was just a bit surprised that Dad was making pancakes for the second day in a row." He shrugged. "I thought Mum had got home early, that's all."

Tia played with the silverware next to her plate. She bit her lip. "Why do you keep saying that?"

"Saying what?" Buzz tried to push down his rising irritation. Why were Tia and Dad acting so strangely?

"About Mum getting home early," Tia snapped. "At best it's cruel and at worst you're deluded. Buzz, we haven't heard anything from her in months." She shook her head. "And as much as it might pain you to admit it – Dad has been making us pancakes every Saturday since Mum left because he is doing the best he can. You're trying to wind him up and I don't think it's fair."

Buzz's skin began to prickle into goose bumps. "Tia, Mum called us yesterday. We were sitting right here having breakfast. Dad was making pancakes."

Tia threw her hands up in exasperation. "Yesterday, I had a piece of toast and met Clarissa at seven forty-five at the top of her road. You were late for school – goodness knows why but I bet it had something to do with my hair dye – I don't even want to know." She pointed a finger at him. "Buzz, whatever joke you're trying out here – stop it, okay? It's mean."

"It's not a joke," Buzz shot back. "Mum called. She called the house. You spoke to her."

That worried, creased line was back between Tia's eyes, and she fixed her gaze at his temple. "How'd you hurt your head?"

"I told you already, after school I was in Tangley—"

With a clatter, Buzz's father placed a plate of pancakes on the counter. "Your brother got lost in Tangley Woods yesterday and tripped and hit his head." He nodded at Buzz. "Eat up while they're still hot," he insisted. But the Prof's eyes said something else. *Do not tell Tia about yesterday.*

A rush of déjà vu blasted through Buzz, so strong that it slammed the breath out of him. This conversation had happened yesterday – exactly like this.

"Are you sure you're okay?" Tia asked her brother. "You don't look so good."

Buzz heard the question and tried to grab hold of it but it slipped further away as he spotted a newspaper folded on the breakfast bar. Kira Bright's eyes looked out at him from the inky page, and above her picture was a familiar headline:

Weather Woman Mystery Deepens. Fog Over Disappearance Refuses to Lift.

The date at the top of the page said Saturday, September 14, but there was no chocolate sauce on the newspaper's front page – not a drop.

Dizzy, he took a deep breath, but it didn't work – the world still spun around him.

"I took him to the doctor yesterday," he heard the Prof say. "She said that he just needed rest, but maybe we should go back to the hospital."

"I'm fine," Buzz said as the world swung back into focus. "Just remind me what day it is?"

"Saturday," Tia and the Prof said at once. They were both looking at him in concern.

"Saturday," Buzz echoed. *Saturday for the second day in a row,* he thought. He scrubbed at his face. *Kira Bright, a dragon, and now a day that's repeating itself.* A burble of something that could be a laugh or a sob climbed up his throat, and only the shrill ring of the telephone disguised it.

"I'll get it." Tia slipped down from her stool and headed to the phone, but Buzz was quicker.

If he was going to live this day twice, be it by dream or hallucination, then he was going to be the one to answer this phone call. *There have to be some perks to losing my mind.*

He snatched the phone from its stand and hit the green button.

"Hello-the-Buzzard-residence," he said in one breath.

"Buzz? Buzz? Is that really you?" a tinny voice on a crackly line said.

"Mum!"

Despite the fact that he had expected it to be her, had wanted it to be her, hearing Mum's voice made his hands tremble on the phone. "I thought I'd never hear your voice again." His mouth was dry. "I've missed you so much Mum."

Tia and the Prof were already at his side, their faces twin masks of astonishment.

At the other end of the line, Mum was silent, and Buzz wondered if her line had failed. But then he heard her swallow hard, as if her mouth was as dry as his, and he realized that she was nervous. "I've missed you, too, love. I'm so sorry to have put you through this – will you forgive me?"

"It wasn't your fault. It was the electrical storm."

His mum gasped. "Did I tell you that already? I could have sworn that—"

"When will you be home?" Buzz asked, cutting her off before she could ask any more difficult questions.

"I'll be getting on a plane first thing tomorrow. And when I'm home everything is going to go back to normal, I promise."

Normal, Buzz thought, and the warm glow of talking to his mother began to fade a little. He'd left normal behind the day he imagined he saw Kira Bright imprisoned by an enchanted rope in Tangley Woods. *And now I'm locked into living the same day again.* Normal felt really far away. Buzz's hand tightened on the phone. *Maybe I'm still asleep,* he thought. *Dreaming away in my bed upstairs.*

"I can't wait," Buzz whispered, and he hoped the desperation is his voice would get lost in the static on the line. He hoped the sooner Mum was back, the sooner his world would return to its axis.

"All right, love, pass me over to your father."

Buzz handed the phone to the Prof, and he could see the flash of annoyance that crossed his sister's face as she realized the phone wasn't coming her way.

She got to speak to Mum yesterday, Buzz reminded himself. *Not that she knows that, because yesterday didn't happen for her.*

"Natasha, are you hurt? Where have you been? We thought … well, you can imagine what we thought." The Prof held the phone tightly, and his knuckles stood out starkly against his pale, freckly skin.

Buzz could hear his mother's voice but not her words as the Prof listened intently.

"Natasha, the line is breaking up. Yes, of course, I'll tell her. I lo—" He broke off and looked at the phone in frustration. "She's gone."

"But I didn't get to speak to her." Tia's voice was a little hoarse.

"I'm sorry, but it sounds like she had to move heaven and earth to make the call and the line was temperamental."

Tia nodded, her throat working furiously.

The Prof was looking at Buzz in puzzlement. "I don't know how you knew, but you were right. Your mother really is coming home."

CHAPTER TEN

A NEW GAME PLAN

Buzz walked onto the field, waiting for the dream to fade or the hallucination to shatter, but Saturday kept on running just the same. The Prof seemed to have forgotten all his threats to take Buzz back to the hospital, and Tia had been busy setting out a list of chores to get the house ready for Mum before heading to work. Buzz had slipped out while neither of them were paying attention, determined to go to the football match because it was still the only thing that made any sense.

Coach Saunders raised an eyebrow. "Good of you to turn up, Buzz. More than you managed yesterday."

"Sorry about that, Coach," Buzz said, almost on autopilot.

Coach Saunders winked. "Lucky for you, you're kind of integral to my game plan, so I'll let you off this time." Coach pulled a crumpled piece of paper from his pocket and waved it under Buzz's nose. "With this we can't fail."

Buzz hesitated. Yesterday they had been well and truly crushed by Theo's team. But that was only because Theo had stolen the game plan – it hadn't been a fair match. If this really was a rerun of the previous day, then surely he could have a bit of fun and change the result.

"Coach, about your game plan . . ."

"Hmmm?" Coach smoothed it open and looked at it intently. "What about it?"

"Do you think I could have a look at it?" Buzz asked. "I mean, maybe I could add a few things."

Coach chuckled. "Don't get me wrong, laddie. You're great at strategy." He tapped his nose. "But this game plan is on a need-to-know basis. I like to call it my Super-Secret Grand Game Plan." He chuckled again. "Catchy, right? Now, listen, you just need to focus on your part. You're going to be up front and out wide. Drop back when Max accelerates and don't forget to pass."

Buzz groaned inwardly as Coach continued to talk. He didn't know what to do. There was no proof that the game plan had been stolen, and if he accused Theo, Theo would just deny it or mention the whole dragon thing.

Buzz heard a dull, grating noise and realized that it was him grinding his teeth. The grinding became fiercer as he spotted Theo crossing the field to where his team was warming up on the sidelines and showing off his new pair of trainers before pulling on his football boots. His team were grinning and high-fiving. They looked like a squad who knew they'd won the match already.

Buzz turned to Coach Saunders. "I hate to say it, Coach, but I'm pretty sure the Super-Secret Grand Game Plan is not that secret."

Coach chuckled. "Nice try, but I'm not telling you the game plan yet."

"That's okay. I'll just guess," Buzz replied, and then he proceeded to recall every detail from the match yesterday. He outlined the tactics for each and every player on his team. He even remembered to include some of the motivational stuff Coach had thrown in at halftime. The line about them working together and being more than the sum of their parts had Coach Saunders's jaw hanging open.

Coach held up a hand and begged Buzz to stop. "Am I really that predictable?" he asked forlornly.

Buzz felt a twist of guilt for making Coach doubt himself like this. *But it's for the greater good,* he reassured himself. "Listen, Coach, two heads are often better than one." He smiled encouragingly. "We'll use elements of your game plan, but we just need to disguise the intentions a bit."

Coach Saunders' shoulders straightened, and he looked at his watch. "Right you are, Buzz. We've got exactly seven minutes, so let's get cracking." He took the game plan, scrunched it into a ball, and lobbed it into a nearby bin.

Buzz grinned and in that moment felt a pair of eyes on him. He turned and saw Theo staring at them from across the field.

He wasn't smiling anymore, and that made Buzz grin even more widely.

This do-it-all-over-again day – dream or not – was shaping up to be a lot of fun.

* * *

Buzz saw lights as an elbow crashed into his jaw, and he felt his legs being swept out from beneath him. Buzz hit the ground, hard, as a whistle blew.

It hurt, but there was nothing like leading the match by four goals to take the sting out of these things.

Theo stood over him, his cheeks flushed. "I know it was you, Buzzkill. You switched the plan."

"You mean the plan you stole?" Buzz got to his feet. He wasn't as tall as Theo, but he tipped his chin and that helped a bit.

Theo took a step forwards, but another blow of the whistle stopped him, and Buzz could see that the referee was just a few paces away.

"I'm going to get you back for this," Theo hissed. "I know things about you, Dragon Boy, and soon, so will everybody else." He held his hands up and turned to face the referee, who had now barrelled up to his side.

"Ref, it was an accident. I didn't mean it."

"YOU. OFF. NOW." The referee pointed Theo in the direction of the bench.

Theo stalked off, but not before hurling one last glare at Buzz.

Sam arrived at Buzz's side. "You okay?"

Buzz worked his jaw, wincing. "Right now and for today, I'm just fine."

"That challenge was brutal." Sam shook his head. "Why does Theo hate you so much?"

Buzz remembered what Mrs Robertson had said about Theo's missing brother. And how difficult that was for him to deal with. He shrugged. "Whatever it is, he's never bothered to tell me."

He took the ball that was handed to him by the referee and kicked the penalty. Buzz didn't even need to think about it. The ball found the sweet spot, right in the corner of the net.

The whistle blew for the end of the match, and Buzz felt the air rush past his ears as he was hoisted up on the shoulders of his teammates. They'd won!

* * *

Buzz opened his eyes and stretched his arms above his head, his fingers grazing the wooden headboard. He sat up in bed and swung his legs out from under the duvet, his feet hitting the wooden floorboards and making them creak. He yawned widely and then winced as a sharp pain lanced his jaw.

He cradled the side of face, remembering how Theo's elbow had crashed into it at the match yesterday.

Yesterday. The same yesterday that should have been Sunday but had actually been another Saturday. Buzz had managed finally to convince himself that this second Saturday had been some kind of dream. But if that was the case, why was his jaw hurting?

Buzz sniffed the air and felt his heart rate accelerate. He could smell pancakes.

Not again.

He pinched himself, twisting his skin. If living the same day again and then again was really some kind of hallucination – it was time for him to wake up.

"Ow!" His voice was loud in the quiet room, and all the pinch caused was a red mark on his pale brown skin.

Enough, Buzz thought. *Nothing's been the same since that evening in the woods on Friday the thirteenth.* Answers, if there were any to be had, were going to be there. And Sunna had said the tree would help.

He got ready quickly, laced up his trainers, and tucked his still-broken phone into his backpack before shooting down the stairs.

Tia, dressed in her *Stranger Things* T-shirt, looked up from the breakfast bar where she was tucking into a short stack of pancakes. *Again.*

"Whoa! Where's the fire, Buzz?" she asked, a little crease forming between her eyebrows.

"There's something I've got to go and check."

"But I've made you pancakes," the Prof protested, holding up the jug of batter. Buzz noticed that it was now visibly cracked, and the hibiscus flowers that decorated the surface were little more than blobs.

"Sorry, I've got to go. I promised Sam that we'd have a quick practice before the match."

Prof frowned. "How's your head? I'm really not sure it's a sensible idea for you to go and play, and certainly not without eating something first."

"I feel fine." Buzz snatched a pancake off Tia's plate. "And look, now I've had something to eat." He shoved the pancake into his mouth and gulped it down.

"Firstly, oi! And secondly, what happened to your head?" Tia asked.

"Prof will fill you in," Buzz said over his shoulder as he headed for the front door. "See you later."

Mist rolled over the ground as Buzz left the house and jogged down the path that wended deeper into the forest. The trees stood as silent sentries, witnesses to many things over the years, but most accomplished as keepers of secrets.

He pushed through the woods, the thin blanket of autumn leaves crunching underfoot, and headed for Mornings Lake. The tree had been near there.

Buzz walked along the burbling brook that led towards the lake. The sound of the stream soothed the headache he hadn't even realized he'd been battling, and he felt at peace.

I should have come to the woods sooner, he thought.

It felt so right in this place. His head felt clear, and here, he knew for sure that he had not imagined Kira or the dragon.

And he knew as well that he was not imagining that Saturday was repeating itself on a loop. Something very wrong had happened here on Friday the thirteenth, and the world was not recovering from it. They were time-locked.

Buzz heard the crunch of footsteps behind him, and he whipped around.

"You," he said.

CHAPTER ELEVEN

RATATOSK

"Hi." Mari's voice came out at a whisper.

"What are you doing here?" Buzz demanded.

"The same as you, I'm guessing. I'm looking for that tree." She tugged on her braids, which had been swept into a long ponytail. "I've been searching in these woods for the last two days in a row. Or should I say two *Saturdays* in a row?" She sounded nervous. "It's been kinda trippy, right, reliving the same day?"

"Reliving the same day?" Buzz concentrated on painting a shocked look on his face. "I have no idea what you're talking about."

"You don't?" Mari looked dismayed. "You mean it's just me?" She rubbed at her forehead, and her lips became a worried line.

Buzz was tempted to keep up the act, but he relented. "No, it's not just you. And yes, it has been kinda trippy."

Mari heaved a sigh of relief. "You're getting me back, aren't you? For lying about what happened with Sunna and the dragon." She hugged her arms "I'm so sorry about what happened at my grandmother's house."

"Why'd you lie?" Buzz asked, his anger flickering to life again. "For the last few days, I actually thought I was going crazy."

"Crazy?" Mari repeated. "I hate that word. Do you know what it feels like to be given a label like that? To have your parents spend all their money to send you to a special centre and be monitored and studied and talked at until someone says that you are normal again. Just as long as you promise not to speak any more about the ghosts that you see? Or the fact that you can read people's deepest fears in their faces." Mari's voice was bitter. "If you knew what it really felt like to be called crazy, then maybe you'd lie as well. Maybe you'd do anything to protect yourself."

"You should have told me that. You should have told me that you couldn't tell the truth about the dragon," Buzz insisted. "I would have understood. Instead, you let me turn up at your grandmother's house with my uncle Mark and make a complete fool of myself."

Mari bit her lip. "I'm sorry. I guess I wanted to be Mari for a bit longer and not Scary Mari who sits on her own in the cafeteria. And my grandma gets so worried about me. Forgive me, Buzz." Her brown eyes were uncertain behind her glasses. "Can we start again? No secrets this time."

Buzz rubbed at the back of his neck. Maybe Mari should have told him the truth. But to be fair, all that stuff about seeing ghosts and people's deepest fears sounded even stranger than seeing an actual dragon.

Besides we're the only two people who seem to notice that we're locked into the same day. We need each other.

"Let's go find that tree," Buzz said. "It's the only lead we have."

Together, they followed the brook towards Mornings Lake and between them tried to decide if any of the scenery looked familiar.

"It's strange," Mari mused. "I put the coordinates of the tree into my watch, but we still can't find it."

"So what's going on?" Buzz asked.

"Well, the tree is magic. I suppose I could have guessed my watch wouldn't work."

"No, I mean the Saturday loop thing," Buzz responded, trudging through the leaves. "Why is it happening? And why are we the only ones to notice it?"

Mari grinned in the gloom of the forest. "I'm smart, but I'm not a genius."

"But you have a theory, right?"

Mari shook her head. "Not this time. But I do think the dragon thing, the Sunna thing, and this Saturday lockdown are connected." She rubbed at her forehead. "I think seeing Sunna being taken means we don't get affected this Saturday loop like other people?"

92

"Okay, I've spent the last two days trying to forget everything because I thought I was making it up but Sunna did say something about an unmorrow curse. Is that why we keep reliving the same day?"

"Maybe. I've been doing some research," Mari said. "Sunna said that she'd been a goddess a long time ago, before she went into her deep sleep." Mari reached into her pocket and took out the necklace with its half of the pendant.

Buzz took out his half, and they clipped them together to make the bolt of lightning:

"This is Sunna's rune mark, her insignia," Mari said, placing it around her neck. "It means sun." Her eyes were wide. "I didn't remember the name before, but Sunna is the Norse goddess of the sun."

"Holey pyjamas!" Buzz exclaimed, and he wasn't even embarrassed that he'd used the phrase. Nothing else was really going to cut it. "But if Sunna is the sun, what is that star 92.96 million miles away? You know – the one that kind of powers our whole planet?"

"You're the son of a mythologist, you have absolutely no clue when it comes to mythology, and yet you know exactly how far away the sun is!"

"I'm full of contradictions."

"Clearly." Mari shook her head. "Anyway, I didn't say that Sunna *was* the sun. It was the people who worshipped her that made her the symbol of that star 92.96 million miles away. They made her a day guardian too, just like she said. Sunna is just a person with superpowers. I think that might be true of all these gods."

"Okay, so Sunna and her other superpowered day guardian mates fell out with this Loki guy and imprisoned him, but now he is free and has kidnapped Sunna in revenge."

"Not just for revenge. He wants her powers and the powers of the other gods who wronged him, remember?" Mari pushed her glasses up her nose. "Those powers are in the Runes of Valhalla. We need to find them before Loki does."

"But what does any of this have to do with us all being stuck in a Saturday loop?" Buzz asked.

"Yer can't have a Sunday if that day's guardian is gone from your realm, bird brains," a gruff voice said from above their heads. "Everything is stuck, stuck, *muk*, *muk*."

There was a sound of rustling leaves and more *muk*, *muk*ing, which seemed to reverberate in the chest of whatever creature was generating it. Then, scrabbling down the trunk of an old oak tree, came a squirrel.

It stood in front of them, blocking their path. Its large, clever, dark eyes watched them carefully. The squirrel's red, bushy tail was held high, but Buzz noticed immediately that the tip was missing, leaving behind a raw-looking stump.

A memory came back to him. A flash of red fur hurtling through the air, forcing him to move out of the way of the dragon's rapidly descending tail.

"You were there when Sunna was taken," Buzz said. "You saved my life."

"It's me job. Apologies that it's taken so long to find yer. Been recovering from me injuries." The squirrel gave a theatrical bow. "Ratatosk at yer service. Agent of the World Tree. *Muk, muk.*"

"Nice to meet you, Ratatosk." Mari bowed low, her long ponytail almost grazing the ground. "Sunna said the tree would help us, and she was right."

Buzz noticed that Mari was positively beaming, and it occurred to him that she didn't look even remotely thrown by the fact that they were talking to a squirrel.

"What do you mean when you say everything is stuck?" she asked Ratatosk. But the squirrel was not listening. His nose was twitching. His whiskers were quivering. And then, in a streak of burnt umber, he was away into the undergrowth.

"Wait!" Mari and Buzz exclaimed at the same time, but all they were greeted with was silence.

CHAPTER TWELVE

HIM UPSTAIRS

"Ratatosk," Buzz called. "RATATOSK!"

"All right, all right. Keep your ruddy hair on," Ratatosk yelled back from the dense undergrowth. "I'll just be a sec."

They heard the scrabble of claws, and then a stream of earth shot out onto the path as the squirrel began to dig away. In no time at all, Ratatosk gave a *muk, muk* of pleasure and appeared back in front of them with a large cobnut in his little paws.

He filled his furry cheeks with air and blew on the nut to try to rid it of any dirt. Looking pleased with himself, he popped it into his mouth and began chomping away.

Mari gave a small, polite cough, and then a louder one so she could be heard over the chewing. "Ratatosk, what do you mean, stuck?" she asked again.

Ratatosk looked up, his little jaw still working hard. He tried to say something, but all Buzz and Mari actually heard was,

"Numph, numph." Realizing that they hadn't understood, Ratatosk swallowed the last of his cobnut, gave a tiny burp, and rubbed his furry tummy. "Time is locked on Saturday because Sunna has gone from your world and been taken to one of the hidden realms."

Buzz rubbed at his forehead. "But why does Sunna being gone mean we're stuck in a time lock?"

Ratatosk shook his head despairingly and with his hind legs began shovelling the pile of dirt on the path back into the undergrowth.

"It ain't brain surgery. Days of the week each have a guardian," Ratatosk explained, hind legs still working furiously. "Sunday is Sunna's day. But now that she's been taken from your world and to one of the hidden realms by that dragony brute Nidhogg, Sunday can't happen. The days can't move on. That means we're stuck. Stuck in the unmorrow curse." Ratatosk finished with the dirt and sat back on his haunches. "And the longer we remain in the unmorrow, the worse things will get. It's gonna get real messy."

Buzz thought of his mother. He imagined her out there in the Amazon rain forest, waiting for the plane that would bring her home – a plane that would never come if it was Saturday forever. *And I don't even want to know what Ratatosk means by things getting real messy.* Right now, he could only deal with one thing at a time.

"How do we get Sunna back and stop the unmorrow?" he asked.

"Yer need to find the other runes and give them back to the right gods so they can regain their powers. Then they'll be able to stop Loki."

"Okay. But how do we find them?" Mari asked.

"The runes or the gods?" Ratatosk asked, sniffing at his tail.

"The gods," Buzz said.

"The runes," Mari said.

"Are yer having a laugh?" Ratatosk's fur bristled. I can only tell yer one thing at a time. I'm not a magic squirrel, yer know. Do I look like I have two heads, two mouths, two—"

"Okay, okay. Tell us where to find the gods first," Mari soothed.

Ratatosk's fur bristled even more. "That's way above my pay grade." He shook his furry head. "Listen, their god selves will be asleep. Embedded deep down in a person, just like it was with Sunna. The day guardians are going to look like average Joes just like you, Buzz."

"Average," Buzz repeated. "Thanks for that."

"If they could be anyone," Mari mused, "how are we supposed to find them?"

"If yer get the runes, they'll lead yer to yer sleeping gods. If yer don't get the runes, yer only clue will be that the hosts of the day guardians will have stayed close to the tree. Close to these woods."

"So that could be anyone in Crowmarsh," Buzz mused.

Ratatosk nodded. "Some of yer hosts may have an inkling

that something ain't right and that they're stuck in the unmorrow. That might help yer spot them. But more likely, they'll have no idea that they're hosting gods, and so the sleeping day guardians won't wake up until they are reunited with their runes. That's the only way for them to get their power back." Ratatosk lifted his injured tail and gave it a sniff. "D'yer think it's infected?" he asked fretfully. "That horrible dragon crushed it to a pulp."

Mari knelt down and peered at it. "No, I don't think so." She leaned forwards and sniffed it gingerly. "And it doesn't smell bad, either. I think it's all right." Ratatosk beamed at her. "Thanks for looking. I'm a complete hypochondriac sometimes." He over looked at Buzz. "She's very helpful, this one. Let's hope those gods yer need to find will be just as obliging." Ratatosk stroked his whiskers meditatively.

"Okay, so where are the runes, then?" Buzz asked.

Ratatosk crossed his arms "I'm just a squirrel. How should I know?"

"You're the agent of the tree!" Buzz exclaimed. "You're not just a squirrel. Squirrels can't talk."

"Have yer ever listened?" Ratatosk shot back. "I mean *really* listened?"

"No. But—"

"You seem so wise and knowing, Ratatosk." Mari reached out and gently stroked the squirrel's head. "So we just assumed that you'd know. Are we wrong?"

Ratatosk calmed down and nuzzled into her hand. "Well . . .
I did hear that the runes are scattered across the hidden realms
and I'd bet all the cobnuts in this wood that Loki is looking
for them right now." He clasped his paws together. "If anyone
knows where the runes are for certain it will be him upstairs.
Yer know – the lord of all time. Yer'll need to speak to him."

"Him upstairs." Buzz gulped. "As in, the big cheese . . . "

"Saturn, yeah," Ratatosk replied.

"Oh," Buzz said. "That's not who I thought you meant at all."
His brow scrunched. "How are we going to speak to a planet?"

"What in the worlds are yer goin' on about?" Ratatosk looked
outraged. "Why would I be telling yer to talk to a planet? How
would that even work?"

"He means the Roman god, Saturn," Mari said. "You know,
the God of Time?" She stroked Ratatosk's head again and the
squirrel looked up at her adoringly and began to purr.

First, Buzz didn't even know that squirrels could purr.
Second, he didn't know that Saturn was the Roman God
of Time. And third, as much as he was trying to ignore it, he
didn't know why Mari was staring at him with such a seriously
perplexed look.

"Are you sure your father is a mythologist?" she asked after a
moment. "How come you don't know any of this stuff?"

Buzz's cheeks flushed. "I guess he hasn't been that interested
in telling me."

Or you haven't been that interested in listening, the annoying voice in his head replied. *Because you thought it was all rubbish.*

"A mythologist?" the squirrel asked. "What's that, then?"

"A professor of mythology," Buzz responded. "He does a lot of research about myths. Spends most of his time in these woods, actually, looking for evidence about different ancient mythologies and their epicenters."

"I know exactly who you mean," Ratatosk said. "Pale, serious-looking guy with the glasses, always poking about. Sings to himself – his voice kind of stays with you."

"That's him." Although Buzz didn't think he'd ever heard the Prof sing before. He thought Mum was the singer.

"Where was I?" Ratatosk picked a bit of nut from his front teeth. "That's right, Saturn. He and Odin have always been as thick as thieves. Singing each other's praises." The squirrel rolled his eyes. "Strange really, since gods tend to stay with their own kind. Norse with Norse, Roman with Roman, Egyptian with Egyptian. Babylonian with Babylonian. Yoruba deities with Yoruba deities." Ratatosk wrinkled his nose. "But Odin and Saturn were peas in a pod, ruthless as yer like. After Odin had Loki imprisoned and stripped of his powers, he asked Saturn to become guardian of the Trickster's day."

"So that's when it became Saturday," Mari said. "Saturn's day."

The squirrel nodded. "Thing yer got to understand is that Saturn is proper old," Ratatosk warned. "Been around from the beginning. That makes him as wise as time itself. It also makes him a tricky customer to deal with. He likes to play games."

"How do we find him?" The words slipped out before Buzz could stop them, and he braced himself for another scary squirrel telling-off.

"How'd yer expect me to know that?" Ratatosk was so angry he was shaking.

No, hang on a minute, Buzz thought. *He's laughing.*

In fact, the squirrel was laughing so much, tears were running down his furry cheeks.

"I'm just pulling your leg." Ratatosk guffawed. "Yer should have seen yer face. I ain't that fierce, am I?" He tilted his head. "Up the tree we'll go and find the right branch. The tree can take you to any hidden realm there is."

Without Buzz even realizing it, Ratatosk had led them right to the glade where the World Tree waited for them. It was just as big as Buzz remembered, its branches reaching upwards to the sky. The tree was so tall you couldn't see the top, and the ground seemed to fizz with energy beneath his feet. Mari breathed.

"It's so big . We could be climbing for hours." Buzz's knees felt like they were made of clay. "How will we know which branch to choose?" he asked. *Please let it be one of the bottom branches.*

"Yer'll need to tell the tree where yer want to go, and then it will show yer the branch." The squirrel's furry face went grave.

"It's no game travelling between realms. Yer can get lost in more ways than one. Truth is yer most reliable guide, but yer heart must be open to listen to its advice."

Buzz nodded and placed his hand on the tree. "Show us the path to Saturn," he requested, and the bark answered by pulsing with power beneath his fingertips.

Mari grinned at him. "Time to go up!"

CHAPTER THIRTEEN

RIFT

Do not look down, Buzz told himself, climbing further and further up the tree. *Just don't do it.*

But Buzz's eyes couldn't help it. He gazed down past his feet in their battered trainers, through the silver branches and their tangled leaves, all the way to the ground, which looked very, very far away.

He began to tremble, and the rucksack he'd slung carelessly over his shoulder slipped off his arm like soap suds off a plate. "Watch out," he cried as the bag tumbled downwards, taking a swathe of twigs and leaves with it.

He heard Mari curse. "I told you I should have gone first." Her voice came from somewhere beneath him.

Buzz tried to get his breathing under control. "Sorry."

"It's okay." Mari's voice sounded less annoyed. "There was nothing important in that bag, was there?"

"No, not really. Some money. A drink." Buzz didn't want to mention that his mum had bought the bag for his last birthday. A burning pain in his arms made him catch his breath, and he realized that he'd wrapped them so tightly around the trunk of the tree that the bark was cutting into his skin. He wondered how he was ever going to move from this position. His arms were locked into place, his feet were clumps of concrete, and his heart beat so furiously against his ribs that he could almost hear it tapping out a rhythm on the bark.

"Hey, Buzz, you're not moving," Mari called up. "Are you sure you're okay?"

"I'm fine," Buzz insisted. "Just give me a moment." But still his arms tightened around the trunk.

He heard a familiar scrabbling sound, and then Ratatosk was dangling beside him, his tail securing him to the branch while the wind made him sway merrily back and forth.

Just looking at the squirrel made Buzz feel dizzy. "Ratatosk, unless you're a flying squirrel, I suggest you hold on to this tree properly." He said the words through gritted teeth.

"Just take a breath, mate." Ratatosk's voice was soft. "Don't feel bad about being scared. Yer scared because yer want to live. It's nothing to be ashamed of."

"But how am I going to do this?" Buzz asked, and he knew he wasn't just talking about the tree. He was talking about all of it. Finding the runes, waking the sleeping gods so that Loki could be defeated.

And Ratatosk understood that, too.

"Yer'll do it because yer and Mari are the only ones who can do it. Yer'll do it because this world will go kaput if yer don't. Yer'll do it because even though yer haven't realized it yet – yer and Mari were born for this."

Buzz looked into the squirrel's dark eyes. *What had Ratatosk said earlier? Truth is your most reliable guide, but your heart must be open to listen to its advice.*

The concrete he imagined around his feet crumbled into dust, and his arms loosened around the trunk.

"Thanks, Ratatosk. Come on, we've got a Roman god to find." Buzz pushed upwards, his arms and legs working to pull his body further up the tree. Ratatosk was right by his side, leaping from branch to branch.

"Hey, Buzz, slow down," Mari squawked from below.

"I thought you were good at climbing trees!"

"I am, and if I knew it was a race, I wouldn't have given you a head start," she shot back.

Buzz slowed down, but only a little bit.

As he pulled himself up onto the next bough, he saw a sliver of light between the skeletal limbs of the tree. It was a solid silver branch as bright as a sword's blade. It gleamed in front of them. Thin, but as long as the path that led up to his front door. The bark was smooth and cold. At the far end of the branch, the air was split in two, leaving a void. It wasn't a door – not really – but Buzz knew that he and Mari would have to pass through it.

He stepped out onto the metal limb to get a closer look, but his foot immediately slipped on the smooth surface and he fell backwards against the trunk. His arms and legs splayed in a lucky tangle of limbs that somehow kept him from falling.

"Buzz!" Mari cried. "You all right?"

The fear that he thought he'd left much further down the tree rushed back again, but this time Ratatosk was not next to him to calm him down. Buzz swallowed hard, trying to bring back saliva to his dry mouth.

"I've had better days," he said, getting himself into a safer position. He managed to look down through the foliage, and he saw that Mari was below him. But the squirrel was nowhere in sight.

"Where's Ratatosk?" he asked. "I've found the branch."

Mari pulled herself upwards so that she even closer to where Buzz sat. "He said he could hear something from further down the tree. He went to check."

Buzz wrinkled his nose and sniffed the air. "Do you smell that?"

Mari inhaled. "Smoke. It's smoke."

With a swish of leaves being brushed aside, Ratatosk appeared, his sides heaving. His delicate, furry head, which poked up through the foliage, glistened with sweat. "He's back." The squirrel panted. "And he's coming up here."

"Who?" Buzz asked.

"Loki?" Mari said at the same time.

The squirrel nodded. "Loki and his dragon. He saw yer bag, Buzz. He knows someone's on the tree. Yer've got to get out of here."

Buzz felt a bead of sweat roll down between his shoulder blades. "I've found the branch." He pointed upwards. "It's right there."

They heard tree limbs cracking nearby. Ratatosk eyes were wide. "So what're yer waiting for? Go!"

"But—"

"Go! He won't follow you into Saturn's world – not without more backup. He can't be working by himself."

Mari had clambered up past Buzz and was now scuttling along the solid silver limb towards the rip in the sky.

"Hurry up, Buzz." Her voice was almost completely snatched away by the wind that was coming through the rift.

Buzz climbed onto the first part of the impossibly smooth branch but stopped to look back at Ratatosk. "Come on, then," he said.

The squirrel shook his head. "I ain't coming. Someone's got to stop Loki and Nidhogg from getting up here until yer through." His red fur rippled in the wind, and he glowed so brightly in the morning sunlight that he looked like a ball of flame. He raised a paw in farewell even as the smoke behind him began to snake around his body. Plumes of black grasped at him like shadowy fingers.

"Go!" the squirrel demanded again. "I'll be fine." He then

turned and leapt into the heart of the smoke.

Buzz tried to call out the squirrel's name, but the word couldn't get past the knot in his throat. Instead, he pulled himself further onto the silver branch, moving carefully and slowly towards the rip in the sky. Mari was some distance ahead of him now, and Buzz held his breath as she stood up gingerly, balanced for a moment like a ballerina in tortoiseshell glasses.

"I guess this is the bit where we start our quest," she shouted over to him. The wind coming from the rift buffeted her strongly, and she swayed back on her heels. "Cross the threshold and all that."

"What are you going on about?" Buzz yelled. "Just get through the rift before you fall off that branch, will you?"

"We're going through together." Mari's expression was stubborn.

"I'm right behind you," Buzz promised as he pulled himself along the slender limb. He was doing his best to focus on the simple movements of putting one hand in front of the other, but he knew he was making painfully slow progress. "Just go. It's not going to help either of us if you lose your balance."

As if in answer, a gust of wind howled out from the rift and rocked Mari back on her heels once more. Her mouth was an O of surprise as her toes curled around the branch and her arms shot out to balance herself.

She took a quick breath. "See you in Saturn's realm." She edged right up to the rift. "We're going to find those runes!"

And she threw herself into the ripped air. There was no noise. No flash of light. Mari was simply not there anymore, and Buzz was all by himself on the silver branch. He got carefully to his feet and stepped towards the rift. The air coming from it smelt damp and dark, but there was another smell as well and it crept towards him from behind. Smoke. So strong now that it made his eyes water.

"Who are you?" A voice that seemed to burn all the oxygen from the air snarled from behind him. "Why do you seek the Runes of Valhalla?"

Buzz whipped round, instinctively throwing out his arms to keep his balance. A figure who was both solid and not solid had ascended the tree. *Loki.* His cloak glided over the branches in a billow of smouldering mist. Buzz couldn't really see a face through the smoke, but he glimpsed a slash of a mouth and cayenne-coloured eyes that slanted upwards like the flame of a candle.

"Who are you?" the voice asked again. "Are you kin of Odin?" The smoky figure seemed to expand his volume and spread towards him. "Answer me."

"No, I'm not," Buzz shouted back. "Where's Ratatosk?"

The figure crept closer, until the heat coming off him singed Buzz's eyelashes.

"My dragon has a new pet to play with. Come down with me and watch. It's quite a show."

A hand shot out at him, the skin pale and scarred.

Buzz leapt backwards. The wind from the rift tore at his shoulders.

He stared at Loki, straight into the candle-flame eyes. "We're going to stop you," Buzz vowed.

"I look forward to seeing you try." Loki's burnished blade of a mouth opened to show sharp teeth, and then he sprung forwards.

Buzz didn't hesitate. Half falling and half throwing himself backwards, he passed through the rip in the air.

PART II

THE RUNES OF VALHALLA

CHAPTER FOURTEEN

THE CHASE

Buzz felt himself being torn out of the world and plunged into a void. He was falling . . . upwards? He was in complete darkness, and his eyes ached with the strain of searching for any pinprick of light.

"Buzz!" Mari's voice sounded like it was travelling across centuries, and it was tiny and scared. "Buzz?"

"I'm here," he called back.

"I thought you weren't coming." He could swear that he heard tears in her voice. "I wasn't scared, you understand. I just hate the dark."

"I got a little bit held up by a furious trickster god," Buzz explained.

"You met Loki?" Mari almost sounded jealous. "Did he say anything about the rune—" But she broke off with a gasp.

"Mari?"

Silence.

"MARI?" He screamed her name. His voice filling the void but she did not reply.

Then he felt it. Hands guiding him upwards – *or was that downwards?* They reached out from the darkness, covering every inch of his skin, including his mouth. The hands were not gentle. Not rough, either. Just methodical. Hands passing him along the darkness until he was placed firmly on his feet. He felt a pressure on his back that pushed him forwards through another gap in the air and into sunlight. He was standing at the centre of a field filled with rippling wheat. The golden stalks stretched off in every direction, but around the perimeter he could see the sheer face of mountain rocks. They were inside some kind of crater.

Buzz squinted. In the distance he could just about make out Mari. She was racing after an impossibly tall figure who was wielding a scythe and cutting a path through the wheat.

Buzz set off in pursuit, through stalks of gold that were so tall they grazed his chin.

It felt good to be on solid ground again.

He caught up with Mari. *She's fast, but not as fast as me.* Her cheeks were puffing in and out as she ran, but she managed a smile.

"Why are we chasing after this guy?" Buzz asked.

Mari took a gulping breath. "He was here when I arrived. He told me that time waits for no man, then just strode off." She frowned. "It's pretty sexist, actually, as clearly I'm not a man, but I didn't even get a chance to say that because he was already halfway across the field."

"Okay," Buzz said slowly. "So we're chasing this guy so that we can tell him that he is being sexist."

Mari laughed. "You are silly, Buzz. Saturn is also known as Father Time," she explained patiently. "Plus, the Romans believed that Saturn was the god of the harvest as well as time." She pointed up ahead. "Do you see that huge scythe he's carrying? Trust me. He's the guy we need to talk to. I'm sure of it."

"All right, Sherlock, I'm convinced."

Mari grinned. "It is just a process of deduction and dismissal. No big deal. It's what all good detectives do."

Suddenly, the landscape around them changed. A fierce wind picked up, the wheat began to whither, and snow began to fall.

Buzz and Mari continued to run, but it was harder going through the snow, and the cold wind cut through their clothes.

They were at the edge of the field now, where the terrain turned rocky and soared above them.

The tall figure traversed a narrow path that wound up to the sky, his strides slowing. Mari and Buzz were finally gaining on him.

"Go get him." Mari panted. "I'm right behind you."

Buzz dipped his head and charged forwards. The cloaked man was just ahead of him now, and Buzz reached a hand out to grab the cloak. But his hand passed straight through the material. The cloaked man was made of air.

"Hey," Buzz called. "We need to talk to you."

The figure reached the front of the rock face, stepped forwards, and disappeared into the mountainside.

Buzz leapt to the place where the hooded figure had just vanished. His hands combed the mountain face, but it was solid beneath his fingers.

"Where'd he go?" Mari asked, arriving at his side.

"Right through this wall." Buzz pointed at it. "But—"

"What we waiting for then?" Mari strode forwards but gave a little yelp as she crashed into the solid wall.

"But Saturn wasn't solid like us," Buzz finished. "He was just air."

"Well that would make all the difference," Mari said. "No biggie, I've got an idea." She held up her enormous watch and tapped two of the buttons on the side.

"I don't think your GPS is going to be able to help," Buzz said. His eyes darted across the mountain face, looking for some kind of gap or entrance way.

"You sure about that?" Mari asked, as a dark blue ray beamed out of her watch and illuminated the mountainside. An area of lighter blue immediately revealed itself a few feet upwards. "There's our entry. Right on that ledge."

"Holey pyjamas!" Buzz exclaimed. "How does your watch do that? Darth Vader I get, but this?"

Mari lifted her chin proudly. "My classmates were fans of water balloons. Said it was just a bit of fun. Not to take it personally. I designed my watch so that it could assess the density of solid objects."

"So you could spot whether they were carrying water balloons or not?"

"Exactly. It worked very well at recess." She began to scale the mountain face, and Buzz followed. "I even designed a setting so that the ray could burst any hidden balloons. But my parents took me out of that school before I could test that function."

"Just so you know," Buzz said, as they got closer to the area that had been illuminated by the watch's beam on the rock face, "your classmates sound awful."

"It wasn't all their fault." Mari pulled herself onto the ledge. "I have a knack for saying things that freak people out. I know stuff about them. Their secrets."

"It doesn't matter," Buzz said, thinking of Theo Eddows. "Some people just get a kick out of making others miserable. Do we have to save the whole world or can we just save the people we like?"

"I'm not gonna answer that." Mari edged along the ledge and used her watch to light up the rock face again. Now that they were closer, Buzz could see that the surface was completely flat. There was no visible entrance, and he wondered for a second if Mari's watch was quite as advanced as she thought.

Mari began to feel along the rock face, her fingers prodding and probing. "Jackpot!" she said as her hand disappeared into an area that still looked like solid rock. She pushed her self through.

Buzz followed, plunging his arm and then his whole body into the rock.

On the other side, he found himself in a tunnel. The stone interior walls looked like a honeycomb, and each cell flickered with a dull golden light that lit up Mari's face.

"What is this place?" Buzz asked.

"The time tunnel," a voice boomed from deep within the shadowy interior. "In this place you will each see your own timelines, your destinies, your fates."

The voice was retreating. "Walk the tunnel. To survive the challenge, you will need to stay focused. No side routes, no backwards glances. If you make it to my workshop – and if you still want to ask your questions – then I will answer them. Good luck."

Mari and Buzz looked at each other. "Ratatosk did say Saturn liked games," Mari sighed.

"So we just start walking?" Buzz asked.

"I guess," Mari replied. "But I'm gonna walk quickly."

As if in answer, a countdown appeared in each of the cells on the wall.

10

9

8

7

The game is about to begin, Buzz thought. Somehow, he didn't think he was going to like the rules.

6

5

4

3

2

1

CHAPTER FIFTEEN

TIME TUNNEL

Every cell in the honeycombed walls flickered into life. Each one glowed with a different image, like a mini TV screen.

Buzz and Mari felt their way forwards, the light from the screens bathing them in a soft, golden light. Buzz had promised himself he wouldn't look, but this light in the dark tunnel drew him close.

Buzz crept towards the nearest flickering cell and watched, a smile tugging at his lips. He saw her straightaway. His mother. She had her arms open wide, and he saw himself as a small child running into them.

In the next cell, he saw his mother and father dancing around the kitchen together. It looked like the Prof was singing as they twirled around. Buzz was in his highchair, and his sister sat on the floor giggling as she watched their parents.

Buzz couldn't remember ever seeing his parents look so happy together.

In the next cell, he saw himself again. This time at Christmas. He was older – maybe nine or so. The boy wanted to open his presents. He wanted to give the presents he had made but they were waiting for Dad. They were waiting a long time. *Sorry kids, I just had to finish off some stuff*, Dad had said. Buzz remembered that Christmas Day clearly. It was the first time he'd called his father the Prof. No one had thought it would stick, but it had.

Buzz could feel that familiar anger now. That feeling he got every time his father chose his work instead of his family. Every time he forgot a birthday, an anniversary, a school play, or a parents' evening. *Why is he like that? Why can't he be like other dads?*

The next cell showed his house again, but everything in it looked worn and broken. His sister sat at the breakfast bar. Her shock of red hair was tangled and matted, and her skin looked sallow. She was eating pancakes, but they didn't look right. They were covered in fungus and yet she still ate them, chewing steadily.

Buzz's eyes travelled along the wall of cells. He saw his sister again. The kitchen was now covered in a thick layer of grime. She sat at the breakfast bar, and the pancakes on her plate were mottled and actually seemed to crawl. Her face looked haggard – she was old and young all at the same time. She stared into space, never blinking, but a tear tracked down her cheek.

In the next cell, he saw his mother. She stood on a small airstrip looking up at the sky. She was searching for something. Her plane. Her clothes were tattered and ragged, and just like Tia, her eyes looked tired and so, so old.

He saw his father again in a new cell – he was framed by darkness. The Prof was shouting, his face critical and sneering.

Buzz saw himself approaching his father – just a view of his back.

The Prof's expression changed to one of fear as the other Buzz reached for something from his pocket. And all of a sudden there was sound. "Don't do it. Don't hurt me, Buzz. I'm your father."

Buzz could feel his whole body shake, as he watched the other Buzz lift whatever it was he had in his hand.

"Stop, please." Buzz banged a fist against the cell and felt his hand pass through the surface. He pushed forwards. He had to stop the other Buzz but felt a hand on his shoulder.

"You can't go, Buzz."

Buzz whipped around to see Mari. Her face was drawn and her eyes had a bruised, wounded look to them.

"I have to stop him. Stop *me*."

"I don't know what it is you see in that cell," Mari said softly. "I can't see it. I can't hear it. But I do know that you shouldn't go in there. Remember what Saturn said. 'To survive you will need to walk the tunnel. No side routes, no backwards glances.' That's the challenge."

Buzz turned to look at the cell again, but now it was blank. He collapsed against the wall and slid to the ground. "If this tunnel shows my destiny, Mari, then I do something bad in the future."

Mari chewed at her lip. "It might not be what it seems"

"Prof was so scared of me. He asked me to stop and I didn't. I think I was going to hurt him."

Mari sat down next to him, the light from the cells putting her face in and out of shadows. "Buzz, it's this place. This time tunnel has been designed to hurt people. I think that is what Saturn wants – what he expects – but we can't let him win."

"In my timeline, everything I love is gone," Buzz tried to explain. "Everything I love has become rotten. I've become rotten. Am I just supposed to deal with that?"

"Perhaps. Maybe you do what I'm going to do and remind yourself that these are possible futures and not actual ones." Mari wrapped her arms around her legs protectively. "We're in control of our own destinies. No one else."

"What did you see?" Buzz asked. Something in Mari's voice told him that she was barely keeping herself together.

"I saw a world like the one you've described." Mari almost seemed to be talking to herself. "A rotten place. Broken. But I didn't seem to care. I didn't care that my parents looked like zombies or that my grandmother sat in a room that was filthy and festering, because I was somewhere else. And it was dark – a place of death – but I felt right at home. Then ... Then I saw – "

Mari jumped to her feet. "I'm not talking about this anymore. Come on, we're getting out of this tunnel."

"Wait – what were you going to say?"

"Nothing, okay?" She grabbed Buzz and pulled him up by his shirt, and for a moment he was struck by just how strong she was.

"Okay, this is the plan," she growled. "We're going to look into each other's eyes all the way to the end of this tunnel." Her hands tightened on the material. "That is the only thing we're going to concentrate on doing. Are we clear?"

Buzz frowned. "How are we going to do that and walk at the same time?"

Mari put her hands on Buzz's shoulders so that they looked at each other directly and his back was facing down the tunnel. "You'll have to walk backwards." Mari grinned. "It's the short straw, but it was my idea, after all."

Buzz shook his head but found himself smiling despite everything. "Why do I get the feeling I'm always going to be the one drawing the short straw?" Buzz plonked his hands on her shoulders.

"Keep your eyes on mine and we'll get to the end, I promise," Mari replied.

They began to walk, and in the dim light Buzz did his best to concentrate on looking into Mari's eyes. Yet still, at the edges of his vision he could see that the flickering cells in the wall were still throwing up images. His brain kept trying to capture the snippets and decipher what he was seeing. "Buzz, you're cheating," Mari said. "Look into my eyes."

"I'm trying." Something crunched beneath Buzz's foot. "What was that?"

Mari's gaze darted downwards and then back up again. "A skeleton. More than one. Keep walking."

Beneath his palms he could feel that Mari was shaking, and he wondered if he was as well.

"We aren't the first ones to try and get down this tunnel, are we?" he asked.

Mari kept her eyes fixed on Buzz. "No, I don't think we are. But trust me, we're not going to end up as a pile of bones in this place."

They continued to walk, and after a while Buzz didn't even flinch when he felt something crunch underfoot. *Funny how quickly you can get used to something,* he thought. *Even really horrible things.*

Mari began to squint. "Hey, I can see something. Light! I think we're almost at the end of the tunnel."

They walked faster. In fact, they were almost running. Not easy when travelling backwards.

Finally, they spilt out into a chamber and the tunnel behind them began to narrow to a pin-prick until it had disappeared entirely.

Buzz scanned the room. The chamber they were in seemed completely empty except for a heavy door with an ornately carved surface. At first glance, Buzz thought the door had a geometric pattern carved into it. But as he looked closer, he saw that the carving was actually of a man with two faces. The older face looked to the left while the younger one looked to the right. In his left hand, the man held a key, while his right hand was just an empty palm. Mari pushed at the door but it didn't budge.

Buzz noticed a large keyhole. "Looks like we'll need a key."

Mari stared all around. "But there's nothing in here except these doors."

"Then we better knock." Buzz's fingers curled into a fist and he hammered at the door.

"OW!" came a voice.

"Ouch," came another.

Buzz stopped knocking. Under his fist, the two carved faces were scowling out at him.

CHAPTER SIXTEEN

THE GATEKEEPER'S RIDDLE

"Young man, what on earth do you think you're doing?" said the old face.

"Dude, that was seriously uncool," said the young face.

Buzz dropped his hand. "Whoops," he said.

"Whoops indeed." The old face rolled his one visible eye. "The youth of today are so incredibly uncouth and uncivilized. I BLAME THE PARENTS."

The young face yawned. "He's sorry, Janus. There's no need to start going on and on."

"On and on? That's rich coming from you. All you do is go on and on about the things that you wish you could do. 'Oh, I wish I could go surfing, I wish I could go to that music festival.'" Old Janus sighed. "What I wouldn't give to sit down with a nice cup of tea, a biscuit, and a newspaper! Small, civilized pleasures."

"Janus," Mari said, almost to herself. "The Roman god of doorways."

"That's us," the two faces said as one.

"Hi," Buzz said, not quite sure who he should be looking at. "It's nice to meet you . . . um . . . both. Thing is, we really need to speak to Saturn. He said that if we got through the tunnel we could get some answers. And we really need to know where the Runes of Valhalla are so that we can stop Loki. So if you can just open up . . ."

The younger Janus laughed bitterly. "I wouldn't be so eager to see Saturn if I were you. You can't believe a word that guy says. He told us that we'd be his gatekeeper for just a little bit. And trust me, it has definitely been more than a little bit."

"I don't think it is appropriate for you to talk about our employer in such unfavourable terms," Old Janus reprimanded him.

"These are the facts," Young Janus continued, ignoring the other half of his face completely, "he's a dishonest crook who carved us into this door without our permission, and that is not cool. I was happy living my life and he used the old magic to trap us."

"It is an honour to protect time itself," Old Janus intoned.

"There's no honour in protecting that paranoid wreck." Young Janus sniffed. "Still, maybe I'd be paranoid as well if I did what that lot did to Loki."

"Saturn played no part in that," Old Janus pointed out.

"He didn't stop them. And why would he, when his buddy Odin had already promised him Loki's day?"

"Be quiet," Old Janus growled. "You've said enough."

"Make me," Young Janus growled back.

"Exactly how long have you been here?" Mari questioned.

"That's a tricky one. Time is a slippery thing in Saturn's realm," Young Janus explained. "In this dimension all things run in parallel. It could be a year, or it could be a hundred or a thousand, but I know it is longer than I wanted it to be." He pursed his lips. "And he refuses to let us go."

"I'm sorry that he trapped you here," Mari said. "It must be horrible to be a prisoner in a place you hate. But we really do need you to let us through to speak to Saturn."

"Child, I will let you speak to him," Old Janus said.

"That's great," Mari said. "Can—"

"But you will need to pay the price," Old Janus explained.

"The price?" Buzz and Mari repeated.

"I'm afraid so," Young Janus said. "The thing is, any door that has us carved into it is going to be pretty much impossible to pass through unless we give you permission. But even if we do give permission, it always comes with a price. It's pretty standard practice."

"Okay, so what's the price?" Mari asked.

"We can't tell you that, either, I'm afraid," Old Janus said.

"This is impossible." Buzz snapped.

"It is not supposed to be easy." Old Janus's tone was mocking.

"That's the point of having a gatekeeper. Nothing gets through us unless we will it."

"Ah, come on, old guy, maybe we can give them a little clue," Young Janus pleaded.

"We can't, really—" Old Janus said. "It's not in the job description."

"Neither was being trapped in the door," Young Janus countered. "If these kids can stop Loki, then maybe Saturn will chill out and free us."

Old Janus seemed to consider this for a moment.

"Think about the biscuits," Young Janus said.

"And the newspaper," Mari added.

"Small, civilized pleasures," Buzz finished.

"Fine," Old Janus said. "But *I'm* giving them the clue. Understand?"

"Agreed."

"Actually, think of it less as a clue and more as a riddle." Old Janus scrunched up his half of his face in concentration and closed his eye.

"Psst," Young Janus said to Buzz and Mari. "Don't let me down, okay? If you deal with Loki, we might all have a chance of going back to normal."

Normal, Buzz repeated in his head. That would be nice. He was pretty sure normal wouldn't include killing his father.

Old Janus's eyes sprang open. "I am now ready to deliver your riddle." He smirked. "You work out the answer, and you will know what payment we need to receive. But I doubt you'll get that far."

"Okay," Mari said. "We're ready."

Buzz bit his lip. He was good at running and kicking balls into goals. But words were not his thing. It was part of the reason he and the Prof never seemed able to finish a conversation without it turning into an argument. Buzz never had the right words to talk to him.

"I am two-faced but bear only one," Old Janus began. "I have no legs but travel widely. Humanity spill much blood over me. Kings and queens leave their imprint on me. I have greatest power when given away, yet craving for me keeps me locked away. Who or what am I?"

Buzz let out a breath he didn't realize he'd been holding. *The riddle was easy.* He grinned at Young Janus and then Mari. "Don't worry, I've got this," he said.

"You have!" Mari sounded delighted.

"You have?" Young Janus sounded dubious.

"Sure I have. The riddle is talking about you. You are two-faced, and Saturn is craving for your protection, which means that he keeps you locked away in this door."

"Wrong!" Old Janus sounded gleeful.

"Dude, that reasoning stinks," Young Janus said mournfully. "The answer needs to fit with each line of the riddle. That's remedial riddling. Riddling 101. What about the whole bit about having no legs and kings and queens leaving their imprint?

You didn't even try and answer that bit."

"I don't know," Buzz mumbled. "I thought since I'd worked out the first line it didn't matter if I didn't exactly know what the rest of the riddle was going on about." He stopped and wished that the starkly empty chamber had just a little bit of clutter to hide behind.

"And this young man is going to save us from Loki." Old Janus snorted dismissively. "I mean—"

"Leave him alone," Mari commanded. "It was his first riddle and everyone's allowed to make mistakes."

She smiled reassuringly at Buzz and his need to hide somewhere lessened. "Are we allowed another go?" Mari continued. "We were just warming up."

"Well, not really," Old Janus said. "It's not the done thing when it comes to the business of riddles, and we take our role of gatekeeper very seriously."

Young Janus opened his mouth to say something but Old Janus spoke over him.

"However, your first answer was so amusing I must admit that I'd rather like to hear your next attempt. It's your last chance, mind."

Mari turned to Buzz. "Come on, then. Let's solve this thing."

Buzz snorted. "I'm not going to be much help, am I?"

"Hey, don't look so glum. It doesn't matter that you got it wrong." Her eyes twinkled. "This whole thing is just a method of deduction and dismissal, remember. It's what detectives do."

"Right." Buzz rubbed the back of his neck. He knew that Mari was only being nice, but he appreciated it.

"So first, I think we need to slow this whole thing down," she said. "And start right at the beginning." Mari tapped her upper lip thoughtfully. "For starters, what has a face?"

"A face?"

"Yep, the riddle talks about two faces," Mari explained patiently. "But to start with, we need to think about what has one."

"Okay, a person does," Buzz said, feeling silly for stating the obvious.

"Yep, but so do a clock, a mountain, and a wall," Mari added. "So what has two faces?" She looked up at the door. "Other than Janus, of course." She winked at Buzz.

Buzz tried to think, flipping the question over in his mind like a coin . . . a coin . . .

A COIN!

It had two sides to it, two faces, but it only had one head.

"I suppose a person can be two-faced," Mari continued. "There were certainly loads of two-faced people at my school. Jenny Granger was a two-faced snake. Did you know you can get two-headed snakes? They are called—"

"Mari, I've got it."

"Really?" Mari sounded unsure.

"Really?" Young Janus sounded even less sure.

"Oh, goody," Old Janus said. "Go on, then. I'm ready for another good laugh."

Mari leapt forwards and put a finger to Buzz's lips. "Don't you dare say a word."

"But—"

"Don't do it. All good detectives consult with their partner first. Didn't I say that before?" She took his arm and led him a few steps away from the door.

Buzz smiled. He'd never seen Sherlock Holmes consult with anyone other than himself in the TV shows. Frankly, Doctor Watson was just there for window dressing. What was really amazing was that for once, Buzz might actually be the Sherlock Holmes in this situation. He ran though each line of the riddle again, grinning because a coin could answer each part. "So do you want to hear the answer, then?"

"Sure I do." Mari was trying to sound upbeat, but her face just looked nervous.

"A coin," he said. "A coin is two-faced."

"A coin," Mari repeated, her eyes widening. "Of course. A coin travels far even though it has no legs, wars are fought over money, and a king or queen imprints themeselves on a coin."

"And coins are most powerful when they are given away," Buzz finished, "but people like to hoard money. Lock it up in a safe place."

"Wow, Buzz, that is pretty impressive," Mari said. "Don't get me wrong. I'm sure I would have worked that out eventually, but that is very impressive."

"Course you would have done, Watson. Come on, let's go and tell Janus."

"Here they come," Old Janus crowed as they approached. "This should be fun."

Mari turned to Buzz. "I think the pleasure should be all yours."

Buzz bowed gallantly and turned to the gatekeeper.

"The answer is a coin," he said.

Old Janus's imperious look slipped. "Oh," he spluttered. "That's correct. Er . . . well done." The words were clearly choking him.

Young Janus smiled widely. "Great work, dude. Now you've just got to pay us."

"Excuse me?" Mari and Buzz said at the same time.

"You must now pay us a coin to pass," Old Janus demanded, regaining some of his composure. Young Janus was frowning. "You do have a coin, right?"

Buzz thought about his bag with all of his money in it, at the bottom of the tree. "No," he groaned.

"How about you?" Young Janus asked Mari. "Have you got us anything that you can offer as payment?"

She shook her head, but even as she did so, Buzz realized that it wasn't true. Around her neck Mari wore the chain and her half of Sunna's pendant.

"What about the pendant?" Buzz pointed at it. "It's gold."

Mari put her hand to her throat protectively. "But we're keeping it safe for Sunna."

"Yeah, it will be really safe trapped here between the time tunnel and Saturn's workshop," Young Janus pointed out. "Listen, the old boot is right. We're really going to need some kind of payment if you want to pass through this door."

"Old boot!" Old Janus cried. "How dare you, you impertinent, impudent, insolent pup."

"Hey, I'm agreeing with you, and I still get told off," Young Janus said huffily. "It's literally impossible to win with you."

Mari unclasped the chain from her neck and gently tugged off the gold pendant. "Here you go." She held up the pendant to the squabbling faces. "But how exactly am I supposed to give this to you?"

"Hang on," the wooden door began to creak, and the carved, open palm belonging to Young Janus pushed its way out of the door ever so slightly Mari carefully draped the pendant over the raised edges of the hand.

"Thank you." Young Janus's hand retreated back into the flatness of the door and the pendant became a carving in the shape of a lightning bolt.

"You may now enter." Old Janus's voice was almost lost beneath the tremble and shake of the door as it swung open.

"Good luck," Young and Old Janus said as one and Mari and Buzz passed through the door.

CHAPTER SEVENTEEN

THE CLOCKMAKER'S WORKSHOP

The sound of ticking was overpowering as they entered the next chamber. They immediately saw why – the room, with its incredibly high ceiling, was a workshop, crammed full of clocks. All types: grandfather clocks, pendulum clocks, spring-driven devices, digital clocks, sundials, cuckoo clocks, and piles and piles of watches and timepieces.

In the far corner, a man in a long black cloak was hunched over a scuffed wooden workbench. He held a tiny pair of tweezers and a screwdriver but gave a squawk of surprise as Buzz and Mari entered the workshop. Swiftly, he clambered over the pile of clocks, bumping his hip on a sundial, and hopped up onto a raised throne.

He sat down, but then cursed and quickly jumped off his

throne to retrieve his scythe from where it leant against a grandfather clock.

He settled himself back onto his throne. "Welcome," he said in a booming voice. "You are in the presence of Saturn. Please try not to be too awed."

Now that Buzz was closer, he decided that Saturn definitely looked like a god. He had flowing white hair and a beard that only a god could get away with. His eyes flashed like lightning.

"Tell me. What is it you want to ask Father Time?"

Mari coughed to clear her throat. "I would have asked you in the wheatfield but you didn't give me a chance. We need to find the Runes of Valhalla and reunite them with their day guardians. Can you tell us where they are?"

Saturn laughed. "Oh, you are mistaken. That wasn't me in the field. Rather, a projection – your generation call it a hologram, I think." Saturn removed a watch from the voluminous folds of his cloak and began to polish its face. "You can't really expect that I'd sit around waiting for visitors in a wheatfield. I have time to manage."

"But we chased after you?" Buzz said.

"That's the idea. Anyone who comes to my realm is supposed to follow the apparition and, if they're lucky, enter the time tunnel. Most people just end up stuck in that field and die of the cold." Saturn breathed on the watch face and polished even more vigorously. "If they're a bit luckier, they make it to the time tunnel, where they become jabbering wrecks and stay for all time." He looked up at them. "I had been worried that the challenge was too hard but here you are."

"That's just horrible!" Mari exclaimed. "You basically enjoy stranding people in fields or tormenting them in freaky tunnels. Why do you make it so hard to find you?"

"Gods are not supposed to be easily accessible," Saturn said magisterially. "If we were, we'd be just like everyone else."

"What a ridiculo—"

"Okay, time out!" Buzz shouted, feeling an awful lot like a referee. "We really need to find the Runes of Valhalla."

For the first time, Saturn seemed to take real notice of what they were asking him.

"The Runes of Valhalla? But why? They are only to be found if Loki walks free."

"Trust me," Buzz said. "He's free and he's angry."

Saturn jumped to his feet, his scythe falling to the ground. "Loki is free? Then the prophecy is coming true?"

"Yep." Mari looked almost pleased at Saturn's discomfort.

"He must be stopped!" Saturn said. "The trickster cannot be allowed to end the world."

"We know!" Buzz exclaimed, reminding himself to stay calm. "That's why we're here."

Saturn peered at Buzz and then Mari closely. But you're not Sunna. No, neither of you are Sunna. Your auras are all wrong."

"Loki has Sunna," Mari said. "But she told us what we need to do."

Saturn turned on his heel and began to pace along the platform beside his throne. His cloak was a swish of black flaring out behind him. "Poor Sunna," he kept repeating. "Odin could only choose one day guardian to be Loki's watcher." Saturn bent down to pick up his scythe and resumed pacing, the scythe clunking on the ground as he stalked along. "I mean, having Sunna linked to Loki's awakening sounded good at the time. All she needed to do was come and find me and I would help her wake the other Norse gods." He shook his head. "Now the game has been lost even before it has truly begun."

"The game is not lost," Buzz said fiercely. "That's why Mari and I are here. We're going to stop Loki."

Saturn snorted with laughter. "This is no quest for children."

"Oh, really," Mari said. "Sunna doesn't think that and neither does Ratatosk. He said the runes will lead us to the day guardians."

The God of Time was trembling. "You don't understand. Loki is one of the most powerful forces to have ever been unleashed. I'm no fighter."

Mari narrowed her eyes. "Then help us, instead of just telling us we've lost already."

Saturn's hand tightened on the scythe. "Help? That's all I've been doing – ever since Odin dragged me into this sorry mess and asked me to look after the runes and become the day guardian for Saturday." He stopped pacing. "Obviously, it made more sense to split the runes up and so I gave my three sons two each."

"You mean you gave the responsibility to others," Mari said.

Saturn glared at Mari but did not correct her.

"Wow, you're a piece of work," Mari said. "You don't want any responsibilities at all."

Saturn looked thunderous. "Everyone is living their lives on fastforward in your realm," he snapped. "No one has time. That's what they say all day long. *I have no time.*" Saturn's face wore a wounded expression. "So why should I care about your realm when I have my glorious workshop? My clocks are the most loyal of subjects." He waved a hand around the chamber. "You judge me, but it's not only I who has retreated, you know. Many of the other gods have simply disappeared entirely because no one believes in them anymore, and those that are left have taken themselves off to other hidden realms."

Buzz could feel his frustration mounting. "Okay, look, we need to stop Loki and break the Saturday time lock. We need to get the runes back to Crowmarsh. Where are your sons?"

Saturn frowned. "Of course, with Sunna taken, your realm must be deep in an unmorrow curse." He grimaced. "Goodness, things will getting a bit . . . unsettled."

"Unsettled," Buzz repeated.

"Maybe worn down is a better way to put it. The poor souls in your realm won't know what's hit them. It's not natural to live the same day again and again."

Buzz thought back to the images of his home in the time tunnel. How strange his sister had looked. He had to stop the unmorrow curse. "You could fix this," Buzz said. "You're Father Time. Can't you reverse everything so that Sunna isn't kidnapped or Loki isn't freed?"

Saturn's cheeks reddened. "I could do that – of course I could. But I don't believe in meddling."

"Liar, liar, pants on fire," Mari muttered.

"Excuse me," Saturn spluttered.

"Liar." Mari pointed at him. "You can't reverse time. You're not powerful enough."

Saturn jumped to his feet. "I could extinguish you from all time with a click of my fingers," he snarled. "Erase you from the memory of all who have loved you or will ever love you."

Mari crossed her arms. "Prove it."

"Mari," Buzz warned. "Stop winding him up."

"I'll do it," Saturn threatened. His thumb and middle finger were a whisper away from meeting together. "It will take one click. Unless you apologize right now."

"No way, no how." Mari's back was as straight as a flagpole and her chin was tilted high. "Why don't you just start telling the truth?"

"You've made your choice." Saturn's brought his fingers together and clicked.

CHAPTER EIGHTEEN

THREE CLOCKS

Nothing happened.

Mari still stood there, her chin jutting out defiantly.

The god's shoulders dropped, and he slumped onto his throne.

"I can't reverse time," he whispered. "Haven't been able to for years. Not since mortals stopped believing in me." He glared at Mari. "I've got no power, okay? In fact, every time I leave this workshop, I get weaker."

"But you're still a day guardian," Buzz said. "You're in charge of Saturday."

"Yes and I hate it. Each day guardian must be present in your realm for the order of things to be maintained, so have to I pop back every once in a while to make sure I do my part." Saturn snorted. "That's why Odin and the other day guardians chose to put their god aspects to sleep in their mortal hosts so that they could stay in your realm." He waved a hand. "The day guardians are a bit like gravity. You don't notice them most of the time, but you would if they disappeared entirely." The god shook his head. "Truth is, you're right. I never really cared about being a day guardian; I did it because Odin asked. But to be a god was extraordinary. The best." He sighed. "At the time, I thought Odin and his kind were deranged when they put their powers into the runes to rejuvenate. But at least their powers have been preserved. They haven't faded away over time like mine."

"Hang on – so why are we all so worried about Loki?" Mari asked slowly. "Won't he be just as powerless as you? He doesn't have a rune, and he doesn't have worshippers, so he can't exactly recharge."

"You do not have a sympathetic bone in your body, do you, young lady?" Saturn said. "I've just opened up my heart to you."

Mari stared back at him stonily.

"It's hard to know what state Loki will be in," Saturn said. "He's been in the ground a long time, and his worshippers are all gone, but then, he was always different from the rest of us. Loki comes from chaos. That place where fire, water, earth, and air boil as one. That place where everything started." Saturn bit his lip. "Because Loki comes from chaos, he can feed off it as well, and if your world is in the unmorrow curse it certainly has chaos." Saturn hugged his arms, and for a moment he looked like an old man who was no longer sure of himself. "Thank the gods he doesn't know where I am. He'd blame me for stealing his day. Say I was involved in his capture."

Buzz winced. "But he does know where you are."

"No, he doesn't," Saturn said confidently. "My realm is hidden from him. When Odin replanted the World Tree in the Tangley Woods, he ensured that the tree would not reveal my location to Loki."

"Well, we kinda made it visible," Buzz said. "He saw us come here and he knows we're coming for the runes."

Saturn's expression became very still. "What?"

Buzz was going to reply, but a loud pounding at the door stopped him. The whole chamber quaked. Cracks crept across the surface of the door, and dust from the stone wall that encased the entrance rained down.

"He's here," Saturn said. "Loki is here."

"But Janus will stop him from getting in, right?" Buzz asked.

"Janus will do their best, but I was a fool to believe that anyone could keep Loki out. How can you keep chaos out?" Saturn leapt from his throne, sweeping the contents of one of his worktables to the floor. Racing around the workshop, he placed three clocks on the table.

"The runes you seek can be found using these three clocks. Choose one to begin your quest."

The pounding on the door was even fiercer now, and the sound of wood creaking and then cracking filled the chamber.

A voice that hissed and spat like a funeral pyre seeped under the door. "Saturn, is this any way to treat a friend? We have so much to catch up on. And you owe me, old man. You owe me."

Saturn pointed to the first clock. "This is an astronomical clock and will open a portal to the cloud realm, where you will find my son Jupiter, god of the sky. He has the first two runes, which hold the powers of Sunna and Mani." He pointed to the next device. "This is a water clock, which will open a portal to my son Neptune, god of the sea. He has the second two runes, which hold the powers of Tyr and Odin." Saturn's hand moved over to the last clock, which glinted with gold. "This is an ormolu clock. Many call it a death clock." He touched the golden clock gently, his finger tracing the gilded edge. "It's a thing of true beauty, but the men who made these clocks often died for their art because the gold veneer used to embellish the clock killed them with its toxicity. This clock will take you to my son Pluto, god of the underworld. He has the last two runes, which hold the power of Thor and Frigga."

The door gave a splintering crash, and Saturn flinched. "I can't promise that my sons will welcome you. But this is all I can do to help."

Buzz stepped towards the astronomical clock, his eyes sweeping over the weight-driven device with its train of gears, and etched star map. It reminded him of the ceiling in his room.

"Mari, shall we choose this one?" Buzz looked over and saw that Mari was staring at the death clock, the gold reflected in her glasses. "Mari? What do you think?" She still didn't respond.

Buzz shrugged to himself. "We choose Jupiter's realm."

The God of Time stepped forwards and, concentrating on

the star map, pressed two of the shining nodes on the device. A pair of stars shot out of the clock and zipped around the room with a high-pitched ringing noise.

"You each need to catch one of the stars before its light goes out, and then ask it to take you to Jupiter," Saturn said. "Your star will do the rest."

Buzz nodded, his eyes tracking the stars. They were already slowing down a bit, their light fading gradually.

"Mari, come on!" he called as he climbed up onto one of the benches and watched the star drift towards him.

Mari pulled her gaze away from the death clock. Her expression was almost wistful.

"Are you sure we shouldn't start with Pluto?" She said the words as if in some kind of daze.

"Too late for that now," Saturn said. "Your friend made the choice. Now catch one of these stars before it winks out completely. I won't be able to call on more stars before Loki appears." He looked at the door. It was still standing, but only just.

Buzz climbed from the bench onto the table and reached for a star. His fingers just grazed its warm brilliance.

"Come on, Mari," Buzz said, reaching again.

Mari dragged herself from the death clock and leapt onto one of the tables as well.

"Good luck in your quest." Saturn had tidied away the three clocks and was now heading towards the door. "Time is on your side." He smiled. "I mean that."

"Where are you going?" Buzz asked as his fingers closed around a star.

"To let Loki in. Janus should not have to pay for my cowardice, and I'm not sure the door will stand much longer. I'll do my best to throw Loki off the scent."

The star was now in Buzz's grip, and it vibrated in his palm, making his hand tingle. Looking over at Mari, he saw that she had a star in her grasp also. She nodded at him.

"Take us to Jupiter," they said as one.

CHAPTER NINETEEN

STAR TRAVEL

As soon as the words were uttered, Buzz felt himself compress and his eardrums pop. He looked over at Mari and watched in amazement as she was sucked into the heart of her star before realizing that the same thing was happening to him. White light flooded over him, cocooning him, and he shot upwards towards a small aperture that was carved into the high ceiling.

Just before the light got too bright, he gazed down and saw Saturn open the door. A figure of smoke and burning embers stood at the entrance, grinning with a flaming mouth.

Buzz and Mari flew through the hole in the ceiling, through a funnel-like narrowing, and then they were outside. Still they travelled up, until they could see the very edge of space. All that separated them from the inkiness of the universe was a swathe of cloud, and it was here that their stars stopped.

Buzz felt himself start to expand, but the star stayed the

same size, and like a chick hatching from an egg, he burst out of it. He was standing on a rainbow path where row upon row of tall black units balanced on clouds, each one winking with blue lights. Large birds darted in between the units, flapping their huge wings and creating a cool breeze.

"What are those black things?" Buzz asked, turning to Mari, who had shaken off the remnants of her star. "And what are those birds doing?"

"They look like data storage towers," Mari said. "You know, for holding everyone's uploaded photos and music." She watched the flapping wings for a moment. "And I think those birds are trying to keep the units cool."

The birds began to caw excitedly as one of the data storage units shifted from a cloud and onto the rainbow path. Then, on mechanical feet, it clunked over to them.

The top of the data storage unit popped open, and the face of a man was beamed up into the sky. The man was tanned and clean shaven, and he wore an open-collared shirt, with expertly styled hair that was the right side of floppy.

"Welcome to the Cloud," he said in a smooth, laid-back voice. "Where anything that can be stored is stored."

"This is the Cloud," Mari said, gazing about in wonder. "As in *the* Cloud!" She reached out and touched one of the data towers. "We're actually in the place where all our data, all our electronic memories, are kept."

The face flashed perfectly white, perfectly straight teeth.

"I am Jupiter. My dominion is the sky," he said. "If mortals were going to start worshipping something called the Cloud, then you'd better believe that I wasn't going to let an opportunity like that pass. All it required was a bit of retraining." He glanced at the discarded stars on the ground. "What can I do for you? Your mode of transport tells me that Dad sent you."

"We're looking for the Runes of Valhalla," Buzz said. "Your father said that you have Sunna's and Mani's."

"Ah, yes, the runes of the sun and the moon," Jupiter said. "I've been keeping them safe. Loki is free then?"

"He is, and the only way we're going to stop him is by gathering up runes and returning them to our realm," Buzz said.

A frown marred Jupiter's perfectly smooth forehead. "It may not be quite as easy as that."

Buzz scrubbed a hand over his face. *Was it ever easy?* "Why?"

"A virus, called EarthWorm." Jupiter looked miserable. "Not only has he got the runes, he keeps on slithering through the Cloud and eating all my data and files, too. If this continues, people are going to stop believing in the Cloud, and I'll be out of a job. *Again.* A sad, old, forgotten god, just like the others."

"But why does EarthWorm have the runes?" Buzz asked. "You said you've been keeping them safe."

Jupiter looked embarrassed. "Do I have to say?"

"Well, since the runes are the only things that are going to stop Loki from destroying our realm and therefore all the people who worship you, I think so," Mari replied.

"EarthWorm has the runes because he has me," Jupiter muttered. "He swallowed me whole, and the runes were in my pocket."

"Oh, that's just great!" Mari threw up her hands in disbelief.

"But if you've been swallowed whole, how are we talking to you?" Buzz asked. "Are we talking to your hologram?"

Jupiter shook his head. "I backed myself up onto one of the servers, luckily. Thing is, EarthWorm keeps on coming and eating up more and more of my data. He loves chaos and is feeding off the anarchy he's creating. That's what sustains him. He doesn't even properly digest the information he eats. It just sits there in his gut along with me."

"Okay," Buzz said. "If we want the runes, we're going to have to destroy EarthWorm and free you. Is that right?"

"That's about the sum of it," Jupiter said. "But don't underestimate EarthWorm. You need to be smart." Jupiter gave a high whistle, and one of the birds that had been flapping at a data tower hopped over to him. "Guide these two to the junk cloud, please. They don't fly, so stick to the superhighway," he instructed.

The bird bobbed his head and spread his wings, then soared upwards on a jet of air, hovering just above them.

"Hey, we haven't actually agreed to this little quest, you know," Buzz protested.

Jupiter flashed a smile. "What other choice do you have? Are you going to stick around here talking to a huge head for the rest of your life?" Jupiter winked. "You need me free if you want those runes, or if you want me to download you to your next destination."

There was no arguing with that.

Buzz and Mari took off after the bird overhead, sliding along the rainbow path past the rows and rows of servers.

In the distance, they could see a collection of defunct objects spinning in their own orbits – ancient satellites, rocket motors, and flecks of paint that danced like confetti in the wind. The coiled length of an enormous worm rested on an abandoned rocket platform. Its skin was thin and translucent, and beneath it Buzz could see strings of binary code and pulses of electricity.

As Buzz and Mari approached, the worm began to uncoil itself, foot after foot of rippling translucence, and Buzz caught a glimpse of a body in a linen suit lying very still within its belly. *Jupiter. The god wasn't lying.*

The bird above them gave a caw of farewell and wheeled in the sky before beating a hasty retreat back to its companions.

"What exactly is the plan here?" Buzz whispered out of the side of his mouth.

"Haven't a clue," Mari responded.

"But you're supposed to be Sherlock!"

"It's true, normally by this point I'd have a brilliant idea," Mari said. "But I'm drawing a blank on how to destroy a virus worm who just so happens to have swallowed a Roman god."

"Not just any virus worm." Buzz felt the need to clarify.

"A chaos-loving virus worm." He peered at the creature more closely. "Who looks like one of those weird balloon animals that bad clowns make."

The EarthWorm was directly in front of them now and reared up, its head weaving from side to side like a snake.

"Maybe we just talk to him," Mari said, craning her neck to look up at the worm. "I mean, Jupiter tried to fight with him and that didn't work, so maybe diplomacy is a better option."

Buzz and Mari both stood there. Neither saying a word. Neither moving a step closer to the giant worm.

"Well, go on, then," Mari said. "Say hello to him."

"Why me?"

"People don't tend to like me, Buzz." Mari spread her arms wide. "I rub them up the wrong way. Surely the fact that I had to invent a watch that identifies and destroys water balloons is a clue?"

"Well, Theo Eddows hates me," Buzz protested, knowing already that he was going to lose this argument. "He put my phone down the toilet."

"That's one person." Mari snorted derisively. "Pretty much my whole school disliked me. Will you just say hello to the worm?"

"Fine." Buzz stepped forwards and held up a hand. "Greetings, EarthWorm. We come in peace." *Man, I sound like a bad* Star Trek *episode.*

A whirring sound and a series of clicks seemed to come from the worm. "You looking at me, kid?" the worm said after a moment. Its voice was high and thin like the feedback you get on speakers, and then it giggled and the sound was the chugging of a laptop booting up. "Not in Kansas anymore."

Mari and Buzz looked at each other.

"Why is this thing talking in film quotes?" Buzz whispered.

"I literally have no idea," Mari responded.

"'Come a little closer,' said the spider to the fly," the EarthWorm said. "That's one small step for man, one giant leap for mankind."

And now quotes from nursery rhymes and the moon landing, Buzz thought. It had to mean something, but he wasn't sure what.

Buzz took a step closer. "As I said, we've come in peace."

His gaze flicked to where he could see Jupiter through the worm's skin. He pointed to the outline of the god in the worm's belly. "You and Jupiter have not got off to the best start, but we'd like to change that." Buzz flashed a smile. "So, if you could just regurgitate or whatever it is that you do, then perhaps we could all sit down and talk."

"Jupiter mine. My precious." The worm giggled again. "Life is like a box of chocolates. You never know what you're gonna get." The worm's massive head then hurtled down and Buzz only just managed to leap out of the way as it smashed on the rainbow bridge.

"Hey!" Mari said. "That's not fair. We were trying to be nice."

"Nice guys finish last," the worm replied, and his head swung towards Mari and smashed down again.

But Mari was quicker. She was already clambering up onto a pile of space rubble that spun in the air.

The worm gazed down at her and then lurched forwards, its head barging into the base of the rubble, scattering it through the cloudy sky.

Mari flew through the air, hitting the rainbow bridge hard. She slipped along the superhighway like a puck on ice, her hands scrabbling for purchase. She only just managed to grab the edge of the bridge as she went careering over it.

"Mari!" Buzz got to his feet and staggered towards her. "Hang on." The Darth Vader voice of her watch was her only response. "You are approximately infinity miles from Tangley Woods."

The worm made a noise that could only be described as a coo of delight and stopped in his tracks.

"I've been waiting for you, Obi-Wan," the EarthWorm said. *"We meet again, at last. The circle is now complete. When I left you, I was but the learner; now I am the master."*

The worm's eyes flickered more quickly and the whirring noise within him seemed to be increasing.

"Obi-Wan never told you what happened to your father?"

"He told me enough! He told me you killed him!"

"No ... I am your father!"

The worm giggled again, and Buzz could see something that looked very much like joy on its strange face.

EarthWorm likes films, he realized. *All that data he consumed must have contained loads of them.*

The worm was gliding towards Mari, who had pulled herself back onto the bridge. Its strange eyes were looking at the watch on her wrist as the gadget kept on calling out the coordinates to Tangley Woods in its Darth Vader voice.

Mari was trapped on the edge of the bridge. There was nowhere to go.

"Mari, throw me the watch," he yelled.

Mari's mouth dropped open. "I'm about to get eaten by a worm at worst or pushed off the bridge at best and you want my watch." She looked furious.

"Just trust me," Buzz begged. "You do trust me, don't you?"

Mari hesitated for a moment and then nodded. "Of course I do, Buzz." She hurled over the watch to him.

Buzz grabbed it and strapped it to his wrist. Darth Vader greeted him in much the same way he greeted everyone else: with directions.

"Hey," Buzz called. "Fancy this bit of data? Come and get it."

EarthWorm whipped around and shot out towards him.

"Buzz, what are you doing?" Mari cried, leaving the edge of the superhighway and chasing after the worm.

"Stay where you are!" Buzz called back. But Mari did not stop.

Buzz held his breath as the worm reared up over him, its strange black pupils flickering like the cursor on a computer screen, and then it swooped down and swallowed him whole.

CHAPTER TWENTY

INSIDE THE WORM

Buzz expected everything to be dark and sticky and gloopy inside, but the reverse was true. It was like he was in a huge balloon filled with air that was heavy with static – like the sky before a storm. He could smell electricity. Strings of glowing code swept around him and through him. He was weightless, and he whooshed through the worm's body, loving the rushing sensation of freedom and the data that rained down on him, welcoming the facts, files, and documents that exploded behind his eyes.

For a moment, he almost forgot that he had a plan – his mind felt so full of the worm and all that it knew. When he remembered, he felt regret that he would have to leave this feeling behind.

But there is no other way. How could he enjoy his submersion into this amazing world of data if his own world were destroyed?

EarthWorm was a virus, and Buzz was the antiviral software. His hand went to the buttons on the side of the watch. He'd seen which one Mari had pressed before to scan the mountainside for an entrance in Saturn's realm. Now it was time to press the other one.

His finger rested on the button that Mari had designed to burst water balloons. The button that was going to burst EarthWorm. She hadn't tested it. But it would work. *It had to work.*

He felt something bang into his side, and he saw Jupiter floating in the light and air, his eyes closed and his breathing shallow.

It was time. He pressed the button, and a red light beamed out from the watch and hit the translucent side of the worm's body.

BOOM!

The worm was gone, and Buzz was lying on the rainbow bridge, watching bits of code drift off into the ether.

"Buzz?" Mari knelt down beside him. "Are you okay?"

Buzz sat up. He felt better than okay. He felt amazing. Extraordinary, even. Something had changed in him. But he wasn't quite ready to tell Mari that yet. Not until he understood properly what had happened. "I'm fine," he said. "How are you?"

"Much better now that I know you're alive." She tilted her head to one side. "How'd you do it? How'd you explode the worm?"

Buzz unstrapped her watch from his wrist and handed it back to her. "Your water balloon exploder function."

Mari grinned. "It works!" The smile slipped off her face. "Hey, that was pretty dumb, Buzz. I told you I hadn't tested it."

"Yeah, but I knew that it'd do the trick."

"How?"

"Because I know you."

"You trusted my invention," she whispered. "You trusted me." She held out a hand and pulled him to his feet. "Listen, Buzz, I need to tell you what I saw in the time tun—"

A low groan to their left interrupted her. Jupiter lay on the ground, his eyes still closed. They swiftly knelt by his side, and Mari gently touched the god's shoulder.

Jupiter's eyes snapped open. He sat bolt upright.

"Wow, what a trip!" he exclaimed. He looked up at them and jumped to his feet.

He slapped a hand on Buzz's shoulder. "You are the *Homo sapiens* who freed me. Why would you do that?"

Buzz and Mari exchanged a glance.

"We came for the runes," Mari said.

There was not a flicker of remembrance on the god's face.

"You have no idea who we are, do you?" Buzz questioned.

"I have spent several days in the belly of a data-eating worm. I'm going to have an idea about almost everything now."

"What do you mean?" Mari asked.

"Young lady, do you know what happened to Odin when he spent nine days and nine nights as a prisoner of the World Tree?" Jupiter asked.

"Yes. He was given all the knowledge in the world." The answer flew from Buzz's mouth.

Mari frowned at him. "How'd you know that?"

He shrugged. "Must have heard the Prof say it at some point."

Jupiter smiled at him with knowing eyes. "Hanging on that tree was the hardest thing Odin had ever done. By doing it, he was given the secrets of the universe and immense power. But that knowledge came at a price. Odin became distrustful. His infinite knowledge told him that no one could ever be truly trusted. That we all have secrets." Jupiter took two stones out of his pocket. They both had symbols carved into them. "Being inside that worm for all that time flooded me with knowledge. I know now what Odin felt."

He held out a closed palm to Buzz and Mari. "These are for you." He opened his palm to reveal the runes. "I give you these willingly as a thank-you for saving my life."

Mari and Buzz both reached for the runes at the same time, their hands bumping in their eagerness.

"Sorry." Buzz smiled at his friend. "You have one and I'll have the other."

Mari nodded, her eyes wide as she took Mani's rune, which had a diamond symbol carved into it.

Buzz took Sunna's rune and tested the weight of it in his hand. It was surprisingly heavy for such a small pebble, and it felt perfectly smooth except for the grooves of Sunna's lightning bolt insignia.

"Thanks for this," Buzz said, looking up at Jupiter. "But now we need the next two. They are with your brother Neptune."

"Say no more," Jupiter said. "I'll download you safely to his location." He inclined his head. "Give Neptune my regards."

The god of the sky then clicked his fingers, and Buzz felt himself disintegrate into the air. His thoughts exploded like fireworks as his brain rapidly processed what was happening. He had been dematerialized and turned into a wave of energy. He could feel himself flowing downwards, and as he rippled through the air he heard Jupiter's voice.

"The EarthWorm has given us both a gift." The god's words sparked like electricity behind Buzz's eyes. "Don't ignore what you are capable of, don't ignore what others are capable of."

"I don't understand," Buzz said. "What am I capable of?"

"So much. Let me help you see," Jupiter replied. "Remember. People are not always as they seem. History tells us that."

With a crunch of molecules, Buzz felt himself materialize and become whole once more. Mari was there as well, right next to him. They were falling through the clouds, wind whistling past their ears. He looked down to see an immense stretch of blueness below them.

"Buzz, why are we falling through the sky?" Mari cried. "He said we were being downloaded into Neptune's kingdom. This feels like we're just being dropped."

"I think Jupiter is trying to test me," Buzz tried to explain over the whooshing of the air whistling past his ears. "He was in my head. He said something about showing me what I'm capable of."

"What do you mean, capable of?" Mari snapped. "We're capable of dying if we hit the sea from this height. We'll break every bone in our bodies."

Not if you break the surface tension of the water first. The thought popped into his head from a reservoir of knowledge that he never knew he had. *If you break it, you might be able to pass right through.* His hand tightened around the rune that was still in his grip.

"Buzz!" He realized that Mari was screaming his name. "Buzz, why is Jupiter testing you?"

Because he needed me to understand. To see that the worm had given me knowledge. Buzz thought. "It doesn't matter now," he shouted back. "I have an idea." The sea was rushing to embrace them. "Before you hit the water, throw your rune downwards. It will punch a hole through the surface. You just need to follow it through."

"It will never work," Mari said. "Will it?"

The still ocean was incredibly close now, a deadly blue mirror.

"You trust me?" Buzz said.

"Absolutely," Mari replied.

Buzz nodded. "Stay upright, cross your legs, point your toes, and throw the rune – NOW."

They hurled their runes in unison, and Buzz crossed his arms and anything else he could think of. The runes pierced the water like arrows and Buzz and Mari entered the sea straight behind them. Buzz squeezed his eyes shut and held his breath, waiting to hear the cracking of bones. But he didn't. *It worked.*

Buzz hurtled through the water like a torpedo. He waited for the downwards momentum to slow so he could kick upwards, take a breath, but it didn't happen. He was only going in one direction.

Down.

CHAPTER TWENTY-ONE

BENEATH THE SURFACE

Buzz opened his eyes. He was caught in a swirling whirlpool, created by the two runes that continued to race through the water. They were glowing, one with a white, ethereal gleam and the other with a sparkling amber light that reminded Buzz of Sunna's eyes. He'd let her down. Let everyone down. He was going to drown, here, in a sea far from home.

He surrendered to the pull of the runes and their guiding light – what else could he do? The pressure in his chest was almost unbearable now, and he knew that nearly all the oxygen in his lungs had been used up. Yet still they were being pulled downwards by the runes' vortex, far from the surface. Far from air.

He was in a world of silence.

His consciousness shrank to a pinprick of amber and white light and his eyelids drooped.

He would sleep.

Buzz slammed against something solid and yet soft.

He was awake again, his sight shifting from the pinprick of light to a panoramic view. With his last scrap of oxygen, he registered some kind of undulating dome with two rune-sized holes punched into it. Then the whirlpool that had brought him this far pulled him through one of the wounds in the bubblelike shield, tearing it wider, and he was no longer in water but in air. The pressure in his lungs was gone. The water in his nose and mouth had vanished.

The vortex dropped Buzz gently onto a sandy floor and then dissipated with a sigh.

Buzz doubled over and took in a gasping breath.

He felt dizzy.

A little bit sick.

And so very pleased to be alive.

I'm alive.

But what about Mari?

He forced himself to stand up straight and look around. Relief kept him standing, even though he still felt dizzy. He could see Mari just a few feet away, and he waved over at her. She was holding Mani's rune in her hand and looking up at a building – a citadel encircled by seven pillars of white stone. Statues lay abandoned on the ground in front of it, still and watchful.

The light in this dome was dim, but bright enough to see by. Buzz realized that it was coming from several giant, luminous pearls that were scattered about on the seabed. Next to one of them was Sunna's rune. It no longer shone with its amber light – it was just a smooth, grey stone with etched lines once more. He scooped it up.

"Where are we?" Mari called out to him. Her voice echoed around the dome.

"I think you humans call it Atlantis," a voice replied.

A woman in a breastplate made of shells and a skirt of silver and gold coins appeared from inside the citadel. Her eyes were an amazing aqua green, and pinned to her glistening, seaweed-coloured hair was an iridescent train of blue netting.

"Now I have a question. Two, actually." The woman's mouth curved downwards, and Buzz imagined it would take a lot to change that expression. "Who are you and what do you want?"

Mari gave a little wave. "I'm Mari and he's Buzz," she answered.

"Nice to meet you," Buzz said.

"Are you sure about that?" the woman replied.

"We've not come to cause trouble," Buzz rushed to add. "We just need to—"

He trailed off. The woman was not listening. She was staring over his shoulder, her greenish lips pursed so tightly that they were blanched of all colour.

"Your kind are always trouble." She pointed with a webbed hand at the dome above. "And that's rather troublesome as well."

Buzz turned and winced as he saw the two steady streams

of water that were trickling in through the holes caused by the runes.

Two tracks of tears. The thought popped into Buzz's head, and he wondered if it was because this woman seemed so sad.

She gave a high whistle, and a train of soldiers marched out of the citadel, led by a general wearing a helmet fashioned of coral with a plume of sea anemones.

"We have been breached, General Neale," the woman said. "The dome is compromised. Have it patched up for now, and we will get the Beast to breathe us a new shield at the next full moon."

"Of course, Lady Pisces." General Neale bowed so low that the plume of his helmet brushed the sandy floor. His back cracked loudly as he tried to stand straight once again.

"Go get the repair kit," the general told one of the soldiers, wheezing as he finally straightened up completely. Buzz couldn't help but notice how red in the face the general looked. *These soldiers are seriously out of shape,* he decided. The general surreptitiously adjusted his helmet, which had fallen over one eye, shooting a glance at Lady Pisces as he did. But she paid him no attention. She was too busy pacing back and forth, looking up at the damage to the dome.

"So Lady Pisces," Buzz began but she just waved a hand at him dismissively. He was clearly going to have to wait until the dome was fixed before she'd even look his way again. Eventually, the soldier who had gone into the citadel to get the repair kit reappeared with a small chest tucked under his arm.

General Neale nodded at the soldiers who were lined up behind him, and they immediately began to climb onto one another's shoulders. The air was filled with yelping and squeals of annoyance, but after some time there were two swaying towers of soldiers just high enough to begin the process of fixing the holes. Wide sheets of sticky webbing from the repair kit were passed up the balancing soldiers.

They look like two huge, swaying jellies on a plate, Buzz thought. He was sure they'd get the holes fixed, but it was going to take a long time, as clumsy hands kept dropping the webbing, which would float to the floor before being passed back up the tower again.

Lady Pisces muttered something rather rude under her breath, but she stopped pacing and barking instructions at the soldiers and came to stand in front of Buzz and Mari once more.

"We're really sorry about your dome." Mari nodded her head at the two towers of soldiers. "But they're doing a great job."

The lie hung in the air between them like a bad smell.

"What do you want?" Lady Pisces growled.

"The Runes of Valhalla." Buzz decided to get right to the point. They'd already wasted enough time watching the soldiers not fix the holes in the dome, and if what Saturn said was true, and Buzz's world was in danger of dissolving because of the unmorrow curse, then they'd already lost too much time.

"Saturn told us that Neptune has two of the runes, Tyr's and

Odin's," Mari explained. "He was given them for safekeeping until the time they were needed. That time is now."

The woman's sea-green skin paled, but she gave a toss of her head. "Dear Grandpapa," she trilled. "He's ever so old now, isn't he? I'm not sure you can trust what he says. He gets ever so confused."

Buzz frowned. Lady Pieces was doing her best to cover it up, but her whole body thrummed with worry.

"Jupiter didn't say any different." Buzz crossed his arms. "He's already given us the runes he had. Now we need the ones Neptune has been keeping safe."

"Right, I see. So you've already been to see Uncle Jupe, have you?" Lady Pisces fiddled with the netting that draped over her hair.

"He's the one who sent us here." Mari sniffed. "In his own unique way."

"Well, you have been busy. How very endeavouring of you to collect two runes already." She smiled at them, and looked like a completely different person.

Buzz smiled back, relieved that she had cheered up.

"I'll take you to see my father." Lady Pisces strode forwards. "If you'll just follow me."

General Neale appeared at her side. "My lady, I should accompany you."

"Oh, there's no need to do that," Lady Pisces assured him. "I'm completely capable of dealing with our guests."

"As you wish, my lady."

Buzz noticed that the general was looking at Lady Pisces with a mixture of concern and full-blown lovesickness, but Neptune's daughter did not seem to notice.

Mari grinned as they followed behind Lady Pisces. "Poor General Neale. He's got the biggest crush I've ever seen."

Buzz was about to reply, but Lady Pisces's shrill voice cut him off.

"Do keep up," she said. "It is quite a distance to my father's quarters."

They walked past beautiful lagoons and ruined temples rubbed smooth by the sea.

"I assume you can swim," Lady Pisces said, coming to a narrow, inky-blue pool that looked a little bit like a well sunk into the ground.

She dropped into the water, and as she did, her legs fused and became a tail.

Buzz and Mari tried not to stare, but it was difficult. The tail was ridged with beautiful iridescent scales that glinted in the low light of the pearls all around them.

Lady Pisces looked up at them, her aqua eyes stormy. "I'll ask again. Are you sure you need these runes?" she asked as Buzz and Mari stepped to the edge of the water. "My father can be awfully grumpy when he is disturbed." Her palms glided across the water and little bubbles came to rest on her hands, sparkling like diamonds. "Turn back now, and I will offer you a companion who will see you back to your home realm safely."

"The runes are the only things that can save our realm," Buzz replied.

He bent his legs and dived into the pool. He had expected it to be cold, but it was as warm as bathwater. He began to tread water. Lady Pisces swallowed hard and then inclined her head. "So be it. Follow me down."

Mari stood nervously on the edge of the pool. "Um, just a tiny question. How are we supposed to breathe? I mean, I assume you have gills or something, but we don't. We need air to live."

"Gills?" Lady Pisces sounded outraged. "I am not a fish." Her tail thrashed in the water, submerging Buzz in a wave. He emerged from it spluttering. "I am a child of Neptune. He took me in as his daughter and he is the guardian to all merpeople." She titled her chin. "When my father saw that humankind were hunting merpeople instead of revering them – that humans no longer prayed to the great Neptune before sea journeys – he took steps to protect himself and his kin. He took Atlantis and made the merpeople a new realm in the deepest part of the ocean. He made sure that they were safe and had a dome and a supply of air whenever they needed it. Neptune's subjects would never need to surface from the sea again."

"Right, I see now," Mari said. "Actually, I don't. How am I supposed to breathe if we go down that well thing?"

"Just get in," Lady Pisces said. "All will become clear."

Mari, still looking mistrustful, took in a gulp of air and leapt into the water. Pisces dived downwards, and Buzz and Mari followed. Clusters of bubbles streamed their way, attaching themselves to their skin.

I can breathe! Buzz thought. It was like he was surrounded by bubble wrap – the world around him segmented into hundreds of infinitely reflective mirrors.

Down and down they swam, until they spilt out into a wide and still lagoon. Lady Pisces continued to swim, her powerful tail propelling her through the clear waters, but Buzz found the lagoon too shallow. He began to wade through it instead, the water coming up to his waist. "Are we close?" Mari asked.

"Very," Lady Pisces replied.

In front of them, set into a wall at the edge of the lagoon, was an enormous wooden door encrusted with sea barnacles.

Swimming up to it, Lady Pisces took a key that hung from the wall, slipped it into the lock, and turned it. The door swung open by itself.

"Why is your father locked up?" Buzz asked.

"Goodness me, don't you think it is rather rude to question our customs?" Neptune's daughter huffed. "If you want the runes, then here they are. Hurry up and get in." She swam out of the way so that the doorway stood empty.

Buzz hesitated on the threshold. Something was very wrong here, he could feel it.

"Come on, Buzz," Mari said. "Let's get this over with. I don't like this place." She waded through the entranceway.

"Mari, wait!" He leant forwards and grabbed for her arm, but she was already through the door.

"Off you go, then," Lady Pisces said. Buzz turned to her just in time to see the flick of her powerful tail and then he was thrown forwards through the door. It slammed shut behind him and the key turned in the lock.

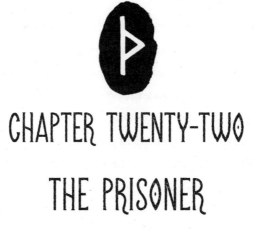

CHAPTER TWENTY-TWO

THE PRISONER

"Hey!" Buzz banged on the huge door. "What are you doing? Let us out." The barnacles that studded the wood stabbed at his hand painfully. "Let us out," he bellowed again.

"Buzz!" Mari's voice wafted from deeper in the cavern. "You've got to come and see this."

"Mari, you might not have noticed but we're prisoners," he muttered.

"Then you've got time to come and look at this."

Buzz's fists unclenched. If Lady Pisces was still there behind that door, she wasn't saying, and she certainly wasn't opening it.

He swam forwards, the water in the prison coming up well past his shoulders. The cavern was gloomy but as Buzz swam further into the interior he could see how small it was. Mari was treading water a few feet away, staring at one of the stony walls. As he got closer, he saw that the entire surface was covered in the most amazing art. Hundreds upon thousands of shells and fragments of gleaming sea glass had been stuck to the wall to form intricate, complicated patterns. A single image was woven throughout the pattern – a winding snake that stretched across the whole wall.

"It's amazing," Buzz breathed.

"Thank you." A softly spoken male voice floated over to them.

Buzz and Mari whirled around. A giant beast with a beak for a mouth was gliding towards them. But progress was slow in such a cramped space. The creature was round, with many tentacles that seemed to have gnarly looking hooks sticking out from them.

Is this really Neptune? Buzz wondered. *He doesn't look much like his brother, or father, but maybe gods can take whatever form they want...*

The squidlike beast came to a stop just a few feet away from them and tried to rise to his full, impressive height, but hit his head on the ceiling of the cavern.

"Ouch," he exclaimed, but Buzz realized that the creature's beak did not move. The word came to him like a strong fragrance on the air.

"Are you okay?" Buzz asked.

The creature nodded. "What's your favourite part of the wall?" he asked them.

"The snake, definitely," Mari replied. "It looks really lifelike, and you've got so much expression in its face." The beast's skin had been peachy brown, but it got rosier and rosier as Mari spoke.

"I worked really hard on that bit, actually," he said. "I wanted to try and remember Jörmungandr's face – every part. It's been such a long time since I've seen it." The creature's skin changed again, becoming a dull grey shade.

Buzz felt the *click clack* of his mind riffling through information. The knowledge given to him by the worm told him that squid communicated by changing the colouring of their skin and releasing chemicals into the water. That had to explain why the creature's words came to him like a scent on the air rather than sounds.

"Are you Neptune?" Buzz asked hesitantly, sure of the answer even as he asked the question.

The creature's skin instantly became a stormy colour, and he raised two of his tentacles as if to smash them down on Mari and Buzz.

"Wait, I'm sor—" Buzz broke off as he realized that the squid was using its tentacles to scrub away tears that had sprung up at the corners of its strange yellow eyes.

"I'm not Neptune. My name is the Kraken, but you can call me Kay." The squid's tentacles dropped to his side, and he seemed to slump downwards, sending a wave their way.

"We're Buzz and Mari," Buzz said even as they had to put their backs against the shell wall to stop from being washed away.

"Neptune has had me here for centuries," Kay went on to explain, his skin becoming duller and duller by the moment. "He keeps me here and forces me to blow giant air bubbles so that his subjects can breathe underwater and remain undetected from humans."

"You created the dome!" Mari exclaimed.

The Kraken nodded mournfully. "And all the other bubbles that flow in the tributaries of Atlantis. I've become a glorified bubble machine, but I used to be so much more than that. I was one of Odin's most trusted ambassadors."

"So you're not here because you want to be?" Buzz questioned.

"Absolutely not," Kay replied. "I'm Neptune's prisoner and his people see me as some kind of mindless monster," Kay said wistfully. "I was free once, sharing my life with Jörmungandr."

"As in Jörmungandr, Loki's child?" Mari asked in surprise. "Myths say he was a giant snake that was cast into the sea by the gods because he was getting too big."

"Jörmungandr is big, but not that big." Kay sounded defensive. "And he'd made peace with living in the water. I was the one to relocate him on Odin's behalf – that's how we met. After that, I left Odin's employment, and Jörmungandr and I were happy living in a loch in Scotland – troubling no one – but then I was kidnapped by Neptune." The squid's beak took on a sneering expression. "Neptune saw his chance when Loki was taken and Odin put himself into the deep sleep. He knew there was no one left to stop him. That he'd get away with it."

"But what about Loki's other children?" Mari asked.

The Kraken waved a tentacle. "They're dead, banished, or simply gone." Kay peered down at them. "Will anyone notice that you're gone? That you're here in a prison with me?"

Buzz and Mari shared a look.

Their world was in the unmorrow curse. Buzz wondered if anyone had even noticed that they were gone.

Kay shook his great head. "You know, the person who put you in here probably thinks I'm going to eat you or something. It's ridiculous. I'm vegetarian. I eat seaweed!"

"Listen, Kay," Buzz said softly. "Our world is stuck in an unmorrow curse but we left our home to look for the Runes of Valhalla. Neptune has them and we need to find him."

"You're wrong," a familiar-sounding but significantly out of breath voice suddenly interrupted. "Neptune doesn't have the runes. Not any more. You need to leave Atlantis. I'll help you."

General Neale stood there, a spear in his hand, and Buzz realized that he must have swum the length of the chamber underwater to appear unnoticed.

Faster than Buzz could even blink, Kay thrust out a tentacle and lifted the general clean out of the water. He squeezed until the general gave a yelp of pain.

"Wait," Buzz called out. "He came to release us. Put him down Kay."

"Yes, that's right." General Neale gasped. "I guessed what Lady Pisces would do and I've come to undo it. Forgive her. She was just scared."

"You are the one who should be scared." Kay was bright red now. "I'm going to crush you. Crush you like Neptune crushed me into this prison."

There was a crashing noise as the door to the prison was thrown open.

"No, stop, please." Lady Pisces was in the doorway to the prison and an imposing looking merman was at her side, a trident tattooed into the greenish skin of his chest.

Mari raised an eyebrow. "Is literally the whole of Atlantis in here?"

"Just the important people," Lady Pisces said. Her voice trembled.

"Neptune," Kay snarled, and General Neale cried out as the beast's grip tightened. "What are you doing here?"

"My daughter asked me to come," Neptune said simply. "She said she'd made a mistake, and she didn't think she could fix it herself."

Lady Pisces fixed her gaze on Mari and Buzz. "The two Runes of Valhalla that you seek are not here in Atlantis. They were stolen by a human but only because I allowed that to happen." She crossed her arms. "A few months ago I swam to the surface. I knew it was forbidden but that did not stop me. I met a man on a beach. He was kind and listened to me, and we continued to meet for many weeks. For a long time, he never asked where I came from, and I never told. Then, he noticed the jewels that I wore in my crown, and I told him that my home was filled with such treasures." A tear trickled down her cheek. "He said he would love to see them – that it would be his way of really understanding my homeland. I brought him our most precious possessions, and he asked me to leave them with him, just for one night, so that he could have the evening to gaze at their beauty. I agreed. But the next morning, he was not there to meet me. He never came back, and Atlantis's treasures were gone." Her face crumpled as more tears began to fall. "I could not find the words to tell the truth to my father." She took another sobbing breath. "So when you turned up saying you needed the runes, I panicked. I didn't want Father to find out. I didn't want him to be disappointed in me."

"Panicked?" Mari repeated incredulously. "You locked us up!"

"I know. It was a stupid, evil thing to do." Lady Pisces dabbed at her eyes. "I'm just so pleased that this foul, ravenous beast hasn't eaten you and your little friend."

"Hey," Kay said. "How many times do I need to say it – I'm ve—"

"Vengeful," Buzz interrupted. A plan was forming in his head and this was not the time for Kay to remind everyone that he was vegetarian. "The Kraken's vengeful and hasn't eaten us yet, but that doesn't mean he won't."

"What?" Mari and the Kraken said as one.

"You'll eat us, right?" Buzz said, winking at Kay.

"What's wrong with your eye?" The Kraken asked, concern

written all over his grey, blobby face. "Have you got something in it? I hate when that happens. Maybe I could blow it out. Do you want me to try?" Kay puckered his beaklike mouth.

Buzz groaned. His plan was not going . . . well . . . to plan. "Don't you remember?" he ground out. "You'll eat us unless they promise to release you."

"Oh right, yeah," Mari said. "You'll crush our bones and roll us up like a pair of burritos. That's what you said."

"I did?" Kay questioned. Then understanding dawned. "Oh, yeah, I did." He paused. "Grr," he added for good measure. Lady Pisces looked at her father imploringly. "Papa, I'm so sorry about the treasures and the Runes of Valhalla, but you have to let the Kraken go before it hurts these two pathetic children."

"Hey, we're not pathet—" Mari began.

"All right," Neptune interrupted. "I will let him go."

"You will?" everyone – including Kay – said at once.

Neptune's expression was resigned. "I kidnapped the Kraken a long time ago," he explained. "I did it because I knew there was no one left to stop me." The sea god's sharp teeth worried his bottom lip. "But Ragnarok is almost upon us. If Odin wins, he's not going to be pleased with my treatment of the Kraken. And if Loki wins, he's not going to be pleased that I stole Jörmungandr's true love. Either way, I think it is time my kingdom and the Kraken part ways. We'll just have to find a way to cope without the creature's protection." Neptune cracked his knuckles. "Besides, my men have become lazy because of the creature's bubbles. With no threat of being seen by humans, there's been no impetus to train."

General Neale bristled, but he did not argue, and Kay dropped him back into the water with a splash.

Neptune stroked his long, green beard. "As for the runes, if you want them, you will have to find the human who stole them from my daughter, or at least work out where the runes have ended up." Neptune peered at them, his aquamarine eyes as sharp as sea glass. "I don't think such a task is beyond you. This quest chose you for a reason."

"I'm sorry I have made your mission that much more difficult, children." Lady Pisces looked up at Kay. "And I'm sorry for our treatment of you. Somehow I don't think words are enough."

"They are not," Kay replied, staring hard at Lady Pisces and then at Neptune. "Maybe one day there will be a reckoning but it is not today."

"Understood." Lady Pisces turned to General Neale. "And thank you for coming to release them. I can see now you always have my best interests at heart. That means a lot." She gave him a small smile, and the general beamed back in response.

Kay gathered up Buzz and Mari, holding them gently in its tentacles. "Thank you so much little humans. It's time for me to get out of here."

"Glad we could help," Buzz replied.

"And I will help you in return," Kay said. "You may not know it, but Odin made the runes from the stones that surround the World Tree in Tangley Woods. If the runes are in the human realm, they will try to find their way back to the tree, or at least get as close as they can."

"Ratatosk said a similar thing about the runes and the gods always being drawn back to the tree," Buzz said slowly.

"So Tyr's and Odin's runes might have been back in Crowmarsh this whole time!" Mari exclaimed.

Kay nodded. "I'll take you back to Tangley Woods, if you like?"

"Yes," Buzz said. "That's what we should do."

"Hang on. How will we get to Pluto's realm to get the last two runes when the time comes?" Mari asked.

"The World Tree will show you the way," Neptune assured her. "Say hello to my brother when you get to the underworld, won't you?"

Buzz nodded.

The Kraken began to blow and blow until a skinlike bubble surrounded Buzz and Mari. Then, holding the orb carefully, Kay hurtled out the door and up from Atlantis, smashing through the dome and leaving the white-stoned city far below them.

"You mentioned Ratatosk," Kay said as they flew through the water. "He was an ambassador to Odin at the same time I was. Tell me how he is. There is no more honourable creature in all the realms."

Buzz remembered the fingers of smoke grasping at the brave squirrel on the World Tree and how Loki had said that Ratatosk was now just a plaything for the dragon Nidhogg.

"I don't know how he is," Buzz answered honestly. "I really want him to be okay but I don't know that he is."

Kay did not reply. But what was there to say?

The bubble that encased Buzz and Mari finally bobbed out of the water and floated downstream. The landscape that Buzz could spot from inside the orb was immediately familiar. They were back in Tangley Woods. The bubble gently bumped up against the bank of Mornings Lake, and Buzz let out a breath of relief that he didn't even know he'd been holding. Buzz had half expected the woods to be a pile of ash or dead stumps because of the unmorrow. But the forest looked much the same as it had when they'd left.

Kay grazed the bubble with one of his hooked tentacles and it burst, allowing Buzz and Mari to clamber onto the bank. It felt good to have solid ground beneath his feet, and not a rainbow superhighway, a cloud, or an ocean bed.

"Thank you for bringing us home," Buzz said.

Kay bowed his massive, spongy head, the Kraken's yellow eyes blinking rapidly in the light of the forest. "It was my pleasure. You gave me my freedom, and for that I will always be in your debt."

"There is no debt here," Mari insisted.

Kay held up a tentacle and wagged it disapprovingly. "I beg to differ. I owe you my freedom, and so my life. I hope I will be able to repay the favour one day." Kay smiled. At least,

Buzz thought it was a smile. It was difficult to tell the expression on the face of a giant squid thingy.

The Kraken closed its eyes and breathed in deeply. "I think Ratatosk is alive," Kay said after a moment. "I can't know for sure, but the forest is telling me that he lives."

Buzz felt a spark of hope.

"Good luck finding Jörmungandr," Mari said.

"You'll find him," Buzz said. "He's still in that loch in Scotland. Exactly where you left him. People call him the Loch Ness Monster nowadays but I know he was sighted last on July sixteenth."

"Why thank you, Buzz." Kay had gone pink all over again. "Thank you." The Kraken held up a tentacle in farewell and dropped soundlessly back into the water of the lake. Buzz watched the dark shape disappear, pleased that Kay and Jörmungandr would be reunited once again.

True love always found a way.

CHAPTER TWENTY-THREE

THE RETURN

Mari was frowning at her watch.

"What's wrong?" Buzz asked.

"The date," Mari replied. "We climbed the World Tree on Saturday, fourteenth September."

"Yeah," Buzz said. "That feels like a lifetime ago."

"It wasn't quite a lifetime," Mari murmured. "But my watch is saying that it was more than two weeks ago. It's now technically October first."

"Two weeks? But how—" Buzz broke off, remembering what Young Janus had said. Time moved differently in Saturn's realm.

"Saturn," he breathed.

"Good old Father Time," Mari added.

"I can't believe we've been away for two weeks. Do you think anyone's noticed?" Buzz asked.

"It's been two weeks of Saturdays, remember," said Mari. "For them, for my grandmother, only a few hours will have passed since they saw us last." She peered out through the trees. "What does a world that's been worn away by the unmorrow curse even look like?"

Buzz shrugged. "We need to see if the runes stolen from Lady Pisces have come back to Crowmarsh like Kay said." He rubbed the back of his neck, his whole body ached. "Do you think that guy might have tried to sell the treasures from Atlantis, then?"

"Criminals gotta eat." Mari wrinkled her nose. "Let's see if the runes have surfaced online." She tapped at the screen of her watch, trying to walk at the same time. She frowned. "There's no Internet. I can't get a signal at all."

"We're in the woods. Coverage can be a little patchy."

Mari shook her head. "It worked before when we were here."

Buzz felt the still unfamiliar sensation of his mind sorting through the reams and reams of information that had passed through him in the EarthWorm. "The 2038 quandary," he said.

"2038?" Mari repeated.

"It's a bit like the millennium bug," Buzz said. "The theory is that computer systems are going to stop working in 2038 because they won't be able to recognize it is a year." Buzz paused, trying to think of the easiest way to explain what was in his head. "When these systems were set up, they were never designed to cope with dates beyond the year 2037," he continued. "Maybe a similar thing is happening here. Computers can't cope because of the unmorrow curse. All the dates are out of sync and don't make sense."

"Sure, it's possible, I guess." Mari was looking at him in amazement. "But how do you know about the 2038 bug?"

"Doesn't everyone know about it?" Buzz replied.

"No," Mari said. "They don't." She peered at him. "You're different, Buzz. You know stuff you didn't know before. Even the fact that you knew the date of when the Loch Ness Monster had last been seen. What's going on with you?"

Buzz opened his mouth to explain but he found that he couldn't. Jupiter's warning came back to him. *Remember. People are not always as they seem. History tells us that.*

"You wouldn't understand," he said instead.

"Try me," Mari countered.

Buzz wanted to tell her about his strange transformation, but it was like the more he knew, the less he trusted. And he couldn't help wondering about what she'd seen in the time tunnel. *It had really rattled her – should I be worried?* Perhaps if he knew, it might help him to share his own secret.

"Okay, I'll tell you my secret if you tell me what you saw in the time tunnel. That's the deal."

"Deal?" Mari repeated, she stared at him in disbelief. "We're friends, Buzz. I would gladly tell you what I saw in the time tunnel, I wanted to tell you what I saw, but I don't make *deals* with friends just so that I can get an honest answer. That's not how friendship works."

Buzz felt his cheeks go hot. Mari was looking at him as if he was some kind of poisonous toad. "You lied to me before, Mari, in front of your grandmother and my Uncle Mark. Don't forget that." He shoved his hands in his pockets. "You can't blame me for being cautious."

Mari's mouth opened and closed in surprise for a moment, as if she were a fish snatched out of water. Then she turned on her heel and stalked through the forest. "I said I was sorry about that," she shouted over her shoulder. "I thought you understood why I lied when your Uncle Mark came round? I thought you trusted me now?"

Buzz hurried after her as a light drizzle began to fall and was soon matching her step, stride for stride. "I do trust you. I've just got a lot going on in my head at the moment. I'm sorry."

"Oh, forget about it," Mari said. "Maybe you're being the smart one. Didn't Jupiter say that Odin didn't trust anyone a hundred percent? And he had all the knowledge in the world." She pushed her glasses further up her nose, and Buzz noticed that one of the lenses was cracked.

"Hey, how did you break your glasses?"

Mari stopped, took off her glasses, and examined them. She looked really different without them, and for the first time Buzz noticed that one of her brown eyes was much darker than the other.

Mari gave a bark of laughter. "Now, let me see." She tapped her chin thoughtfully. "Maybe it was when I dove out of the way of a massive data-eating worm, or when I hit the sea after falling a great height or got dragged through a giant bubble."

"Okay, silly question," Buzz conceded.

"Perhaps, but it reminds me of the old Buzz. He was full of silly questions."

"Mari," Buzz began.

She held her hands up. "It's okay. I don't want to have another fight. We need to save our energy."

"You're right," Buzz said. "How are we going to find out whether the stolen runes have turned up if we don't have the Internet?"

"We'll just have to do our research the old-fashioned way." Mari put her glasses back on. "Does your library have a microfilm reader?"

Buzz went to shake his head – but then he realized that this wasn't quite true. He'd heard his sister moaning about some kind of microfilm thingy a few months ago to the Prof.

"I think they still have one," Buzz said. "And I know exactly the person who'll be able to tell us for sure. What time is it?" he asked.

"Three p.m." Mari responded. "It's going to get dark soon."

"My sister has a Saturday job at the library," Buzz explained. "If we can get there, I'm sure she'll be able to help us."

* * *

The Crowmarsh public library was an imposing Edwardian building, red-bricked and narrow. The walls were normally impeccably clean, but graffiti was now scrawled all over the brickwork and they glistened from the rain that was lashing down.

"None of it matters," Mari read. The words were painted in red, yellow, and green, and caged in a thick black outline. "They're right, you know," she said, hugging herself to keep warm from the storm that was brewing.

"What?" Buzz's hand went to push the door, its broken windowpane like a jaw filled with ragged teeth.

"If we don't find the runes and reunite them with their true owners. None of it will matter." Mari's voice was a whisper as her fingers traced the graffiti. "The world will end. Death will win."

Buzz felt the hairs on his arms stand on end. Mari's voice sounded so cold. "But, we're not going to let that happen, are we?"

Mari's fingers came away from the letters as if the paint were suddenly red hot. "No, of course not."

Buzz pushed open the door, and the smell of old books assailed his nostrils. He loved that smell normally. It was pretty much the only thing he liked about his father's study. But today that book smell was almost overpowering. It smelt like the books were rotting.

A lone figure sat at the entrance of the library, behind the counter. It was his sister. Her legs were crossed at the ankles and propped up on the desk, and Buzz noticed how scratched and muddy her calves looked. Like she'd walked through Tangley Woods and got caught in the brambles. Her hazel eyes looked glassy and bloodshot, and her bright red hair was matted and wild. The tea she'd been drinking had been knocked over and was dripping onto the floor, leaving a brown, sad-looking puddle that was soaking into the carpet.

Behind her, the normally immaculate library was in complete disarray. Books were torn and scattered across the floor. The windows were all open and sheets of newspapers whipped around the room like angry birds of prey, while rain flooded in, soaking furniture, hardcovers, and paperbacks alike.

"Let me shut these windows for you," Mari said to Tia, coming up to the counter.

Buzz's sister ignored her. She just sat there looking out into space.

"Um, hello, Tia." Mari waved a hand in front of the older girl's face.

"Go easy, okay?" Buzz said.

"Sorry, you're right. She's not herself." Mari backed away sheepishly. "I'll leave you to it. Where do you think the microfilm reader might be, if it is here?"

"In one of the reading rooms. You go check, and I'll ask my sister and see if she says any different." Mari nodded, and Buzz watched her go. "Tia," Buzz whispered. "Tia," he said again more loudly.

Tia gave a start. "How can I help you?" she croaked, sitting upright in her chair. Her throat sounded sore, and her lips were so cracked that they bled. She was staring right at him, but Buzz knew that she wasn't really seeing him.

"It's me. Buzz," he said.

"Buzz?" Tia stared at him. "Buzz," she said again, as if searching for a memory. Recognition entered her bleary eyes. "Where have you been?"

He was surprised that she'd noticed he'd been gone. He opened his mouth to tell her about Sunna and Loki. Ratatosk and the time tunnel. Janus and Saturn and Jupiter and the EarthWorm. The Kraken, Neptune, and Lady Pisces. But Tia was not really looking for an answer. She just kept on talking.

"I was all by myself at breakfast this morning," she complained. "Dad wasn't there, either." She twirled one of her matted curls. "It's Saturday, you know. He's supposed to make pancakes. That was the deal with Mum gone. For us to at least pretend that things could be normal."

Buzz's lips twitched upwards. Tia sounded completely outraged. She almost sounded like herself again.

His sister's shoulders slumped. "But I guess none of it matters. Not really." Her finger was now yanking at her curl rather than twirling it. "I made the pancakes myself and they tasted funny, but it doesn't matter. None of it matters."

An image from the time tunnel dropped into Buzz's head. It was of Tia eating pancakes that were old and rancid. The future he'd seen was coming true.

"Tia, I'm going to help you," Buzz promised. "But first I've got some really important research to do."

"The Internet isn't working, I'm afraid," Tia interrupted as if on autopilot. "And I can't really check out any books because the computers are acting up." She flung back the hatched lid of the library desk so violently that Buzz only just managed to leap back and save his fingers from being crushed. "Just take what you need. Everyone else is. I'm going home." His sister strode past him and out the door without even a backwards glance.

"Hey, wait." Buzz went to follow her, but Mari appeared at his side and grabbed his arm.

"If you want to help her, the best way is to find the runes," she said.

Buzz tried to pull away. "I can't just let her walk out into a storm. She's not herself."

"It's just another Saturday for her," Mari insisted. "And it will start all over again tomorrow if we don't gather the six runes together and find those sleeping gods. Come on, I think I've found something on the microfilm."

Buzz allowed himself to be dragged away. *Our house isn't too far from here,* he told himself. *And it's the safest place for her.*

Mari led him to an ancient-looking machine in the corner of one of the reading rooms. A newspaper article was captured there. "Have a read of this," she said. "I think you're going to like it."

Buzz scanned the page of the article.

"Hey, this is about my Uncle Mark," Buzz said. "It says that he was the undercover agent in a sting operation to take down a ring of antique thieves." His finger went to the screen. "'Among the haul was a collection of stone carvings that many are saying are ancient and rare runes.'"

"Kay was right," Mari said. "Ratatosk too. The runes tried to make their way back to the tree. To Crowmarsh."

"We need to get to the police station," Buzz said. "Uncle Mark will know where the runes are now."

Mari nodded.

They raced for the door and spilt out into chaos.

CHAPTER TWENTY-FOUR

DEEPEST FEARS

Buzz and Mari were hiding. They could see a ring of people through the leaves of the hedge. The mob were circling a lamp post, their heads craned back to stare up at something. They didn't seem to mind the rain that pelted them.

A couple of people in the crowd were holding tomatoes that were well beyond their use-by date and taking aim at whatever was up the lamp post.

Mari poked her head up over the hedge. "There's actually someone up there," she said. "They must be terrified. Who knows how long they've been trapped?" She shook her head. "We've got to do something."

"We *are* doing something," Buzz hissed back. "We're trying to find the Runes of Valhalla and the sleeping gods so we can stop Loki, remember?"

"Of course I remember," Mari snapped. "But we can't just

leave that person up there."

"Yes, we can. We need to find Uncle Mark."

"And we will, but someone needs our help now," Mari said. "Just look."

Buzz poked his head over the hedge and could just see the bottom half of a boy clinging to the lamp post. He wasn't wearing any shoes, and his trousers were dripping with rotten fruit and vegetables. The faces of the people circling the lamp post wore manic, delighted expressions. They howled up at their prey.

"Okay, so what do we do?" Buzz asked.

"We scare them away."

"How do we do that?"

"Leave that to me," Mari said, and she emerged from behind the hedge.

"Mari," Buzz called under his breath. "Come back."

She ignored him and walked out into the crowd.

"You like to scare people, do you?" she asked, addressing the mob. "You think it's entertaining to terrify someone?"

"We do, actually," said a voice that Buzz knew almost as well as his own.

Samraj? No, it couldn't be.

Buzz emerged fully from the hedge, and now he could see the whole mob clearly. His best friend, Sam, was there right at the head of it. Some of the members he recognized from school, others from around town. Children, adults, and the elderly stood together in the rain, shouting at the kid trapped up the lamp post.

"Sam, what are you doing?" Buzz asked. "This isn't you. You're not a bully."

Sam had walked right up to Mari, a dripping tomato in his hand. He stared at Buzz as if trying to place him. "Hey, Buzz," he said after a moment. "Where were you this morning? Why didn't you come to the match?" He wagged a finger. "Coach Saunders didn't bother to come either." He jerked his head towards the lamp post. "Unfortunately, our resident pain in the neck did make it, although he kept on complaining that things didn't feel right."

Buzz stepped in between Mari and Sam, so that he was now directly beneath the lamp post. Looking up, he found himself staring at the figure of Theo Eddows.

Theo scowled back at him. "Bog off, why don't you?"

If Buzz could ignore how scared Theo looked under the scowl, he might have enjoyed this moment. But he saw the lines etched around the other boy's mouth too clearly – saw the trembling in his arms He wasn't sure how long Theo could hold on. At the top of the lamp post he could see a pair of white trainers, their laces tied together and looped over the top of the light. He felt a wave of pity for Theo. *He really loves those shoes,* he thought. That was clearly how the mob had got him up the lamp post in the first place. Now they were using him for target practice.

Buzz looked back at his best friend. "Sam, I'm sorry I wasn't there this morning. Come on, let's get out of here and go and play a match now. You can ask your friends to come as well." His gaze travelled over the motley crew of young and old – it would be quite a game.

Sam was staring at Theo again, his fingers tightening on the rotten tomato in his hand. "I don't know. Using Theo as target practice is definitely more fun than football." He held out the tomato to Buzz. "Do you want to have a go?"

"Ha! Right," Buzz heard Theo goad from up the lamp post. "As if Buzzkill is any good at hitting a target."

Buzz stared at the tomato. It looked really appealing.

Mari snatched the tomato from Sam's hand and threw it to the ground. "Okay, Sam, since you like games and scaring people, how about we play a little game of our own?" Mari pushed Buzz to one side so she could square up to the other boy.

Sam crossed his arms "Sure, why not?"

"The game is called *Guess Your Greatest Fear*," Mari said. Sam laughed. "You're going to guess what my greatest fear is?"

"Yep, your deepest, darkest fear. And then I'm going to share it with everyone here."

Sam snorted. "I'd like to see that. I'm not scared of anything."

Buzz frowned. He knew for a fact that wasn't true. Sam had a full-blown phobia of custard thanks to an all-you-can-eat buffet, a dare, and an unfortunate incident with a trifle that had resulted in Sam being banned from that restaurant for life. *But Mari's not going to know that,* he thought. *How could she?*

Buzz stared first at his oldest friend and then at his newest, and somehow he knew that Sam didn't stand a chance.

Mari looked deep into Sam's eyes, concentrating hard. After a moment, she raised a single eyebrow.

"Custard," she said. "You have a mortal fear of custard?"

There were some sniggers from the crowd.

Sam's normally tawny skin blanched of colour. "How . . . how do you know that?"

His eyes slid over to Buzz. "Did you tell her? How could you?"

"I didn't—" Buzz began.

"Oh, please," Mari interrupted. "Buzz didn't tell me a thing. This is what I do best. I read people's fears. Scary Mari – that's what they call me at school you know."

Buzz remembered that Mari had told him this just before they went into the time tunnel. "*I know stuff about them . . . Their secrets.*"

Mari looked out into the mob. "You." She pointed a finger at a tall, lean man. "Your greatest fear is that no one likes you because you don't like yourself." The man flinched and took a step back. Her finger travelled over the rabble and rested on a man in a tweed jacket. "Your greatest fear is that your family will find out that you've spent all your money at the races."

The man in tweed looked defiant. "It doesn't matter," he said. "None of it matters anymore."

The woman beside him, who had been busy hurling bananas at Theo, went very still. "Oh, but it does." She crushed half a banana into the man's forehead and then turned on her heel and walked away. The man chased after her, splashing through the puddles in the street.

Mari's finger came to rest on a young woman in a fuchsia pink dress. "And your greatest fear is that you're just a pretty face. That no one cares about what you think. Even worse, you're too scared to tell them any different."

The woman gasped, her heavily mascaraed eyes swimming with tears, and then she fled from the crowd.

"Anyone else?" Mari's eyes glittered fiercely, and she was breathing heavily.

People were shaking their heads, not meeting Mari's gaze.

"Then I suggest you get out of here – quickly." Mari's hands were planted firmly on her hips.

The crowd began to back away as one, many looking at Mari as if she were a wild animal that might pounce on them at any moment. In no time at all, the whole mob had scattered just as the storm clouds seemed to.

All except Sam. He lingered for a moment, his face miserable. "I think I'm going to go home," he croaked. "Maybe lie down on the sofa and watch some TV."

"That's a great idea." Buzz put a hand on his best friend's shoulder. "Go home and watch some Saturday night TV."

Sam turned and trudged off. "It doesn't matter. None of it matters." The words weren't much more than a whisper, but Buzz heard them.

"It does matter," Buzz called after him. "And this Saturday will be over soon and everything will get back to normal, I promise."

"Hey," a voice said from behind him. "Just so we're clear. I won't be saying thank you."

Buzz turned to see that Theo had climbed down from the lamp post. He was covered in tomatoes, potato peelings, and rotten apples, but his precious trainers were around his shoulders, and he looked pleased to have two feet on the ground once more.

"I expect the minimum from you, Theo, at all times," Buzz answered. "So no, I don't expect a thank-you."

Theo curled his lip but then turned to Mari. "You, on the other hand, are awesome. You've got to tell me how you did that whole deepest, darkest fear thing. That is a seriously cool trick."

Mari beamed with happiness.

She actually beamed.

"You really think so?" she said.

"Absolutely," Theo enthused. "I'm sticking with you."

"Mari, this is Theo," Buzz snapped. "You may recognize him as the charmer who threw my phone down the toilet at school."

"Nice to meet you, properly, at least," Mari said, and she held out her hand.

Theo took her hand and shook it eagerly. "The pleasure is all mine. You're really at our school?"

Mari smiled and nodded. "Just for a test-run day. Did you

know there are nearly 332,000 genetically distinct bacteria on the human hand?"

Theo pulled a face and dropped her hand. "I did not." He surreptitiously scrubbed at his palm.

"Okay, we've got somewhere to be." Buzz steered Mari away. "Theo, why don't you get out of here and start looting or eating rotten fruit or something?"

"Off to fight a dragon, are you?" Theo asked.

"Something like that." Buzz didn't even bother to look over his shoulder.

"Can I help?"

Buzz stopped and swivelled round. "Excuse me?"

Theo had knelt down and was pulling on his trainers, his face hidden from view. "Listen, Buzzkill," he said. "Things have been seriously trippy around here recently. I've been getting the worst case of déjà vu. I mean, I feel like I have lived this day twenty times already, but no one else seems to have noticed. And each time I live the same day, things around here are getting worse. My friends and family have all gone feral on me – worse than usual. I keep on walking over to those woods that you love so much. It's like I'm being pulled towards something, but I don't know what to do when I get there. And I feel like I'm being followed. I saw this strange geezer in the woods. He was bright and kind of shimmery and I just knew I had to run."

"No way." Mari's mouth hung open. "Buzz. He's one of them."

"One of who?" Theo absently picked at his teeth and then examined his findings with interest.

"No, Mari, no." Buzz knew he sounded scared, but that's because he was.

"Think about it," Mari insisted. "Ratatosk told us that all the sleeping gods – Sunna, Mani, Tyr, Odin, Thor, and Frigga – would have enough influence over their hosts to ensure they stayed close to the tree. Stayed in Crowmarsh."

"So?" Buzz questioned. "That doesn't mean Theo is one of them."

But Mari was staring at Theo, a grin spreading over her face. "Ratatosk also said that the hosts of sleeping gods wouldn't be affected by the unmorrow curse like normal mortals – they'd be more resistant." Mari bounced onto the balls of her feet excitedly. "He's one of them. We've found our first sleeping god!"

PART III

THE AWAKENING

CHAPTER TWENTY-FIVE

THE SAFEST PLACE

"Uncle Mark!" Buzz cried, racing into the Crowmarsh police station. "Uncle Mark?"

There was no answer.

The police station was deserted. A cold wind followed them into the room, and cupboard doors swung mournfully on creaky hinges. Files lay scattered on the floor, and the light overhead flickered as if the bulb was taking its last few gasps at life.

"Yo, Uncle Marko," Theo cried, walking over to the stairs that led up to the next floor. "Come out, come out, wherever you are."

"He's not your uncle," Buzz said, following Theo to the staircase. He looked up the stairway. He thought he'd seen a flicker of light up there, but the entire floor above was in complete darkness.

"Technically, he's not your uncle, either – he's your

godfather," Theo shot back. "Whatever, he's not here." He nodded at the wide entrance to the police station. "Come on, let's go to that ash tree you were talking about so that I can get my Thor on."

Buzz massaged his temple, trying to rub away the headache that was threatening to explode there. During the walk over to the police station, he and Mari had given Theo the full story of what had happened since Friday the thirteenth. They told him about the unmorrow curse, the runes, the sleeping gods, Loki, and the end of the world as they knew it. Typically for him, Theo had only really listened to the part that he thought directly concerned himself, and that was the part about going to the underworld and getting Thor's rune and powers.

"You're not necessarily going to be Thor, you know." Buzz tried to keep his voice even. "You could be Tyr, Odin, or even Frigga."

He isn't Sunna or Mani, Buzz knew that much. They'd given Theo the moon rune of Mani to hold, and exactly all of zilch had happened.

"There's no way I'm going to be a girl." Theo sneered. "And to be honest, I don't want to be this Odin guy or Tyr, either."

"You don't want to be Odin – the All-Father, the great and powerful destroyer?" Mari sounded amazed. "He's the big kahuna, you know."

"All I know is that he's not Thor," Theo replied stubbornly.

"Well, Tyr isn't too shabby, either," Mari continued. "He

used to be worshipped as the chief of the gods until Odin superseded him in people's beliefs. Tyr was the god of justice and a great warrior."

"Thor, god of thunder," Theo repeated, not listening to a single word Mari was saying. "The name just sounds right. Man, I can almost feel the hammer in my hand. What's it called again?"

"Mjölnir," Buzz said.

"Mjölnir," Theo repeated. He snatched up an umbrella from the corner of the room and began to swing it like a mighty hammer.

Buzz rolled his eyes. "Put that down before you hurt yourself. We don't even know for sure that you've got a sleeping god inside you."

Theo grinned. "I'm special. Mari said it."

Buzz opened his mouth to argue. But there was no denying that Theo wasn't being affected by the unmorrow curse like other mortals.

Theo smiled smugly. "Listen, we don't know where your Uncle Mark is, but we do know that Thor's rune is in the underworld. We also know that we need to speak to some guy called Pluto, so let's get going." Theo steered Buzz towards the door. "Once I have my powers, I will be able to sort out this whole Loki mess for you, and you can go back to knitting or whatever it is you do in your free time."

"He's right, Buzz," Mari said softly, walking by his side. "There is no guarantee that your godfather will even know where those runes are now – the article we read was from a few weeks ago. Maybe we're better off going for the runes that we already know the location of."

Buzz heard a creak behind him and whipped around to see Uncle Mark walking down the steps with a cup of tea in his hand. Buzz could see straight away that his godfather's eyes did not have the glassy, vacant expression that he'd observed in Tia or Sam. If anything, Uncle Mark looked even better than usual. Fitter and stronger.

"Uncle Mark, you're here," Buzz said. "Why were you upstairs with no lights on?"

"Lightbulb blew," Uncle Mark replied, the cup of tea sloshing over his hand as he swiftly put it down on a nearby counter. "Where have you been, Buzz?" Uncle Mark took two steps forwards and folded Buzz into a hug. "I've been so worried."

Buzz hugged his godfather in return, but a big question was already tickling at the edges of his brain. He stepped back. "How long have I been gone, Uncle Mark?" Uncle Mark frowned. "It's hard to say for sure. On the one hand, it feels like it's been at least a couple weeks, but on the other hand?" He shook his head. "The whole world is upside down. Nothing makes sense." He gave a hysterical laugh. "It's Saturday every day."

"So, you've noticed that we're locked down in a Saturday loop?" Mari asked.

"Of course I have," Uncle Mark said. "And I've noticed that all sense of decency has gone out the window, and that food rots right in front of your eyes. I patrol these streets, and I can't believe what's happening. And no one other than me seems to notice." He looked at Buzz. "Have you seen your father?"

Buzz shook his head. "Just Tia, and she's like a zombie."

"It's probably for the best that you haven't," Uncle Mark said. "Your father is not much better than your sister. He didn't seem to care that you were missing. He couldn't see that we were living the same day over and over again. It didn't matter what I said."

Mari turned to Buzz. "Are you thinking what I'm thinking?"

Buzz nodded. Uncle Mark was exhibiting signs just like Theo. *He's another sleeping god.*

"Uncle Mark, we've got something to tell you," Buzz said. "And it's going to sound whacky." Uncle Mark stared back at him steadily. "It can't be any more whacky than what I've experienced recently. You'd better tell me everything."

And so Buzz and Mari did.

"So, you think I'm a sleeping god." Uncle Mark said the words softly, as if he was afraid someone might overhear. "That I'm one of these day guardians?"

"Yes," Mari said.

"But not Thor," Theo added. "I'm Thor."

Uncle Mark ignored him. "And you've come back from Atlantis to try and find those runes that were mentioned in the newspaper article. The ones that we uncovered during the raid."

Buzz nodded. "Any idea where they might be now?"

"I have more than an idea." Uncle Mark walked over to a safe in the far corner of the room. He swiftly punched some digits into the keypad.

The door swung open, and inside the safe Buzz saw two runes sitting on a black cloth. One was shiny and smooth, and the other looked a little rougher and duller.

"I don't understand," Buzz said. "Why have you still got these? The raid was weeks ago. Are they being held as evidence?"

Uncle Mark shook his head. "One of the curators from the university got in touch and said that the runes were to stay in the area so that they could be put on display at the city museum. We were told to look after them until they could be collected," Uncle Mark explained. "With this whole unmorrow curse thing, they have been in our possession far longer than they should have been."

"We're not complaining." Mari dragged Theo over to the safe. "Pick up the runes," she ordered.

"I don't want to," Theo whined. "I don't want to be Odin or Tyr. They both sound like complete and utter losers." He nodded his head over to Uncle Mark. "Make him pick them up first."

Uncle Mark was standing very stiffly, and if Buzz didn't know better he would have sworn that his godfather was furious. *Maybe he's just nervous about the whole sleeping god thing,* Buzz thought. *I'd be nervous if I thought a sleeping god was inside me, too. What if they didn't want to go back to sleep after they'd been awoken?*

"Theo, I'm the one who put the runes in the safe in the first place," Uncle Mark pointed out. "But I've no problem handling them again, even if you do think that Odin and Tyr are losers." He picked up the runes, rotating them in his palm.

Nothing happened. He held out the two runes to Theo. "Your turn."

Theo grimaced but held out his hand, flinching as Uncle Mark dropped the runes into his palm. He squeezed eyes shut and held his breath, but after a moment he cracked an eye open. "I'm still me, right?"

"Unfortunately," Buzz said.

"Yes!" Theo punched the air. "Project Thor is still a go." He chucked the runes back to Uncle Mark, who slipped them in his pocket.

"Hang on, did it occur to you that my uncle Mark might be Thor?" Buzz asked.

"Yeah, right, Inspector Marko is probably that moon guy, Mani. It was his rune you got me to hold on the walk over here, right?"

Buzz nodded.

"Theo's got a good point," Mari mused. "Nothing happened with him when he held the rune, but it might with your godfather." She reached into her pocket and passed Mani's rune to Uncle Mark. He held it in his palm and stood very still, but nothing happened.

Buzz's disappointment curled through him like smoke. So

far they had four runes, potentially two sleeping gods, and not a single superpower between them. They had nothing. *And all the while, Loki was probably out there seeking the other sleeping gods of Crowmarsh,* Buzz thought, *or giving them to the dragon Nidhogg.* And the increasing chaos outside would only be fuelling Loki's powers.

"Hey, Buzz," Uncle Mark said, slipping Mani's rune into his pocket with the other two. "Don't look so down. The runes that Pluto protects will be the perfect match for me and Theo. They have to be."

Buzz nodded. The final two runes that waited for them in the underworld belonged to Thor and Frigga. They had to be the keys to awaken Uncle Mark's and Theo's sleeping gods. With their help, they would be able to find the other sleeping gods in Crowmarsh and reunite them with their runes as well.

Buzz took Sunna's rune from his pocket, feeling comforted by its weight but wishing at the same time that it was Sunna who held the rune and not him. This had all begun with her.

Suddenly the weight of Sunna's rune was gone.

"Hey!" Buzz was pulled from his thoughts in time to see Uncle Mark pocket the rune.

"It makes sense to keep them all together," his godfather explained. "In the safest place."

"Yes, but—" Buzz began.

"Your Uncle Mark's right," Mari said. "We shouldn't split them up."

"I agree," Buzz replied. "So let me look after them."

Theo snorted. "It's me and Inspector Marko who are the gods, remember?" He threw an arm over Uncle Mark's shoulder, having to stand on his tiptoes to do it. "You're just a boy."

Uncle Mark threw off Theo's arm. "And so are you until we find those last two runes. "Come on, Buzz. Show us the way to the tree and let's get to Pluto's underworld."

CHAPTER TWENTY-SIX

THE WORLD TREE

The tree stood in front of them, its silver bark glowing starkly in the evening light. This time, Buzz had found it easily. He wondered if that was because they had the runes with them.

"So how do we do this?" Theo asked.

"We climb the World Tree and search for the branch that will take us to Pluto's realm," Buzz explained, looking up through the canopy. "The tree will reveal the right path to us. Just like it did last time."

Mari stood on tiptoe. "Let's get climbing." She reached for the first branch, but it shrunk back from her before her fingers could even touch it.

Mari frowned and reached for another limb, but the same thing happened again – the branch shied away from her touch.

Mari stared around at them. "You all saw that, right?"

Theo laughed. "I guess the tree isn't a fan of yours. Let me show you how it's done." He leapt up and managed to get a grip on one of the lower branches. "See—" he began, but broke off as the silver limb swung itself upwards and began to shake him like a ketchup bottle.

"Stop it," Theo howled. "Lemme go!"

"You're the one holding on to the branch," Buzz called up through the canopy. "Try letting go of *it*."

For once in his life, Theo listened to Buzz's advice. He squealed as he flipped through the air before landing in a heap on the mossy ground. Theo got slowly to his feet and dusted the dead leaves off his clothes. He examined his elbows. They were grazed but not bleeding. He glared at the tree. "Not cool. You wait until I get my big old Thor hammer." He smirked. *"TIMBER."* The word echoed around the forest.

"Shhhhh," Buzz hissed. "Loki could be anywhere." He felt the hairs on his arm stand to attention even as he said the name. He remembered the smoky stench of Loki. How it had made his eyes water and his throat burn as they faced each other on the silver branch of the World Tree.

"Fine," Theo muttered. "But the tree'd better watch it."

The tree's leaves rustled and made a noise that could only be described as a *humph*, and then an abandoned bird's nest hurtled downwards and landed squarely on Theo's head.

As Theo cursed under his breath and picked the nest out of his hair, Uncle Mark tried to climb the tree but was shaken off. Buzz reached for a branch. He wasn't surprised when it evaded his attempts to grasp it as well. *What exactly is going on here?* Buzz placed his hand on the trunk of the tree and felt it thrum with power. Ratatosk had said the tree would guide them – they just had to listen and follow with their hearts. *Take us to Pluto,* Buzz asked. *Please.*

The ground beneath his feet began to rumble.

"Nidhogg." Mari gasped.

"Who?" Theo asked.

"The dragon," Mari said. "He's Loki's pet, and I think he's coming back."

"No, I don't think so," Buzz said. He could feel the thrumming beneath the tree's bark intensify. The tree was going to guide them. *We just have to be patient.*

The ground split, and Buzz could see a ball of tangled roots. They were translucent except for the tiny pulses of energy that ran along their length, turning them every other second into filaments of pure light.

As the cool air hit the roots, they began to untangle themselves. Some spilt out onto the ground like tendrils of hair, while others knitted themselves together to form a chute of pulsing light.

Uncle Mark was looking at the roots in wonder. He stepped forwards without hesitation and threw himself down the chute.

Theo staggered forwards, pieces of the nest still on his head. "Oi, wait!" He glared at Buzz. "Your uncle Mark is trying to get my Thor rune before me, and I'm not having it." He threw himself down the chute as well.

Buzz stepped right up to the tunnel of roots, ready to follow Uncle Mark and Theo. But he realized that Mari wasn't next to him.

He turned around. Mari was backing away from the tree. Her eyes were fixed on the entrance to the chute as if the roots that glimmered there were snakes.

"Where are you going?" Buzz demanded.

"I don't think I can do it." Mari was shaking. "I can't go there."

"Go where? The underworld?"

She nodded.

"You're scared?" Buzz said, and he realized that he was surprised. Mari didn't seem to be scared of anything. But then, it was one thing to go to the realm of the sky or the kingdom of the sea – the underworld was a place of death. *Maybe the place of my death.* Buzz pushed away the thought. "Mari, I don't know what we're going to find at the end of this chute. I wish we didn't have to go. But we need to stop Loki, we need to—" Buzz stopped. He wasn't being honest with himself or Mari. Yes, he wanted to stop Loki and save the world, but he wanted something else even more. "I need to get my mum home, Mari. She's been gone for months now and will be home on Sunday, but only if I can stop the Unmorrow Curse."

"Why have you never told me that before?" Mari demanded.

"Because I'm scared it won't happen. But I know it definitely won't if you don't come with me."

Mari smiled sadly. "I wouldn't be so sure of that, Buzz. In the time tunnel, I saw myself make a really bad decision. I saw myself help Loki."

"So what? You told me that what we were seeing possible futures and not actual ones in those screens. That we were in control of our own destinies. Do you remember that?"

Mari nodded.

"Then you've got to take your own advice," he insisted. "I trust you, Mari. You'll make the right decision when the time comes." And as he said the words, he realized just how true they were. He really did trust her. He wasn't going to be like Odin, mistrusting those around him just because infinite knowledge told him to. He grinned. "Besides, you have to listen to me. I'm the Sherlock now. That worm made me really clever."

"Yup, I guessed that!" Mari rolled her eyes. "I just didn't understand why you wouldn't tell me."

Buzz shrugged. "Jupiter told me never to ignore what others are capable of."

Mari frowned. "Did it occur to you, Sherlock, that maybe Jupiter was telling you to look out for the good that people are capable of? Humans can be full of bravery and forgiveness and not just cruelty or deviousness, you know."

"Oh, yeah, right," Buzz said.

"Wow, you really do need me." Mari shook her head and sat down at the entrance to the chute.

Buzz could see that she was shaking.

"Come on, let's do this," she said.

"It's all right to be scared, Mari," Buzz said.

His friend whispered something under her breath in response and then flung herself into the chute.

Buzz could have sworn she said, "Even if I'm scared that I won't want to come back?" But he couldn't be sure: the wind was already roaring in his ears as he hurtled down the root-lined shaft and became part of the light.

CHAPTER TWENTY-SEVEN

DEEPER UNDERGROUND

The vivid lights of the roots dimmed to a glow-worm glimmer as Buzz travelled along the chute, and now that the burning brightness was gone, he could pick out the details of his surroundings. The roots that cocooned him still pulsed with light, but if he focused on individual areas, Buzz could see that they also pulsed with names, written in the tiniest neon script. He whooshed past hundreds, thousands, millions, and billions of names.

Onward he flew, until the chute levelled out and the roots began to curl around him and pull at his clothes, slowing him to an almost complete stop. He had to crawl through the last few feet of the twisted root chute on his hands and knees.

He emerged onto a narrow jetty, which jutted out into a river that curved like a crooked smile. Uncle Mark, Theo, and Mari stood waiting for him, their outlines stark against a sky that was the colour of crushed apricots.

"Come on, slow coach," Theo bellowed.

Buzz got to his feet and saw that the soupy water of the river was bubbling and burbling. As the water lapped at the edge of the jetty, he thought he saw something shadowy swirling in the wash.

The air in this new land was as thick and sticky as marmalade, and he was sweating after only his first few steps along the jetty. *There it is again.* Out of the corner of his eye, he caught a fleeting glimpse of a shadowlike creature that glided beneath the surface of the swampy water. More shadows joined it. They seemed to be gathering eagerly around the jetty.

"We're not going for a swim, are we?" he asked, as he joined his companions. "Because we have company, and they don't look friendly."

Mari was looking at the creatures as well, her face thoughtful and even a little sad.

"They look pretty harmless, actually," she insisted. "Not made of much. Just silt and mist. But they seem so . . ."

"Creepy," Theo finished her sentence.

"No, that's not what I was going to say." Mari gave him a withering look. "Melancholic."

He looked at her blankly.

"Sad," Mari explained. "They look sad."

"No swimming for us, Buzz. We have a ride." Uncle Mark pointed further down the jetty to a small boat that was tethered at the end – it would just about hold all of them. Its hull was as shiny as a beetle's back, and as they got closer Buzz realized that the hull was actually made out of some kind of gemstone. *Black onyx, perhaps.* Its two sails shone as if they had a fine dusting of diamonds and sapphires over them.

"Great, we have a boat made out of jewels," Theo said, as they continued to get closer. "Will it even stay afloat?"

"We'll find out," Buzz replied. "The boat has to be here for a reason."

"'We'll find out,'" Theo mimicked and threw up his hand. "Why, that just fills me with confidence. Buzzkill."

Mari stopped and planted her hands on her hips. "Firstly, don't call him Buzzkill. It's not nice, and we're all on the same team now. Secondly, you wanted to come on this quest, remember? Thirdly – and I hate to break it to you, *mate* – but being on a quest sometimes means figuring things out as we go along." She nodded her head over to the boat. "That goes for sailing that thing."

Buzz had never sailed before but felt his mind race as he sought the information he needed. *Here it is,* he thought in relief. *Everything I need to know about sailing a boat.* "Don't worry. I think I know how to sail it. Get in."

Mari winked at him and clambered in.

Theo got in as well, while Uncle Mark and Buzz untethered the boat from the jetty.

"Since when can you sail?" Uncle Mark asked. "Can't

imagine your dad taught you."

"You'd be right. He didn't." Buzz didn't feel like saying any more than that.

Stepping into the boat, Buzz positioned himself at the back next to the tiller and the spare oar. The others sat in front of him.

They had to wait for it, but eventually a gust of warm air caught the sails, and the boat drifted through the quagmire. Buzz steered them towards the bend in the river, and before too long the jetty was out of sight.

But not the shadowy creatures.

They circled the boat, gliding in and out of its path, the keel of the boat sometimes passing right through them and splitting them in two.

As the boat came around the bend of the marshy river, an enormous palace reared up into view. It was hewn out of the same impossibly shiny black stone as the boat, but the structure did not have a single window or door that Buzz could see. The palace floated in the middle of the marsh, bobbing up and down like a rubber duck in a bath.

"That's where we go," Mari said. "I'm sure of it."

"But how do we get in?" Theo questioned.

Mari shot him a glance.

Theo shook his head, ruefully. "Oh, right, that's it. We'll figure it out."

They circumnavigated the palace slowly but could see

no way in – only the vicious shininess of the black stone that reflected the orange sky back at them. Buzz's eyes ached from the glare.

Then he saw it. A narrow strip of mottled stone jutting out from the base of the palace. *A docking station. No, correction,* he thought. *A* very narrow *docking station.* It would just about hold all of them if they stood shoulder to shoulder. Above it he could see the edge of a large iron wheel and some script etched into the stone wall that was written in a language he didn't recognize.

Buzz turned the tiller, steering the boat in so he could draw up alongside the stone edge, but all he felt was resistance, as if the boat was sailing through mud. "I can't get in any closer," he called out to the others. "I think the current is too strong."

"It's not the current." Uncle Mark pointed over the side of the boat. "Look."

Buzz peered into the water. The swarm of shadow creatures that had been following them since their departure was now a horde that completely surrounded their boat and held it still. They were stuck.

"What do they want?" Mari asked. "Why are they trying to stop us?"

Their boat began to rock from side to side as if in answer.

"They don't want to stop us." Theo stood up in the boat and looked around wildly. "They want to eat us." Shielding his eyes, he looked at the lip of stone that jutted from the palace. "Come on, if we jump, we'll be able to make it onto that stone ledge."

"It's quite a risk, Theo," Uncle Mark said. "What if you miss? What if you hit the wall?"

"It's better than staying and being dinner." Theo scrambled backwards and prepared to jump.

"Will you sit down?" Mari was holding the sides to keep the boat steady. "You're making the rocking worse."

Theo shook his head.

"You guys say you figure things out." Theo's eyes were fixed on the stone ledge. "That's what I'm doing." He accelerated down the boat, Mari and Uncle Mark just managing to get out of his path as he sped past them. He took a running jump, his arms and legs cycling through the air.

Despite himself, Buzz was impressed. Theo had great momentum.

Buzz frowned. *Oh no, his momentum is a little too good.* "Watch out," he cried.

Theo crashed into the wall with a yell of pain and slid down onto the ledge. Even from his position on the boat, Buzz could see that Theo's temple and whole right cheek were grazed and bleeding, and he was only just managing to sit upright.

The boat was rocking even more fiercely now, and there was a cracking sound as two holes, one on either side of Mari, were punched in from outside the hull. Water began to well up through the wounds.

"We're out of options," Uncle Mark said. "We're going to

have to jump. Just like Theo."

Mari nodded, her hands a blur as she bailed water out of the vessel. But the river's invasion could not be stopped, even as she tried to use the old netting in the bottom of the boat to plug the hole between her and Uncle Mark.

"Mari, watch out!" Buzz shouted as a shadow squeezed through a hole and slinked in her direction. The shadow was not solid. Through its body, Buzz could see Uncle Mark, Mari, and even Theo sitting groggily on the palace's ledge. As if it could feel's Buzz's gaze on it, the shadow turned to him and opened its mouth to reveal double rows of white razor teeth. Those teeth could rip and tear.

The creature lunged towards Mari, and Buzz didn't hesitate. He grabbed for the oar by his side and leapt forwards, bringing the paddle down like a club.

The shadow split in two. The pieces of the creature screeched and thrashed, writhing on the ground like fish out of water.

"Go," Buzz yelled. The shadow pieces were already slinking back towards each other. "Quickly, before it re-forms itself."

"What about you?" Mari asked.

"I'm right behind you. I promise."

"Buzz is right." Uncle Mark was on his feet. "We need to get off this boat before it sinks or is overrun. I'll go first, Mari, and move Theo along the ledge to make room for all of you."

He turned towards the narrow stone platform and, like Theo, took a running jump off the boat. Unlike Theo, his leap was expertly executed, and he landed nimbly on the ledge. Uncle Mark put an arm around Theo's shoulders and gently moved him aside. Theo gave a whimper and then slumped against the shiny black wall once again.

"Now you, Mari," Buzz said. The shadow creature was almost whole. Buzz brought his oar down again.

Mari nodded, then tried to mimic Uncle Mark's pace stride for stride. She bent her legs to leap, but as her feet left the stern of the boat, another shadow creature surged through one of the boat's gaping holes. She gave a yell of rage as the shadow curled around her ankle; it stretched and strained to slow Mari's momentum as she flew through the air.

The moment froze.

Then sped up.

Buzz scrambled forwards and used the oar on the shadow that was pulling at Mari. It split in two, one part scurrying back through the hole, the other bit still clinging to Mari's ankle.

She was halfway to the ledge but was losing height.

Don't fall, Buzz begged silently, *Don't fall,* even as he felt something cold and miserable wrap around his ankles.

CHAPTER TWENTY-EIGHT

SHADOWS OF REGRET

Yessss.

Relief flooded through Buzz as he saw Mari get her fingertips onto the stone ledge and Uncle Mark drag her up to safety. But the relief couldn't chase away the coldness creeping up his body. The chill around his ankles had now spread up to his calves, and he looked down to see that the shadow creature he'd whacked twice with the oar had come back for its revenge. It wrapped around his legs. Buzz dropped to the bottom of the boat and began to wriggle and squirm to get the shadow off him. He hit his legs against the edge of the boat, trying to split the creature in two again. The pain of it burned bright behind his eyes and snatched his breath, but he did not stop. He slammed his legs down again on the edge of the vessel.

It was too much for the little boat, and it flipped over into the water.

Water covered his head but he surged upwards, moving his bound legs like he'd seen Lady Pisces move her tail. He broke the surface, the boat creating a small domed roof over his head. Pale orange light seeped in through the holes the creatures had smashed in the boat, and Buzz put a hand through one of them to hoist himself up and stop himself from being dragged down.

He could feel the shadow moving up his body, around his thighs and around his stomach. And more shadows were joining it. He could feel their misery become his. Their sadness was trying push out the things that made him Buzz – that made him believe he was worth anything. He was just loss and hopelessness, and he was being emptied out. The shadows wanted him under the water; they tugged at his legs eagerly. Finally, the pull was too strong to resist. He let go of the boat. He let himself begin to sink.

There was a shuddering noise, followed by the creaking of chains. Then the sound of something huge smashing into the water filled the wooden dome above his head. Then the boat was gone, flipping up and then away on the water as he felt the surge of an underwater current smash into him. The vibration blasted through his whole body, shaking off the shadows that clung to him.

The sense of hopelessness was gone. Like someone had turned on a light and banished all the darkness. He kicked upwards and began to tread water.

"Hey Buzz, over here," Mari called.

He turned around to see that the palace's drawbridge had been dropped and now rested on the water. *That's what the noise was,* he realized.

Mari, Theo, and Uncle Mark stepped over from the ledge and onto the drawbridge, leaving behind the iron wheel and the strange characters carved into the stone behind it.

"Hurry up, then, Buzz," Uncle Mark cried. "The drawbridge won't stay open for long and those shadows are coming back."

Buzz glanced over his shoulder. Uncle Mark was right. The shadow creatures were done with being spooked and were surging back towards him.

He struck out into the soupy water, paddling hard with his arms but not his legs, which screamed with pain where he'd smashed them on the edge of the boat. He grasped the edge of the drawbridge and hauled himself up onto the shiny black walkway. Uncle Mark was at his side in an instant.

"How you doing, buddy?" Uncle Mark asked, helping Buzz to his feet.

Pain lanced through his legs as he tried to put weight on them, and he had to bite down on his lip to stop himself from crying out. "Been better, Uncle Mark."

Uncle Mark slung Buzz's arm over his shoulder, took his weight, and moved them both forwards. "Don't worry. I've got you. You're safe now."

And Buzz knew that he was. Because his Uncle Mark always looked out for him. Just like a father ought to do. Just like his father never did. Ahead of them, Mari was holding Theo's elbow and guiding him into the interior of the palace. He still seemed pretty unsteady, but he was managing to put one foot in front of the other.

Mari threw a smile over her shoulder. "Took your time getting up here, didn't it, Buzz?" Her eyes told him how relieved she was to see him safe.

"Sorry, I got a bit weighed down," he replied. "How'd you get the drawbridge to open?"

"It was your godfather," Mari responded. "It was quite extraordinary. He managed to decipher the words next to the wheel gate so we knew exactly how to open it. Two clicks right, two clicks left, and—"

"It was nothing," Uncle Mark interrupted. "Just a lucky guess, really."

"Hardly," Mari replied. "You read the words. I heard you mumbling them under your breath. I didn't recognise the language at all."

Buzz felt his eyebrow rise. He didn't know his godfather could speak any languages other than maybe a bit of French. It was the Prof who was good at things like that.

"What language was it?" Buzz asked, and then, remembering the stories of Uncle Mark and the Prof growing up at Buzzard House realized he knew the answer. "Latin, right?"

"Yes," Uncle Mark said.

"No," Mari said at the same time. "No," she said again after a pause, sounding even surer. "I can read Latin, and those words weren't in that language."

Mari and Uncle Mark stared at each other for a moment, the already warm air thickening with tension. Then Buzz's godfather laughed. "No, you're right. It wasn't proper Latin. It was more a version of the language. Dog Latin, I think they call it. Do you read that as well?"

Buzz was still leaning on Uncle Mark as they walked along a narrow stone corridor, and he could feel that his godfather's body was almost rigid.

A frown lined Mari's forehead. "I don't. Still, it's very odd that I didn't recognize any of the words next to the wheel gate. Are you sure that—"

"What does it matter?" Theo's words were just a little slurred. "You're all doing my head in with this Latin rubbish, and my head hurts enough already."

Buzz heard the creak of chains once more. Suddenly, the light that had flooded the corridor was snuffed out with a crash as the drawbridge slammed shut. For a moment, they stood in complete darkness, and then a beam of blue appeared to light the way in front of them.

Buzz grinned in the low light. "Have I told you how much I love that watch, Mari?"

Mari laughed. "You're not the only one. Come on." She walked forwards, lighting the way down the corridor. Buzz, Uncle Mark, and Theo followed.

The corridor twisted and turned like a maze as they went deeper into the belly of the palace, but eventually Buzz saw a door made of metal that sat beneath a stone arch.

"Ready," Mari said.

Uncle Mark nodded and pushed at the door. They found themselves on the threshold of a great banquet hall. The walls were smooth, glossy, and black, just like the boat had been. In the middle of the room was a huge table laden with golden jugs and pomegranates and figs. Candles flickered and danced on towering silver candelabras. The impossibly smooth table was made of the same black rock as the walls, and so were the thronelike chairs that sat at either end. Buzz realized that everything in the room was made of onyx.

"Greetings." The voice was soft, dreamlike almost. "Welcome to my kingdom."

CHAPTER TWENTY-NINE

PLUTO AND PERSEPHONE

Buzz squinted in the low light and realized that the two chairs he had thought were empty were in fact occupied. In the first chair was a man with clay-coloured skin and a toga as black and fluid as an inkblot, and in the second chair was a woman with hair the colour of poppies and marigolds. They both rose to their feet as Buzz and his companions stepped closer.

"You must be tired, hungry, and thirsty," the lady said. She waved her hand at the table. "Please do help yourself."

Buzz's mouth began to water, and he reached out for a fig. He couldn't remember the last time he'd eaten. The fruit was heavy in his palm and looked sweet and ripe – overripe, even. He could smell that as he brought the fig to his mouth.

He felt the sting of Mari's hand slapping the fruit from his grasp. The fig spun through the air and hit the onyx wall with a wet squelch.

"I thought the worm made you smart?" Mari's eyes blazed. *Yep, blazing is the only way to describe it,* Buzz thought. Her eyes actually looked like candle flames, and it reminded him of something, the memory staying just out of reach. *It doesn't matter. It's a trick of the light. The candles on the table reflecting in her glasses.*

"You don't eat anything when you're in the underworld." Mari's warning pulled him back to the moment. "Once you do, you can't leave. It's a well-known part of the myth."

Buzz tried to access the information but it wasn't there. None of it was there. All the data given to him by the EarthWorm was gone. *The shadows leeched it out of me,* Buzz realized. He remembered now that feeling of being emptied when the shadows had held him in the water. Amazingly, though, he didn't feel sad that the knowledge had gone. He was just relieved to be himself once more. He heard a slow clapping. It was coming from the lady with the poppy-coloured hair.

"Well done, my dear, you have an excellent memory for stories." She shook her head. "I suppose you are thinking of the tale of how I came to be Pluto's wife." She picked up a pomegranate. "Poor Proserpina, Persephone to some, she ate a few pomegranate seeds and then she couldn't leave. And that's why we have winter. It is a myth. So ridiculous how truths about people get warped." She turned to her husband. "I live in the underworld because this is where my heart is. Not because I ate some silly fruit." She placed the pomegranate back on the table. "The underworld has been given a terrible reputation. You mortals are told it's a place of suffering and misery, but everything that grows on earth starts here." She pointed upwards. "Starts in the soil above our heads, enriched by the minerals that surround us. This is a place of life, not death."

"Those shadow things in the water say different," Theo said.

Buzz nodded. "I felt their sadness. When one captured me, I felt its misery."

Pluto rubbed at his chest as if in pain. "Those shadows are people's regrets," he explained. "When people die and pass on to the next phase of their existence, they always come with regrets." Pluto lifted a golden pitcher and poured what looked like water into a golden goblet. "It used to be that the River Styx would cleanse people of these regrets and carry them away to evaporate. But the Styx has stopped flowing freely, and is now polluted by regrets. Regrets that have quite an appetite."

"Excuse me. This is all very interesting but Loki is free," Uncle Mark began. "Sunna has been captured and so we have come for the Ru—"

"What happened to the river?" Mari interrupted. "Why has it stopped flowing?"

Pluto sighed. "The problem lies with Hel."

"Hell?" Theo repeated. "As in, like, fire and demons with pointy sticks?"

"No, as in Hel the goddess," Pluto explained. "Loki's

daughter. She was queen of the underworld, and it was her responsibility to keep the mouth of the River Styx and the channel that leads from it clear of stones and debris."

"Hang on, but isn't *she* the queen of the underworld?" Theo asked, pointing at Persephone. Persephone gave a trill of laughter.

"Depends on who you talk to. You see, whatever land you are from, however far our kingdoms are from one another, we all pass into the same place at the end. It does not matter what mortals called the place when they were alive. It is all one and the same. And such a vast place cannot be ruled by one. The responsibility needs to be shared." Persephone frowned. "But Hel seems to have given up her responsibility. No one has seen her for centuries, and she has let her kingdom become miserable, parched, and, yes, a bit brimstone-y."

Pluto absently ran his finger around the edge of the goblet. His long, ironlike fingernail created sparks as he did so. "Mortals who have accidently caught a glimpse of her kingdom cannot be blamed for reporting back that Hel's domain is a place of fire and lawlessness. That is the truth. But once upon a time it was a green and verdant landscape. Hel was a fair and good queen, and her kingdom was a place of harmony. The whole of the underworld relies on the River Styx for its nourishment, and that begins in her kingdom."

"So why can't you just go in there and move the stones that are blocking the mouth of the river?" Mari asked. "It sounds like Hel would be around if she could be. You should help her kingdom."

"All the gods and goddesses of the kingdom signed a sacred treaty an eternity ago," Pluto explained. "None of us are allowed to interfere in one another's kingdoms. I wish it was not the case, but it is."

"Okay," Uncle Mark said. "This is all very interesting, but we need the final two Runes of Valhalla. The ones that belong to Thor and Frigga."

Theo nodded so vigorously, Buzz thought he might lose his head. "Yes, especially the Thor one. Do you know where it is?"

Pluto and Persephone shared a swift glance, and then the Lord of the Underworld lifted his golden goblet and drank deeply from it. He wiped a hand across his mouth.

"When my father, Saturn, gave me those runes, he asked me to protect them." Pluto took another swift gulp from his goblet. "This is what I have endeavoured to do."

Buzz stared hard at Pluto. The lord of the underworld looked sheepish and, more than that, guilty.

"Where are the runes, Pluto?" he asked.

"The thing you must understand," Pluto continued, "is that I always expected Sunna to be the one to retrieve the runes." He looked down at his feet. "And so I hid them in a place that only a god or goddess could possibly survive."

Buzz's mouth went dry. *This doesn't sound good. Not at all.* "Where are the runes?" he asked again.

"In the Dread Caves," Persephone answered.

"The Dread Caves," Mari repeated. She kept saying the words, almost as if trying to recall a memory. Turning them over in her mouth like a pear drop.

"The Dread Caves," Uncle Mark said, and his voice broke on the last word. He coughed to clear his throat.

"Will everyone stop repeating each other and tell me what the Dread Caves are?" Theo demanded.

"The caves lie on the boundary between my kingdom and Hel's," Pluto explained. "They make real the thing you dread most." The Lord of the Underworld was still looking at his feet. "Often the thing that you dread is your greatest weakness, and the caves are designed to find that weakness and break you." Pluto raised his head and met Buzz's gaze. "You must understand that dying is the greatest fear for many – it is what they dread most. This is why the caves exist in the underworld."

"It might be all right, my dear," Persephone said, not sounding at all convinced. "There are four of them, and their auras are strong. If they work together they may just survive. You shouldn't blame yoursel—"

"You said the Dread Caves are where our greatest fears come to life," Mari interrupted. "Does that mean we will have to face four fears to get the runes?"

"What? No way," Theo squeaked. "I'm not facing *your* greatest fears. I have no idea what kind of messed-up stuff is in your head."

Pluto played with a pleat in his toga. "The caves will decide how to test you. To be honest, not that many people have actually ever come back in one piece, so it's hard to know how the caves make their decisions."

"How many is not many?" Buzz asked.

Pluto was now looking at his long silver fingernails as if they were the most interesting things he'd ever seen. "Um, well, none."

Theo shook his head. "You know, considering you're a god and have lived for like, forever, those caves were a momentously stupid place to put my rune." His fists clenched. "You've made it impossible."

"Impossible was the idea. I wanted to keep annoying mortals like you away from them," Pluto snapped back. "The Dread Caves would be nothing to Sunna, goddess of the sun." He rubbed at the corners of his mouth. "Still, it is clear I have been somewhat overzealous in the protection of the runes, and so I will help you."

"You're going to come with us?" Uncle Mark didn't sound pleased.

Persephone put a hand on her husband's arm possessively. "He's going nowhere."

Pluto patted her hand. "Of course not, dear. I don't want to end up like poor old Charon, do I?" His expression was pained. "He was the finest boatman to ever ferry the dead," he explained. "I asked him to put the runes in the Dread Caves, thinking he had nothing to dread and so nothing to fear, but he came back rather changed."

"Scared by his own shadow," Persephone added. "He sits in his chamber now and refuses to come out. It is a terrible thing."

"And I don't want the same thing to happen to you lot," Pluto finished. "So I'm going to offer you some gifts to help."

CHAPTER THIRTY

UNDERWORLD GIFTS

Pluto walked over to a massive onyx trunk that stood in the corner of the room and threw open its lid. Piles and piles of strange objects filled the interior.

Pluto hummed to himself as he perused the contents, silver fingers skipping along the objects until they came to rest on something of interest.

It was hard to see what the god was gathering up, but eventually he walked back to the table and laid out the objects.

Buzz could see a broad sword, a curved horn made of bone, a slingshot, and a helmet.

"I give you these gifts to help you in the test ahead," Pluto said.

"What are they?" Mari asked

"Now, that would be cheating." Pluto wagged a finger at her. "These objects choose their owners, but I promise I will tell you what your gift does once it has chosen you."

Theo leapt forwards and picked up the helmet, which appeared to be wrought from solid gold. "I choose this. I bet it's worth thousands. Plus, I've been thrown about by a tree and smashed into a wall in the last hour alone. I think it will be useful."

"Not sure it's smart to sell a gift from the underworld on eBay," Buzz pointed out, relieved that Theo had gone for the shiny thing instead of the slingshot.

"True," Mari agreed. "And I bet it's really heavy. Are you really going to be able to wear it?"

Theo looked at the helmet as if he'd made a terrible mistake. "Can I change my mind?" he asked.

Pluto shook his head. "Afraid not. Trust your instincts. Why don't you try it on for size?"

"Whatever." Theo shrugged, shoved the helmet on his head, and instantly disappeared.

"The helmet of invisibility," Pluto said. "A powerful gift that will keep you safe and keep you hidden whenever your wear it."

"Hang on a second," Theo demanded. "Are you telling me that no one can see me?" His voice came from somewhere in the middle of room.

Buzz nodded, annoyed that he'd failed to choose the helmet first. Still, even now the slingshot seemed to call to him. The silver wood appeared to be made from a single forked tree branch, and rows and rows of eyes had been carefully carved along its length. At the top of the wooden fork rested a leather pouch, which was strung with some kind of sinew. Buzz could almost hear the creak of the leather that would come when he pulled it back, and his finger itched to touch one of the shiny pebbles that lay on the table and—

"Ouch!" He yelped as his hair was yanked from behind.

He swung around to face his attacker but could see no one.

"Whoa, this is so cool," Theo crowed. His voice was somewhere near Buzz's ear, but he still wasn't visible. "You really can't see me, can you? Imagine how useful this helmet would be at school."

Theo pulled Buzz's hair again.

Buzz leapt forwards and picked up the slingshot, along with one of the pebbles next to it. He still couldn't see Theo, but somehow the slingshot was guiding his hand, and before he knew it he'd released a pebble.

There was a deep clunking sound and Theo suddenly appeared, the helmet toppling from his head.

"Hey! You hit my helmet." Theo knelt down and picked it up. "You dented it."

"Well, you started it," Buzz shot back.

"How did you do that?" Mari asked. "How did you know where to shoot?"

Buzz was staring at the slingshot in his hand. "It just knew, and I trusted it."

"And so the slingshot of Yggdrasill has chosen its owner." Pluto looked pleased. "It will never miss its target."

Only the horn and the sword lay on the table now.

Uncle Mark was staring at the sword, the gold of the hilt reflecting in his eyes. His finger traced the flat of the blade, and then he lifted the weapon. He twirled it around his head so that the metal was just a blur of silver.

"Cool sword," Theo said. "It turns anyone into an awesome swordsman, right?"

"Wrong," Pluto said. "That is the sword of justice. It is the sharpest blade ever to be forged, but it will not inflict injury on a person who is innocent. It will defeat any sword held by someone unworthy."

Buzz gazed at his godfather. Uncle Mark wasn't really listening to Pluto – he was far too busy twirling the sword above his head, practising his parries and thrusts.

Since when does Uncle Mark know how to use a sword? Buzz wondered. *Or speak ancient languages that even Mari hasn't heard of?* It was like Uncle Mark was a different man. *Or maybe his sleeping god is just closer to the surface than Theo's?*

"I guess the horn is all mine, then," Mari said, not sounding terribly excited.

"After a fashion," Pluto replied. "I do want you to take this with you on your quest. But you are to give it to Hel if you find her. She is the only one who is to use it. Tell her it will move the stones and make the water flow again."

"So my gift actually belongs to someone else." Mari raised an eyebrow. "Thanks."

"These are my gifts to *all* of you. And I have one more." He took up the golden pitcher and poured water into four goblets. "The water in these cups is from the River Styx. It is pure. Untarnished by the shadows of regrets which plague the river now."

"One sip will heal all your wounds," Persephone continued. "It will restore you to your truest and strongest form, and you'll need that for the fight that is to come."

Uncle Mark lowered his sword. "I thank you for the gifts and for you offer of water, but I have no injuries and no wish to be restored to anything other than what I am."

Persephone nodded. "As you wish."

"Your loss, Inspector Marko!" Theo strode forwards and snatched up a goblet, downing the water in one go. He grinned even as the wounds on his head and cheek began to heal. "Wow, that tastes *amazing*. No way is that water."

"I assure you it is," Pluto said. "There isn't much pure Styx water left in my kingdom, but what remains is the sweetest nectar you will ever drink."

Buzz reached out for one of the goblets, the longing to be free of pain in his legs almost becoming a pain in itself. Since meeting Sunna in the forest, his body had been dropped, drowned, and dragged through the realms of the gods. Buzz hadn't looked at his legs since getting on the drawbridge but only because he was scared that he'd see bone. And those were only the physical pains.

I just want to be fixed.

He brought the cup to his lips but stopped as Mari's warning about not eating or drinking anything in the underworld came back to him. His eyes slid over to her and saw that she also had a goblet in her hand.

"Persephone said it was just a myth," Mari said. "This is real life and we need to be ready for what's coming." She gulped down the water.

Buzz closed his eyes and did the same.

The taste of the water was extraordinary, and his tongue was alive with flavours he didn't even know existed. As the water flowed down his throat, warmth rushed through his body, and even his fingertips tingled with heat. It was like the feeling of crisp sheets still warm from the dryer; it was the scent of his grandmother's bread. It was a hug from his mother. It was a word of praise from his father. He felt the muscles in his legs begin to loosen, and his wounds heal over. He felt the headache that had been with him for days finally leave as well.

"Look at my hand, Buzz." Mari flexed it and waved her right palm in his face. The rose bed of blisters from their first encounter with Sunna was completely gone. Her arm dropped, and she began to look around her. Her eyes were large as she turned around in a small circle. It was as if she was taking in her surroundings for the first time. "It's funny," she said. "I'm getting such a strange sense of déjà vu." She put her hand to her temple.

"Are you all right?" Buzz asked.

She looked at him, her face thoughtful. "I'm not sure. I have this feeling like I know this place, but when I try to think about it, my brain feels like it is being scrambled."

"What have you done to her?" Buzz demanded. "She was fine until you gave her that water."

"You've drunk that water. So have I," Pluto insisted. "All it does is restore."

"Buzz, I'm fine," Mari insisted.

"We've delayed long enough," Uncle Mark said. "It is time that we get those runes."

Pluto quickly took an empty vial from the folds of his toga and filled it with some water. He placed it into Mari's hand. "Since you weren't best pleased with your gift, take this with you as well. I think some more water would do you a world of good. You're not fully restored yet."

Mari looked at the vial and then slipped it in her pocket. "Thank you." She took a candle from the table to help the light the way.

"Which way is it to the caves?" Buzz asked.

"I will take you there," Pluto promised. "Follow me."

CHAPTER THIRTY-ONE

THE DREAD CAVES

Buzz watched Pluto's retreating figure, and then he looked back at the caves. They sat there waiting, a vast yawning mouth with no teeth.

"The Dread Caves," Uncle Mark muttered. His hand tightened on the hilt of the sword of justice. "Come, we have delayed enough. The runes wait for us."

Mari led the way, holding her candle up.

The light from the flame threw their shadows up onto the wall – monstrous and unworldly companions that followed them deeper into the cave.

The sound of approaching footsteps echoed in the darkness.

"Someone's coming." Theo was shaking. His hands tightened on the helmet. It was his comforter, Buzz realized. The only thing that was keeping him from freaking out completely. The footsteps were replaced by a heavier tread and then that faded as well to be replaced by low growl.

Buzz took the slingshot from one pocket and released a smooth, shiny pebble from the other. He wondered whether his aim would be true once again when the time came. Then, Buzz heard the sound of embers crackling, and he smelt a bonfire scent.

Loki, he thought. *The god of chaos was coming.*

Mari sensed it, too. She stared into the darkness, and soon, a figure emerged from its depths. Loki's cloak of embers whirled around him, and the fiery slash of his mouth curved into a smile when he saw Mari. "Come, my dear," the smoky voice crooned. Loki reached out a hand. Mari held his gaze for a moment and then turned away and placed Pluto's candle in one of the grooves in the cave wall. "I think I'm going to need both hands to fight," she said.

As Loki stepped closer, Uncle Mark took a step back and dropped his sword. "I don't understand. Are you even real?"

Loki only stared at him. His candle-flame eyes giving nothing away.

"Does it matter?" Theo asked. He was trembling. "We've still got to fight him, and he's not even a *him*. He's a thing. How do we fight something made out of fire and smoke? We've got no chance." He lifted his helmet to his head, ready to disappear, but stopped as the figure of Loki began to flicker in and out of focus like a camera lens searching for clarity. The smoky outline of Loki blurred even more and then was gone, morphing into someone else entirely.

A young man with long, greasy hair and clothes that were almost threadbare stood before them. His skin looked sallow and his gaze was hooded.

"Joe?" Theo whispered. "Is that you?"

"Who's Joe?" Mari whispered.

"It's Theo brother. The one who ran away," Buzz replied.

"Where have you been?" Theo snarled. "Mum and Dad have been going out of their heads." Theo chewed his lip. "They're so unhappy."

"And you make them so happy?" Joe smirked. "We both know you're not the son they want around. They don't even notice you most of the time. They're just wondering where I am. Wishing I was home." He shrugged. "You're invisible, Theo. Always have been. Why don't you just leave?"

Theo was staring at Joe, his eyes glassy. Buzz could see his pain as clearly as a cut on the skin. "You're right," Theo muttered. "I don't want to be here." And with that, he brought the helmet down on his head and disappeared.

"Theo! Wait. Don't listen to him," Buzz cried. "We need to stick together."

"But I can't," Theo said. "I can't stay in this place. I can't see him. It hurts." His voice already sounded like it was halfway out of the cave. "You wouldn't understand."

"I do," Buzz said. "My mum was missing just like Joe. The not knowing is the worst bit."

"But everyone feels bad for you," Theo's voice was snappish.

"They just think my family is a waste of space. It's like I'm not allowed to be sad that Joe is gone." These last words sounded very far away now.

And Buzz realized at last, too late, why Theo was always so horrible to him.

"Theo, come back," Mari cried. "Please."

But there was no reply. Theo had gone.

Joe's face split into a smile as he began to morph once more, and then the boy was gone and the Prof stood in his place.

"Prof?" Buzz said. "What are you doing here?" But he knew the answer. His father always did put dread in his heart. Dread every time he saw him, because Buzz knew he wasn't enough for his father. Neither were Mum or Tia. And Buzz wished that it was different. He wanted his dad in his life, but the Prof's obsession with the Tangley Woods always got in the way.

"Buzz, I know you're quite the expert when it comes to silly questions, but please appreciate that I'm busy," the Prof replied, his eyes raking the cave. "The answer is here somewhere, I know it. You mustn't distract me."

His father's criticism stung, but Buzz lifted his chin. "This illusion is not going to work." His assertion bounced off the walls. "You're not going to run me out of this cave." Buzz could hear the raw pain in his voice and knew that the caves could hear it as well. He'd have to do better if they were going to leave him alone. "He doesn't care about me," Buzz shouted. "I get it. But I care about him and I always will because he's my dad. You,

on the other hand, are just an illusion, and I'm finished with it."
He took his slingshot from his pocket.

The Prof's eyes went round with fear. "Don't do it. Don't
hurt me, Buzz. I'm your father." *This is exactly what I saw in the
time tunnel,* Buzz realized. *I thought I was killing my father, but
I'm just ending an illusion.* He fired the pebble. The Prof slumped
onto the ground. Then the image of him began to twist and
turn. Skin turned to fur, and Buzz's father was replaced by a
giant wolf.

The beast stood in front of them, his silver fur shimmering
in the candlelight, and Buzz found that he was not scared of
the animal just awestruck at the magnificence of him. The wolf
took his breath away. It froze him to the spot.

The wolf padded towards them and then lifted his muzzle to
sniff the air. Buzz hadn't thought that wolves could smile, but
this one did. A wolfish, lopsided grin that got bigger and bigger
as the beast stared at Mari. He opened his mouth and made a
yelping noise as if in greeting.

Mari frowned. "I know you, don't I?" she whispered. "But
how?" She took a step towards the beast, but Uncle Mark
barged past her to stand before the wolf.

"Fenris." The hissed word was one of pure hate, and Uncle
Mark gave a roar as he charged towards the wolf, his sword
held high.

"No!" Mari threw herself forwards. "No. Don't hurt him."

Buzz sprinted after her, just managing to grab her arm before she put herself between the descending blade and the wolf.

"Uncle Mark, stop!" he cried.

But his words were drowned out by Mari's scream as the blade slashed down towards the wolf's pelt.

Buzz felt something twist in his own gut, knowing that that it was too late to save the wolf.

Then he saw something amazing.

The blade bounced off the wolf, leaving no wound and no blood. It was as if the creature was made of steel.

The wolf was low to ground, hackles raised. He watched Uncle Mark with amber eyes that were full of fury, and his body was tightly wound, ready to spring. The wolf's back arched, and Buzz noticed two familiar stones embedded along the creature's spine. They were nestled in the wolf's fur, the area around them red and raw. *The last two runes.* "Easy, Fenris," Mari murmured. "Easy."

The wolf bared his teeth at Uncle Mark but did not attack. Mari's voice seemed to be dampening his fury.

"Mark, this wolf is not our enemy." Mari's brown eyes flashed fire behind her glasses. "He's an innocent. That's why your blade won't work."

"Innocent?" Uncle Mark was circling the wolf, his sword clasped tightly in his palm. "He bit my hand clean off. That was his thanks when I tried to keep him safe."

"Your hand?" Buzz asked, wondering if his uncle had hit his head or something. "You've got both hands."

"In this lifetime, perhaps," Uncle Mark muttered. "But I haven't forgotten what that beast did. What I lost." His face twisted with bitterness. "'Who wants to worship a one-handed warrior god?'" he said in a falsetto voice. "That's what my followers said. And just like that, I was finished." His jaw clenched. "Replaced by that charlatan and travelling salesman, Odin."

Uncle Mark's hand flexed on the sword's hilt. "But now is my time, and I will have my revenge on those who wronged me. The whole world will kneel at my feet and worship me." *Oh no,* Buzz thought. The Dread Caves were really getting to his godfather, giving him hallucinations. With a cry, his Uncle Mark charged forwards once again. Fenris rose to meet him, snapping out with open jaws and a blur of teeth. Not breaking his stride, Uncle Mark somersaulted upwards and slashed his sword downwards. The blade scraped across the wolf's back in a shower of sparks as it connected with the runes. With a pop, they were released from the wolf's pelt and flew into the air, landing by the cave wall.

"Are those what I think they are?" Mari asked.

Buzz nodded, his gaze marking the spot where the runes had landed. "I think so, but Uncle Mark hasn't even noticed. These caves are making him hallucinate. We need to stop this fight, get those runes, and get out of here."

"This blasted sword is useless." Uncle Mark slashed out at the cave wall, and his blade passed through it like butter, cleaving off a chunk of stone. Uncle Mark scooped up the rock and hurled it at Fenris.

The wolf gave a howl of pain as the rock smacked into the side of his massive, shaggy head, and Uncle Mark took his chance. He darted forwards, flipped the sword upwards, caught the blade between his two palms, and then brought the hilt down on the wolf's muzzle like a club.

Fenris howled and his massive paw swung out and swatted Uncle Mark away like a fly. Buzz saw his godfather somersault through the air and hit the cave wall with a sickening crunch.

Uncle Mark groaned as he slid to the ground, and then lay very still.

CHAPTER THIRTY-TWO

RESTORATION

Buzz ran to his side. *He's still breathing.* But Uncle Mark was in a very bad way.

Buzz turned to Mari. Fenris had flopped down onto the ground as well, whimpering softly. Blood seeped from the wounds on his head and muzzle, and his eyes were unfocused. Mari was kneeling beside him, the vial of water that Pluto had given her at the wolf's lips.

"Wait," Buzz said. "My uncle needs that."

Mari rested a hand on the wolf's giant, shaggy head and stroked it. "Fenris deserves it more."

"He's just a wolf, Mari," Buzz snapped. "And you don't get to decide who lives and who dies. You're not a god."

"He's more than a wolf. I can feel it." Mari's eyes looked uncertain and a bit scared. "And I *do* decide because Pluto gave me the vial. He said that it was mine to use." Buzz took a breath.

Getting angry with Mari was not going to help anyone. "Please, Uncle Mark has been there for me my whole life. And he's hurt. You've got to help him."

The confusion in Mari's eyes was gone. "The body may belong to your uncle but that's not who is here with us."

"What are you talking about?"

His godfather coughed as if in answer, and Buzz could hear a worrying rattle in his chest. "Just before your Uncle Mark got knocked out he vowed that he would be worshipped again by humanity, and told us that he got his hand bitten off by Fenris. Mari sounded exasperated. "In myth, that's exactly what happened to the God of Justice, Tyr – the day guardian for Tuesday." Mari continued to stroke Fenris's head. "Don't you see? The god Tyr has been awake in your uncle Mark for a while now. But instead of telling us that, he's been pretending to be your uncle, accessing Mark's memories so that you'd trust him."

Buzz shook his head. "We're in the Dread Caves. Pluto said that this place has a bad effect on people. That's why Uncle Mark is saying strange stuff."

Mari's expression was the most serious he'd ever seen it. "Your Uncle Mark is not here, Buzz. He's been replaced by a god with a grudge against Odin who's been trying to pull the wool over our eyes."

Uncle Mark groaned. Droplets of sweat were beading on his forehead.

"Mari, give me the vial, ple—"

"I didn't piece it together right away," Mari said. "But Tyr is another angry god just like Loki, and we need to be careful. We don't know what his plan is." "But he can't be Tyr," Buzz protested. "He held the rune and nothing happened. We were there."

"But that was not the first time Uncle Mark would have held Tyr's rune, is it?" Mari countered. "He held it weeks ago, when the runes were discovered in that raid. Don't you see? Uncle Mark's sleeping god probably woke up then."

"But why would he lie?" Buzz asked. "Why wouldn't he tell us what'd happened to him?"

"Exactly," Mari said. "Tyr is hiding something."

CHAPTER THIRTY-THREE

TYR

Buzz's thoughts were like biting ants nipping away at his brain. If what Mari said was true, it meant that Uncle Mark, or rather, Tyr, had been lying from the start of this whole mess on Friday the thirteenth. Lying about looking for the World Tree and not finding it. Lying about knowing nothing about Sunna or Loki. *There has to be a reason*, Buzz told himself. *But we'll never find out what if we don't heal him.*

Uncle Mark coughed again and blood splattered onto his lips. They were running out of time.

"Mari, you want the truth," Buzz said. "And I can't let my godfather die. So how about this? Give half the vial to Uncle Mark and half to Fenris. Give them both a chance to live."

Mari hesitated for a moment, gazing first at Fenris and then at Uncle Mark. Finally, she pulled the stopper from the vial and trickled some of the water into the wolf's mouth before passing the vial to Buzz.

He dribbled what was left of the water into his godfather's mouth.

Uncle Mark groaned and curled himself into a ball on the floor, but Buzz could already see that he was breathing more evenly.

Fenris gave a low whine and lifted his head from Mari's lap. The wolf looked warily at Uncle Mark and then touched his muzzle with his paw. It had already begun to heal, and the bleeding had stopped. He made a yelping noise.

"It was the water," Mari said. "It healed you."

The wolf yelped again.

"No, I don't think it will leave a scar." Mari giggled.

"You understand him?"

Mari's eyes widened in surprise. "You don't?"

Buzz shook his head.

The wolf lay his head on Mari's lap and yelped again. "He says he missed me. That he's been in a dark place, in the chaos, for a long time, but that we have brought him back and he's thankful." She listened carefully as the wolf continued, staring down at him. "He does not want to fight Tyr anymore. He wants to thank him for cutting away the runes. They didn't belong there."

"Mari, who does he think you are?" Buzz asked. "What does he mean when he says he missed you?"

"I don't know," Mari said, stroking the wolf's head. "And I'm not sure he'd understand the question if I were to ask."

Buzz turned to check on his godfather's progress, but Uncle Mark was gone. And so were the runes.

The sound of metal slashing against stone reverberated around the cavern.

Uncle Mark stood at the mouth of the cave. A fierce, gold light radiated from his skin. He was much taller as well. His sword was raised up high, and he smashed it into the giant stalactites that hung overhead.

Buzz scrambled to his feet. "Hey, what are you doing?" he cried.

"I'm sorry, Buzz," his godfather said. "I know Mark would want to keep you safe. He loves you very much – it is written all over his memories. But this is the way it has to be. You will be staying here, forever. A victim of an unfortunate cave-in."

Buzz took a step forwards.

"I would think very carefully before you take another step. This stalactite could fall at any moment."

Buzz stopped and looked up. Several of the giant stalactites were hanging on by moss alone. They just needed a little push.

"So, I was right." Mari was glaring at the god. "You are Tyr."

Tyr inclined his head. "I was doing a good job of disguising my god self until you gave me that water. But there is no hiding from the truth now that I'm fully restored."

"You can't leave us here," Buzz said.

Tyr shrugged. "You are a risk to my plan. A plan that has been hard fought for." He watched the stalactites sway like wind chimes.

Buzz gazed at them also. The gentle sway of the biggest stalactite was almost hypnotic.

The god gave him a crooked smile. "I'll make you a deal," he said. "I will talk with you for as long as this big stalactite hangs. That way, you die with some questions answered, at least. I owe Mark that much for the use of his body. I can hear him squealing at the back of my mind, and this might shut him up."

Mari rolled her eyes. "Could you be a bigger cliché? The villain who tells us all just because he thinks the heroes are about to die?"

"Is that what you think you are? Heroes?" Tyr laughed. "Heroes tend to win the day, and right now I'd say you were definitely losing. And I don't think you're going to die in this place. I *know* it. You have no food. You've used up all your water. And who knows what other fears may creep up on you in these caves."

Fenris gave a low growl and got to his feet, but Mari put a hand on his shoulder, and the wolf sat back on his haunches.

Tyr's eyes narrowed as he looked at Fenris. "It's a shame that I don't have the time to deal with you, wolf-breath, but I have expended enough energy on you. Besides, it makes little sense to kill Loki's son, however furry he might be. It would put an unnecessary strain on our relationship if he were to find out. He does so love his children."

"Loki?" Buzz said. "But you're a day guardian. Why are you working for the enemy?"

"Working for him?" Tyr spat. "He works for me. I freed him, and he has been executing my orders ever since." "Just how long have you been planning this?" Mari asked. Tyr put his head to one side. "Not long. My awakening was accidental. It only happened because Mark came into contact with my rune." He shrugged. "Some would call it fate. Wiser people know that the runes will always try to find their way back to their owners." Tyr's blade grazed the edge of the stalactite teasingly, and it began to sway a bit more.

"When I realized that I was awake but none of the other day guardians were, I took my chance. I freed Loki, and together we planned to finish Odin and the others for good." Tyr's face took on a pleased expression. "Odin stole my worshippers and became Father of the Gods and now he will pay."

"He didn't steal them," Mari said. "People stopped believing in you. There's a difference."

"It was his fault," Tyr snarled back. "Odin took my throne away, but I knew that I could take as well. I could take his powers. I could take the powers of the rest of the day guardians. But I had to find all the sleeping gods first. And find their hidden runes." Tyr smirked. "Odin was so predictable. I knew he would have made it Sunna's mission to ascend the World Tree and retrieve the Runes of Valhalla if she was ever awoken because Loki was unbound." Tyr frowned. "But when I had Loki capture Sunna, she would not tell him where the runes were hidden. Sunna the stubborn she should be called."

Tyr peered at the stalactite. "Wow, this thing is clinging on much longer than I expected. My throat is getting quite parched with all this talking." He raised his sword to strike at the stalactite again.

"Wait! How did you find the sleeping gods?" Buzz asked quickly. It was a question designed to distract Tyr, but Buzz had been wondering this. "Sunna was meant to use their runes to track them down, but you didn't have the runes – we did."

Tyr lowered his sword. "It's a funny story, actually. You see, removing Sunna from the human realm and creating the unmorrow curse made it a lot easier to identify the other sleeping gods in Crowmarsh. Like Theo, they were all aware that something was wrong. They all started asking questions, and ultimately, they all came to ask their trusted town policeman for help." Tyr gave a cackle of laughter. "It couldn't have been easier. They came to me, and I gathered them all up. Now they are prisoners with Sunna until they have served their purpose."

"What purpose is that?" Buzz asked. "Why haven't you just killed them?"

"Oh, I will do that," Tyr assured him. "But first they must each activate their rune. Once each rune is triggered by their touch, I will be able to drain the stones of their power and become the most powerful god that has ever existed." He grinned again. "And thanks to you, I now have all six runes." He jiggled them in his pocket. "It's time for me to go and finish this."

Tyr swung out with his sword again, but just before it

271

connected, the god's eyes rolled to white and then back again. His face seemed to blur and the sword stopped in midair.

"Buzz, it's me, Mark. You've got to help me." His godfather gave a small sob. "I wish I was stronger. I wish I could have told you what was happening." His chest began to rise and fall rapidly. "You need to get out of here and find the others. Tyr and Loki are holding all the day guardians and this really mouthy squirrel in Hel's kingdom. It's the same prison that held Loki."

"It's not your fault Uncle Mark," Buzz said. "I'm going to fix this. All of it."

"If anyone can do it, buddy, you can." Uncle Mark's smile was proud and then his eyes rolled in his head once more and Tyr was back.

"Honestly, mortals! They are so annoying. They never stay where you put them." The god curled his lip. "At least you got to say goodbye." He struck out with his sword and jumped back.

Buzz covered his face with his arm as the biggest stalactite dropped with a crash. Others followed it and soon the mouth of the cave was completely filled in.

"So, here we are," Mari said after the echo of the crashing stalactites faded.

"Here we are," Buzz repeated.

"Tell me you've got a great idea?" Mari asked.

Buzz shook his head. "All that knowledge that the EarthWorm gave me is gone."

"You never needed that worm to give you good ideas, Buzz."

Mari walked up to the stalactites that now filled the mouth of the cave. She reached out and touched it. "There has got to be a way to get out of here," Mari said. "Theo's out there by himself, we need to warn him that Uncle Mark – I mean – Tyr will be looking for him."

Buzz's eyes went to the horn that hung from Mari's shoulder. "Hey, there might be a way," he said. "Doesn't that horn move rocks or something?"

Mari followed his eyes, and she grazed the horn with her fingers. "But Pluto said I was to give this to Hel to make the water flow. It belongs to her."

"Hel isn't here," Buzz said. "Hasn't been in the underworld for centuries from the sounds of it. If she was around, she would have freed her father from his prison. It was in her kingdom, after all."

Mari frowned. "I don't know. It just feels wrong to use it when it doesn't belong to me. What if something bad happens?"

Fenris launched to his feet and began to yelp furiously at her, wolf saliva going everywhere. Fenris was a big wolf. The yelps were big yelps.

Mari covered her ears. "All right, all right," she shouted over the wolf. "Say it, don't spray it, Fenris. Fine, I'll do it."

Fenris stopped yelping, and Mari shrugged the horn off her shoulder.

"What was he saying?" Buzz asked.

"He says that this horn is mine to use and to stop stalling

because we've got to find Tyr and stop him." She put the horn to her mouth and blew. No sound came out but instead Buzz could see a wave of movement on the air. It crashed into the fallen stalactites and the rocks began to vibrate. Soon the rocks were just a black blur, and then just a pile of dust on the floor.

"It worked." Mari stared at the empty cave mouth. "I actually made the horn work."

Fenris padded out of the cave and put his nose to the ground. He gave a low growl.

"He's got Tyr's scent," Mari explained. She climbed onto Fenris's back and held out her hand to Buzz. "Come on, I promise Fenris doesn't mind."

Buzz stared at the giant wolf and gulped. "I've never travelled by wolf before."

Mari laughed as Buzz climbed on. "It's definitely not the strangest thing we've done today. Let's go catch a god."

CHAPTER THIRTY-FOUR

STAIRCASE TO HEL

Fenris galloped along the length of the tunnel that climbed steeply upwards, his giant paws slapping against the rocky ground whilst Buzz and Mari clung to his fur. The dry, warm air of the tunnel glided across Buzz's skin, while grit thrown up by the wolf's massive strides stung his eyes and coated his teeth. It was like being on a roller coaster. *A really furry roller coaster,* Buzz thought. Still he felt safe on Fenris's wide, muscled back even as they headed towards danger.

They spilt out into a cavern that arched above them like a vaulted cathedral. It almost looked like they were inside a volcano. The walls were completely covered in patterns of striped, solidified magma and carved into one side were steps that climbed up to what had to be the mouth of the volcano. Through it, Buzz could see stars that burned brightly in an indigo sky.

"Is it just me or are we in a volcano?" Mari asked.

"No, I thought that as well," Buzz said, as he and Mari climbed off Fenris.

"It's awesome!" came Theo's voice. Then a short, sharp whack filled the air, like a hand being slapped over a mouth.

"Theo? Are you here?" Mari's hands were on her hips and she turned in a slow circle.

Theo did not appear.

"We heard you," Buzz said. "We know you're there."

Still Theo did not appear.

Buzz took out his slingshot and a pebble. He rolled the pebble in between two fingers. "Do you really want me to use this again to find you?" Buzz asked.

But before Theo could reply, Fenris bounded forwards and released his massive pink tongue, slurping at the empty air.

"Eww," Theo cried. He suddenly appeared, helmet in hand and with wolf saliva dripping off his face.

Mari laughed. "Nice to see you, Theo."

"Yeah, yeah," Theo grumbled.

Buzz looked at him closely. Apart from the dripping cheeks, Theo looked much better than he had the last time Buzz saw him. Gone was that look of fear and despair that had been in Theo's eyes in the Dread Caves. He just looked put out that he had been licked by a wolf.

"How did you find your way here?" Buzz asked.

"I travelled wolf style. I was sitting right behind you. Not very observant, are you, Buzzkill?"

"You were invisible."

"Excuses, excuses," Theo responded.

"Hang on – if you got on Fenris's back, then that means you must have been right by the Dread Caves when Mari freed us."

Theo nodded.

"So did you see Tyr trap us in those caves?" Mari asked.

Theo hesitated but nodded his head again.

"And you didn't do anything to stop him?" Buzz asked.

Theo wouldn't meet his eye. "Listen, I was there for pretty much the whole thing. I heard everything that Tyr guy said, and can I just say that he is seriously angry."

"Don't change the subject," Mari said. "You watched Tyr block us into those caves and didn't do anything to stop him."

Theo looked sheepish and defensive, both at the same time. "What exactly was I supposed to do about an angry god who now also has my rune?" Theo spread his arms wide. "Yes, I let him block you in. Yes, I watched him run off at super-fast god speed. Yes, I cut up my hands trying to move those rocks out of the cave mouth."

Buzz glanced down and saw how bloody Theo's hands were.

"Mari, we should give him a break," Buzz said. "Staying hidden from Tyr was probably the smartest thing Theo's ever done."

Theo snorted. "The smartest thing would have been me keeping my mouth shut so that you didn't know I was around."

"We're on this quest together," Buzz said. "Whether we like it or not."

"And that's working out great." Theo rolled his eyes. "Uncle Mark seemed like a nice guy, he was on our quest, and now he's a power-crazed Norse God. As far as I see it, you can't trust anyone."

"So what are you doing here?" Mari asked. "Why did you follow us?"

"Because I want my rune," Theo said. "And once I get it, I'm out of here."

Fenris padded over to the steps, his huge head gazing upwards at the mouth of the volcano. For once, Buzz understood perfectly. Hel's kingdom was up there. The day guardians, the runes, and even little Ratatosk waited for them.

Buzz stepped onto the stairs. "If you want your rune, it's going to be up there. But you're going to have to fight for it." For a moment, Buzz was reminded of his English teacher, Mrs Robertson. She said he was too quick to give up when things got hard. If only she could see him now.

"I guess it can't be as bad as the Dread Caves." Theo tossed his helmet up in the air and caught it.

They began to climb the stairs, the steps whisper soft and smooth beneath their feet. As they rose higher, Buzz saw that the walls of the volcano were pockmarked with holes that seemed to lead off into other magma chambers. Buzz could see flashes of movement in these caverns – could feel eyes watching them – and he remembered what Pluto had said about Hel's kingdom becoming a lawless place. His hand tightened on the slingshot, ready for any trouble.

But whoever was watching them was content with just that and let them pass. *Maybe they're hiding,* Buzz thought. *Hiding from Tyr and Loki.*

As they walked upwards, Mari reached out to touch a deep channel that ran alongside the stairs. When her fingers came away, they were just a tiny bit damp. "Do you think this is the channel Pluto was talking about?" Mari asked. "The one that is supposed to be bring the water to the River Styx from Hel's kingdom?"

"Could be," Buzz said. "Rain would fall onto the lip of the crater, then flow down this channel."

"Then into the branches of the rivers that run into the underworlds," Mari said. "It's just like Pluto said. Something is stopping the water from flowing down channel, and Hel is not here to fix it." Mari's hand went to the horn that still hung from her shoulder. "I wonder where she is."

Fenris butted his head against her side and looked at her with mournful eyes, as if he could sense Mari's concern.

Mari smiled. "Don't look so sad, fella," she said. "You're the upbeat one."

They were almost at the top of the stairs now, the wide open crater revealing an arc of sky only a few feet above their heads. The last step led them directly onto a strip of rock that appeared to lead into another magma chamber.

"Theo. Put your helmet on and go and tell us what you see," Buzz said.

"Alright, Boss." Theo rolled his eyes and then promptly disappeared.

"Do you think that was a good idea?" Mari whispered. "What if he doesn't come back? What if he just gets his rune and runs off?"

"Then better we know that now, before we go in there."

"Oh ye of little faith." Theo appeared again at their side, his hair flattened by the helmet. "Don't worry, there's no way I'm getting my rune back by myself. This is going to have to be a team effort."

"What did you see?" Buzz asked.

"A dragon. A really big dragon, and he was playing catch with this squirrel. The squirrel was not impressed. Had quite a mouth on him."

"Ratatosk!" Mari exclaimed. "He really is alive!"

"Then I saw Loki," Theo went on. "He was placing the runes on this strange circle thing, and Tyr was standing in the middle of it, telling him to hurry up."

"Anything else?"

Theo scratched the back of his neck. "Yeah, I think I saw the other day guardians—" Theo broke off. "You better come and see for yourself. Let's just say there's some familiar faces."

Buzz nodded. "Let's go."

"Wait! Won't Loki and Tyr see us?" Mari asked.

Theo shook his head. "Don't worry. I've found another path that will take us above their heads. They're right down in the bottom of the next chamber." Theo showed them the new path and they came to a narrow platform that jutted out proudly.

The magma chamber below was bigger than the ones Buzz had glimpsed on their climb up the stairs. In the centre of the room, he could see a raised circular pedestal on which Tyr stood. He was surrounded by a radial of carved-out channels that looked like a sunburst. Each ray of the sunburst led to one of the six runes that rested around the edge of the pedestal.

All the runes except two were glowing with an intense brightness. Tyr's rune had already been used up, Buzz reminded himself, and Theo's rune hadn't been activated yet, but clearly all others had. The tiniest amount of liquid light was already beginning to gather in the channels that flowed up the sunburst towards Tyr. In one corner of the cavern, Buzz could see Ratatosk and the dragon. Ratatosk looked exhausted, and the dragon looked bored of his game of catch.

In the other corner, Buzz could see Saturn. He wasn't even tied up and looked like a bad photocopy of himself. Loki stood beside him, watching Tyr on the pedestal with a crooked smile on his face. Buzz spotted Sunna on the other side of the chamber. She was tied to a post by a blue lasso of fire. It was identical to the one that had tied her to the World Tree in the Tangley Woods. But Buzz didn't think it would be turning back to normal rope anytime soon.

Next to her, also lashed to a post, stood Coach Saunders. Buzz could tell it was him, even though he looked different. He was taller and stronger, and with a silver moonlit aura radiating from him.

He has one of the sleeping gods inside him, Buzz realized. *Scrap that.* The god was no longer asleep.

Next to Coach Saunders, Buzz saw Mrs Robertson. She was changed as well. And then, next to her, he saw . . . he saw . . . the Prof.

"Dad?" he said out loud.

"Shhh!" Theo put a hand across his mouth. "I told you that you needed to come and have a look. Your dad is a god – that's pretty cool, right?"

"That's your dad?" Mari asked, pointing. "He looks totally awesome. I mean, much more than the others. He's almost too bright to look at."

Mari was right. Out of all the gods, his father shone the brightest. He was Odin . . . He had to be.

"We've got to help them," Buzz said. He pushed his surprise, his questions about what this meant for his father's future, deep down. They needed a plan.

"Right." Buzz turned to Theo. "You're going to turn invisible, go down there, and free the day guardians."

"What? I should get the runes."

"Use your helmet to break the blue fire that's holding them.

If you break the beam, they will be able to escape."

Buzz put a hand on Fenris's head. "I need you to deal with the dragon." He pointed at the scaled beast who was breathing jets of fire at Ratatosk. The squirrel was managing to jump out the way but not for much longer. The wolf stared at the dragon with hard eyes. He understood. Buzz took his slingshot out of his pocket. "I'm going to deal with our Tyr problem."

"You're going to shoot him?" Mari questioned. "But your Uncle Mark is still in there somewhere and—"

"Don't worry. I'm not going to hit him. I'm going to hit the runes off the plinth. Mari, I need you to catch them and give them to the proper day guardians.

Mari nodded. "Once they have their powers back, they can help us stop Loki and Tyr."

Theo gave a slow smile. "Nice game plan, Buzzkill. Coach Saunders would be proud."

Down below, Tyr still stood on the pedestal, and Loki was watching motionless as more of the runes' power pooled and then flowed through the sunburst channels.

"Why is it taking so long?" Tyr snarled.

"Patience," Loki's smoky voice reassured. "Good things come to those who wait."

"Those runes don't belong to you," Odin's voice boomed from the Prof's mouth. And it sounded like the waves and the wind. "Their powers are not yours to take."

Loki whirled to face the All-Father. "You no longer get to

choose what is right and what is wrong, Odin. That is for others to decide now."

"I know you have no reason to trust me," Odin implored. "I tore your family apart while I was still mad in my grief for my son Balder. I locked you up here in this place and told myself that the only way forward was the way of the prophecy. The way of Ragnarok. I told myself that everything had to end."

"Odin, you didn't just tear apart my family. You ripped out my heart," Loki snarled. "My children were killed, banished, and scattered. And what about my daughter? My sweet Hel. This was her kingdom, and you made it my prison. Then you destroyed her."

"She would not stop until you were free," Odin admitted. "But I did not destroy her. I sent her away. To a safe place."

"Enough," Tyr snarled. "Do you really believe him, Loki? Odin killed her. Just as you can kill him once I have all the power from the runes."

"Buzz," Theo hissed. "This is our chance." Theo was looking down at the gathered gods. "While they're arguing. I'll free Sunna first. As soon as I do, Mari come down with Fenris to catch the runes. Right?"

"Right," Buzz said. "Good luc—"

"Don't wish me luck, I won't need it." Theo shoved the iron helmet on his head and disappeared.

Buzz watched. Waiting for Sunna to be freed.

"You okay, Buzz?" Mari whispered. "I mean your dad is Odin."

Buzz shook his head. "Odin is Odin, and my dad is my dad. They might share the same body, but my father is not really here." As he said the words, he felt a twist of sadness at the thought of that. His head filled with all the words that he'd never felt able to say before because the anger always got in the way.

Stop it, Buzz. He concentrated on the figure of Sunna, and then he saw it. The flash of Theo's face as he took off his helmet and used it to break the lasso of fire.

"Go," Buzz said.

Mari climbed onto Fenris's back, and the wolf leapt down into the magma chamber with a howl.

CHAPTER THIRTY-FIVE

THE BATTLE

Buzz watched as Fenris landed on the ground in one elegant movement, and Mari scrambled off his back and rolled out of the way as the wolf turned to face the dragon – teeth bared and hackles raised.

The dragon opened his mouth with a screech and let forth a jet of fire, but Fenris was quicker. He pushed back on his hind legs and leapt high over the dragon's head. Landing behind Nidhogg, Fenris managed to pounce on the dragon's lower back. With a guttural growl, his claws dug into the creature's scaled flesh.

The dragon screeched with pain and beat its massive wings. He rose off the ground, and began to climb into the air, thrashing wildly. The wolf would not be dislodged – Fenris's claws were too deeply embedded.

Yet still Nidhogg rose.

Looking down from his concealed position on top of the platform, Buzz could see that both Loki and Tyr were staring up at the battle between the wolf and the dragon.

Glancing across the chamber, Buzz saw that Theo had now released Sunna and Coach Saunders. Theo worked in the shadows, while Loki and Tyr continued to look upwards at the battle between Nidhogg and Fenris.

Ratatosk had joined Mari and they were crouched low, hidden by the pedestal, waiting for the runes to start flying.

Time for the next part of the plan. Buzz grabbed his slingshot and launched the first pebble, sending it hurtling towards the plinth. It hit Sunna's rune dead on and sent it spinning off into Mari's waiting hands. Buzz fired off another two pebbles in quick succession, both finding their targets as Pluto had promised they would. Mari and Ratatosk gathered up both runes and ducked behind the pedestal once more.

Three down, three to go, Buzz thought, but the pedestal vanished as the dragon and the wolf suddenly filled his view.

Fenris was still clinging grimly to the dragon's back, desperately trying to claw his way upwards towards the dragon's neck. With another beat of its wings, the dragon was now completely at Buzz's eye level, and it opened its mouth in a screech of fury as it saw Buzz.

Nidhogg let forth a new jet of flame, and Buzz threw himself out of the way, slipping off the strip of rock he'd been balanced on. He plummeted downwards but then felt his whole body snap back up as the slingshot in his hand caught on a piece of jutting rock.

Looking up, Buzz could see small holes where the dragon's flame had scorched the magma wall and melted it. It looked just like Swiss cheese. Nidhogg hurtled towards him. He was so close, Buzz could see Nidhogg's slanted eyes and black pupils ringed with red.

Buzz felt his hand loosen on the slingshot. What would be better? To fall to his death or be smashed to pieces by a dragon? *Holey pyjamas. It's not much of a choice.*

Fenris give a furious howl, and Buzz watched as the wolf swung his body away from the dragon and towards the damaged magma wall. The dragon gave a screech of surprise and went careening off course, smashing into the wall and breaking it apart. Both Fenris and Nidhogg tumbled through the gap and out of sight.

Thank you, Fenris, Buzz thought, even as the slingshot gave a creak of protest and then the sinew snapped. Buzz was falling once more, knowing that this time it really was over.

Oof. Buzz landed, but it wasn't on the ground. It was in someone's arms He glanced up as he was placed on the ground and found himself looking at his father.

Correction: *Odin,* the All-Father. His dad was tall, but never this tall. Buzz had to tip his head back to look at him.

"Um, thanks," Buzz said.

"You're welcome," Odin said in a voice as deep as the valleys.

Odin's face blurred and the expression became awkward and slightly stiff. It was exactly the expression that the Prof wore whenever he wanted to talk about something big.

"Dad?" Buzz asked hesitantly.

"Buzz." His father folded his arms around him. "Oh Buzz, I've been so worried about you. I'm sorry I didn't believe you before. You need to know that."

"How come you're here? I mean, how come Odin is letting you talk to me?"

His father frowned. "Odin shares my mind. He knows how worried I've been about you. Just as I know how sorry he is that any of this happening."

Buzz thought about poor Uncle Mark and how Tyr had been controlling him completely for weeks now. How his godfather had fought to talk to him.

"Odin," Sunna cried. "We need you." Buzz turned to see that Tyr was off the pedestal, wielding his sword against the day guardians. His father kissed Buzz on the forehead. "I'd better let Odin take over from here. You must get those runes. I don't think Odin and the others can fight Tyr for much longer without their full powers." His father's face blurred once more as Odin took control. Buzz watched as Odin charged at Tyr, distracting him from Coach Saunders, who was cornered and defending himself with just the jacket he wore. Tyr swung out at Odin but the All-Father dodged and ducked as Tyr tried to cleave him in two.

Buzz scanned the chamber. *The guardians need their runes.* Where was Mari?

Finally, he found her. She was staring at Loki. But she didn't look scared. She looked joyful. Ratatosk was at her side, his jaw hanging open.

Buzz felt something in his chest twist as Mari held out her hand and gave Loki the three runes that had been shot off the pedestal. The trickster god nodded and turned and walked away with them.

"In the time tunnel, I saw myself make a really bad decision. I saw myself help Loki." Mari's words came back to Buzz then. *She warned me and said she'd make the right choice.* Buzz's hand went to his slingshot, ready to stop Loki, but he remembered that his weapon was gone. Broken and smashed on the floor somewhere.

He raced to Mari's side. "What have you done!" he cried. "Why did you give him the runes?"

Mari looked at him, but her features looked blurred somehow and she shimmered. "Because he's my father, Buzz. Loki is my father, and Fenris is my brother."

"Mari?" Buzz questioned.

But Mari shook her head. "'Tis no Mari you speak to. I am Hel. This is my home." She put a hand on his arm. "Loki is going to help us."

Buzz stared at Mari. *No, Hel.* "Loki is the trickster god," he hissed. "Mari told me that the very first time I met her."

Buzz felt the scrabble of claws on his left leg as Ratatosk clambered up him and came to rest on his shoulder.

"I told yer once that truth is to be yer most reliable guide if yer to survive any quest." The squirrel's whiskers were quivering. "I heard what Loki said. We have to trust him to help us. Help his daughter."

Buzz gazed at where Loki was now stepping away from the pedestal, all the runes now back in place around the edge.

"I have them, sire," Loki called out to Tyr. "The runes are all here."

Tyr backed away from Odin and pointed a finger at the All-Father and at the rest of the day guardians. "Your time is at an end. Once I have harvested your powers from the runes, I will end you all, and I won't need a sword to do it."

Tyr bounded to the plinth and jumped up onto it. The runes began to glow once more, and light flooded into the channels.

"Yes," Tyr cried. "Give me the power!"

There was an explosion of light. It filled the whole chamber, and then there was darkness.

CHAPTER THIRTY-SIX

AFTERMATH

Buzz opened his eyes. Black spots danced in his field of vision, and his mouth felt powder dry. He sat up, not quite believing that Tyr hadn't made him disappear in a puff of smoke yet or punished him in some other fiendish way. Ratatosk was rubbing his eyes and gazing around the chamber. Hel was doing the same. She glowed brightly now, and her face filled with relief when she saw that Buzz was all right.

There was a groaning noise, and up on the plinth, Buzz saw Tyr. He looked different. Smaller, more vulnerable. He looked just like Uncle Mark.

Wait, Buzz told himself. *It could be a trick.*

"Loki," Odin's voice boomed. "What has taken place here?"

Buzz turned to see that all the day guardians were already on their feet. If Buzz thought they had the look of gods about them before, it was nothing compared to now. His father, Coach

Saunders, Kira Bright, and Mrs Robertson were all well over seven feet tall, and they didn't just have golden gleams to them, their skin was crusted with the metal. They were so radiant it was almost impossible to look at them, and Odin shone the brightest of all.

"I reversed it," a husky voice said from the shadow of the plinth. A man with flowing red hair, and eyes like candle flames stepped into the light. "Tyr thought the power of the runes was going to flow into him, but I made it flow outwards, stripping him of his powers as well."

"Why did you do it?" Odin asked. "After all the bad blood between us. Why did you turn on Tyr and give us our powers back?"

Loki smiled a lopsided smile. "It was always my plan to reverse the runes' power surge – I designed the pedestal, after all. Tyr was a fool to think that I would give away all that power. I'm the trickster god after all."

Loki stepped forwards, took Hel's hand, and brought her to her feet. "Until I saw my daughter, here again in her kingdom, I planned for all that power to be mine – to use it to destroy the day guardians once and for all. I did not care that it would plunge the world into a permanent unmorrow curse filled with chaos." He touched Hel's cheek. "But my daughter asked me to make this all stop. To stop the Ragnarok from ever happening. And so I did. I changed it so that the power from each of the runes flowed away from Tyr and into you all." Loki looked over to where Buzz's godfather lay on the pedestal. Uncle Mark's eyes were flickering open. "Tyr's powers have been shared between myself and Hel. He will not be coming back." Loki stared at Odin. "This is my way to atone for what happened to your son Balder. It was an act of mischief that went wrong and I am sorry for that." Loki looked at Odin, the flame in his eyes no longer deadly hot. "I misjudged you. I always believed that you had killed Hel. I was wrong."

"I, too, must atone, Loki," Odin said. "Yours is not the only fault. The great prophecy said that you would be the start of the Ragnarok and you would be the end. To stop it from coming true, I thought about killing you. But I could not. Because even after all the hurt we had caused each other, you were still my friend." Odin sighed. "So I imprisoned you in Hel's kingdom. The only place that could hold you." Odin looked at Hel. "That left me with a problem. You. There was no way you would stand by and let your father be kept a prisoner, and so I had to get rid of you. I forced your god self into a deep sleep and as it was with the day guardians, your god self was passed down the generations. And the whole time your father was a prisoner in your neglected kingdom."

Theo staggered to his feet then – looking groggy. He was nowhere near seven feet tall, and his skin did not gleam. "Um, what happened to me?" he asked plaintively. "I don't have any powers at all, and look at the rest of you. I'm supposed to be Thor."

Mrs Robertson gave a deep laugh as she stepped to the

pedestal and picked up her rune, which looked dull and spent. It immediately turned into a mighty hammer. "You are mistaken. I am Thor, my dear."

Theo's mouth dropped open. "So who am I?"

"Well, I am Mani, god of the moon," Coach Saunders said. He pointed to Kira Bright. "And that's my sister, Sunna."

"I am Odin," Buzz's father continued, "and Tyr and Thor have already been accounted for. So that makes you Frigga." Odin's eyes twinkled. "Goddess of the harvest and family." He crooked a finger at the pedestal and the one rune that didn't look spent, and it hovered over to them. "The reason you haven't changed into your god form is that Tyr never got you to awaken your rune. Would you like to waken it now?"

Odin held out the rune, but Theo shook his head in disgust.

"No thanks. I'm fine just the way I am." He folded his arms across his chest.

Odin nodded. "So be it. Frigga would prefer to sleep, that I know. Besides, I have an inkling as to who I can give some of Frigga's power to and then I will leave the rune to recharge again in case Frigga ever needs it." He beckoned over to Saturn, who sat propped up against a wall. "Come here, old friend. I want to give you something."

Father Time began to shuffle over. It was going to take a while. "So, Theo isn't Thor, he's Frigga. And Frigga's powers are going to Saturn, and you are Hel," Buzz said to Mari. "I don't even know how to get my head around it."

Hel's features blurred for a moment, and then Mari pushed her glasses up her nose. "I'm a host for Hel, Buzz, just like your father is Odin's host. Hel's been there the whole time under the surface. A little of her blending with me. That's why I could guess people's greatest fears. The same thing has been happening with your dad, I think. That's why he was so obsessed with Tangley Wood. That was Odin's obsession, not your father's."

Buzz let that sink in. If what Mari said was true, then his father's neglect of their family made a lot more sense.

"When did you realize you were the host for Hel?" he asked.

"Just before she took control," Mari replied. "She asked my permission. Said it was the only way to stop her father." Mari shook her head. "I think Pluto had his suspicions about my true identity. That's why he gave me the water from the Styx. It woke Hel up, restored her. That's why he gave me the horn as well." She looked around the magma chamber. "This used to be her home, and it really was a wonderful place, Buzz. I share her memories and she shares mine." She sighed. "Looking back, there were lots of clues. The fact I could understand Fenris was a big one." Her eyes went wide. "Fenris, where is he?"

Mari's features blurred again and Hel was in control once more.

"Father," she called. "We must find Fenris. He was fighting Nidhogg. He might be hurt."

Mani scooped up his rune and cast it to the floor. It

immediately transformed into a mighty chariot. "I'll find him." He turned to Loki. "Let this be my way to atone for my part in imprisoning you."

"Do not harm the dragon," Loki requested. "He was only following Tyr's orders."

"So be it," Mani said. "I will bring them both back safely."

"Let me come, too, brother," Sunna said, and she smiled at Buzz as she climbed in. *"Thank you,"* she mouthed.

The chariot climbed upwards, passing through the gap made by the dragon's exit.

Buzz went to the pedestal. Uncle Mark was now sitting up.

"Are you okay?" Buzz asked.

"I've had better days, buddy." Uncle Mark smiled. "But I'm so pleased that you are all right. How's your dad?"

Buzz looked over at Odin. He was still busy with Saturn.

"I don't know," Buzz said. And it was true – he didn't know what would happen to his father now that Odin was fully awake. He looked quite happy over there in his host's body, explaining that Loki would once more be the day guardian for Saturday and Saturn was free of his duties as a day guardian.

There was the sound of galloping hooves from above, and Mani and Sunna landed back on the floor of the chamber, with both Fenris and Nidhogg riding in the back of the chariot.

The dragon had his eyes closed but was breathing. The wolf appeared battered and bruised but smiled as he looked at Loki and Hel. The three of them came together. Heads dipped in towards each other as they hugged. *A strange-looking family*, Buzz mused, but a family nonetheless. And Buzz wanted his family back.

"Odin, I need to speak to you," Buzz requested.

"Of course, Buzz." Odin strode over to him. "Your father is very lucky to have you for a son. He has always thought that, even if he has not been able to express it. For that I am sorry."

Buzz felt his throat tighten. He tried to speak but nothing came out. Odin looked at him kindly. "My obsessions and concerns even in my sleeping state affected your father. Magic does not always stay inside the lines." Odin bent his head. "You are brave and smart, and the gods owe you a debt of gratitude. Whatever you want, you will have."

"Whatever I want?" Buzz said. "That's easy. I want my father back. The same goes for Kira Bright, Coach Saunders, and Mrs Robertson. They all have families."

Odin rubbed his chin and looked around at the rest of the day guardians. He shrugged his massive shoulders. "Humanity has long since forgotten me. I am happy for my power to pass back into my rune. I will put myself in the deepest of sleeps and allow my god self to be passed down the bloodline once more. From host to host as has been the way for centuries. The same will happen with Frigga but I cannot speak for the others."

Sunna, Mani, and Thor exchanged a glance, and then Sunna spoke.

"Our time has passed. We know that. Let us sleep once

more, and if we are ever needed, we will come back."

"So, it is decided," Odin said. "We will put our powers back into the runes, but we will need someone to keep them safe." He looked at Buzz. "Will you be the runes' new guardian?"

Buzz gulped. It was a big responsibility, but he was up to the challenge. He nodded.

"Then it is time for us to return to Crowmarsh and bring our hosts back to safety. Once we are in the mortal realm once more, we will go back to sleep." Odin placed a hand on Buzz's shoulder. "Stay close. Your father would not be impressed if I were to lose you. He feels you have been lost to him for too long. He wants to fix that."

Buzz held out a hand for Ratatosk, and the squirrel leapt onto his palm and up his arm. He then looked over at Hel and asked the question that he'd been dreading. "Are you going to let Mari come home with us?"

A tear trickled down the goddess's cheek. "I don't know what to do. This is my kingdom, and it has been neglected for so long – I have a responsibility." She looked around at her family. "I don't want to leave my father and my brother, but Mari's family is still in the human world." She shook her head. "Neither option gives us both a happy ending."

Loki wrapped Hel in a hug. "Don't cry, my daughter," he said, even though Buzz could see tears in his eyes, too. "You are forgetting something. You are a goddess and I am a god. Gods live for a very long time."

He pulled back from her and looked at her intently. "Let Mari go back and live her life. I will look after your kingdom, return it to its former glory, and wait until your mortal life has come to its natural end. Then I will welcome you back, and you will be Hel once more."

"And my god self won't be passed to the next generation?" Hel asked. "You promise?"

"I cannot make this promise." Loki looked at Odin. "But he can."

"When your life as Mari is at an end, when you are old and grey, I promise that you will come back to your kingdom as Hel." Odin's granite face cracked and he looked mournful. "I am sorry that I took you away from your home and cast you into the human world. It was a selfish act. One I will never forgive myself for."

He traced a symbol above Mari's head. "Your spirit will no longer be a nomad of the mortal world. You will come back to your kingdom and rule it with your father. This I promise. This I vow."

Hel nodded and then looked at Buzz. "Before we go, I have something I need to do." She slipped the horn off her shoulder. "We are going to get the River Styx flowing again. It is going to wash away all the regret. And all of you are going to help me."

EPILOGUE

Friday, 13th July

"Hey, I'm pretty sure these are edible." Buzz knelt down to look more closely at the cluster of mushrooms poking up from the undergrowth. They were growing in a perfect circle, which was about 40 centimetres in diameter.

"Crikey," his father said, kneeling down to look at the mushroom circle as well. "We're going to need to take action." He slipped a notepad and pen out of his pocket and began jotting something down, all the while reciting something under his breath.

"What're you writing?" Buzz asked.

His dad suddenly looked self-conscious. "Song lyrics."

"Song lyrics?" Buzz repeated. He was used to his dad going off on strange tangents, but this was extreme even for him.

His dad tucked the pen behind his ear and swiftly looked over his shoulder. Buzz's mum and Tia were still a few metres away. They were busy looking up at a tree. "Okay, I'll explain," his dad whispered. "In Celtic mythology, mushrooms found in this circular formation are called a fairy ring. Some people believe that they are caused by fairies and elves dancing in the moonlight." He looked over again at his wife and daughter to check their position. They hadn't moved. "Fairy rings often bring bad luck to those that disturb them. But a song, the right song, can reverse that. And I think I have just remembered all the words."

Buzz frowned. "Dad, I'm not sure—"

"You don't believe me," Buzz's father interrupted. He looked disappointed. "I know you don't love mythology, find it boring and silly, but I thought—"

"Boring?" It was now Buzz's turn to interrupt. "Silly? You were there when we managed to save the world from Tyr and met the Norse gods, right? How could I ever think mythology was silly after that?"

His dad grinned. "Yeah, I guess. I forget that it wasn't just me who changed because of what happened in that volcano. You did as well. Our whole family did." His cheeks flushed as if still uncomfortable with displaying this much emotion. "I like that I can talk about mythology with you, Buzz."

"So do I." Buzz smiled. These last few months had been funny and strange and amazing for him. He had got to know his dad all over again. His father still loved mythology, could still get distracted by a rare book or an obscure journal, and he still loved these woods, but he loved his family more. It was like the part of him that obsessed about his work had gone into the deep, deep sleep with Odin. His dad was his own person now. The choices he made were his own as well, and he chose to put Buzz, Tia, and Mum first.

"Dad, listen, all I was going to say was that maybe we should save ourselves the hassle of the song, et cetera, and find ourselves some different mushrooms – seriously, I don't want some irate elves and fairies coming after us. I'm done with magical beings with a grudge."

His dad laughed and ruffled Buzz's hair. "These mushrooms are called Saffron Milk Cap and they are your mother's absolute favourite. There's no way I'm walking away from them." He tapped the notepad. "Trust me. This song will cover us."

"I'm not singing," Buzz insisted. "No way."

"Fine," his dad said. You walk 'round the circle nine times and I'll do the singing.

"Why nine times?"

"Um, I could make up a reason but to be honest I don't know. This is what you do when you find a fairy ring.

Buzz began to walk around the fairy ring and Dad began to sing the song. It was in a language that Buzz didn't understand but the low richness of Dad's voice seemed to explain it to him. It was a song asking forgiveness.

"Why are you singing Dad?" Tia asked, arriving at the fairy ring. Her face was unimpressed.

"I'm sure he has a very good reason to be singing in—" Buzz's mum paused. "Exactly what language is that?"

"One of the old Celtic ones," Buzz's dad replied, finishing the song.

"Well, it was lovely sweetheart," Buzz's mum said. "I'm so glad to hear your voice again." She reached out and touched his cheek.

Buzz's dad smiled with pleasure. "Now, Natasha, have you seen what we've got here?" He nodded his head at the mushrooms

"Saffron Milk Cap!" Buzz's mum gave a squeal of delight and plonked her basket next to the ring of mushrooms She then brought out a little curved knife and gently began cutting the mushrooms away from the earth. "These are going to be wonderful with a bit of thyme and black pepper," she said.

Dad bent down and tenderly kissed her on the forehead. "Not half as wonderful as the cook."

Mum giggled. Buzz knew that on one level it was revolting to have parents mooning over each other like lovesick teenagers, but deep down he loved it. He knew that Mari felt the same way about her parents. The unmorrow curse had been hard for them but somehow her parents had come out the other side as a team. A very much in-love team. Mari thought it had something to do with all the extra time her parents had spent with each other, even if they didn't realize they had been on some kind of lockdown together.

"Remind me why we can't get mushrooms from a supermarket like a normal family?" Tia asked, arms crossed.

"Because we're cooking a special meal for Buzz's American friend and her parents. And then there's Uncle Mark. He's bringing around his new lady friend. I want to push the boat out."

"Don't forget Theo and Sam. They're coming as well."

"This day just went from bad to worse," Tia grumbled. "It's official." She flopped down to sit on a tree stump.

"Hey! Watch where yer parking that behind of yours," a very familiar voice griped, and a blur of fur shot out from the tree stump and into the undergrowth.

Buzz coughed, hoping it might distract her, but Tia was looking properly spooked.

"Did you hear that?" she asked.

"Hear what?" Dad replied.

"A really grumpy voice." She frowned. "I think it might have belonged to that red squirrel I saw before, Mum. The one I tried to show you in the tree."

Mum came over and touched Tia's forehead. "There's no red squirrels in this forest – they're all up in Scotland. It's all that exam pressure, isn't it? You are getting an early night tonight."

"What, no way," Tia said. "I'm not a baby." The two of them began to squabble.

"Close call," Buzz's dad mouthed.

"I know," Buzz whispered back. He'd need to tell Ratatosk to be more careful in the future.

All afternoon, Ratatosk had been showing them all the best

places to find mushrooms, but the squirrel had promised to stay out of the way while Tia and Buzz's mum were about. After all, they didn't know that talking squirrels existed or that Dad had a sleeping god in him or that Buzz had helped to save the world. They just knew that Saturday the fourteenth had been strange for a lot of people across the world. They'd heard it was due to some kind of pressure change in the atmosphere. No one really understood the phenomenon, but people had gone back to normal the next day. Perhaps because it was easier that way.

For a while, Buzz and his dad had planned to tell the truth about everything that had happened, but when Mum got home, all she wanted was normal. She'd actually said that. "Give me a hug and give me normal," she'd begged. "I've heard and seen enough strange things to last me a lifetime." So Buzz and his dad hadn't said anything. Not about the runes that were in a box under Buzz's bed. Not about how they'd got the River Styx flowing again. And not about how all the hosts of the day guardians had made a pact never to speak again of what had happened to them.

Time passed.

Friday the thirteenth was here again, but Buzz didn't care.

Because everyone was happy. Everything was normal. Everything was just great.

TO BE CONTINUED . . .

ACKNOWLEDGEMENTS

I was obsessed with Acrostic poems when I was a kid. I still love them now. Writing them is somewhere between a riddle and a tale and much the same can be said about writing a novel . . .

UCLan Publishing you have made my dreams come true by bringing this novel home. You are all ACE.

Nasrallas thank you for being my family.

Mum for your unwavering love. For your unwavering belief. For your strength and tenacity in building a home for my brother and I.

Oxford University and the tutors of LMH who taught me so much and still support me today.

Remembering too, every English teacher I've ever had and

the very special Mr Lewis who introduced me to a love of the Romans and their mythology in primary school.

Reading memories are strong of warm libraries and warmer librarians throughout my life.

Old friends, thank you for the cups of tea, the shoulders to cry on and for always being my biggest champions.

Wonderful agents of David Higham – Caroline and Christabel. I would not be without your advice and wisdom even if my journey takes me down many different paths ...

IF YOU LIKED THIS, YOU'LL LOVE…

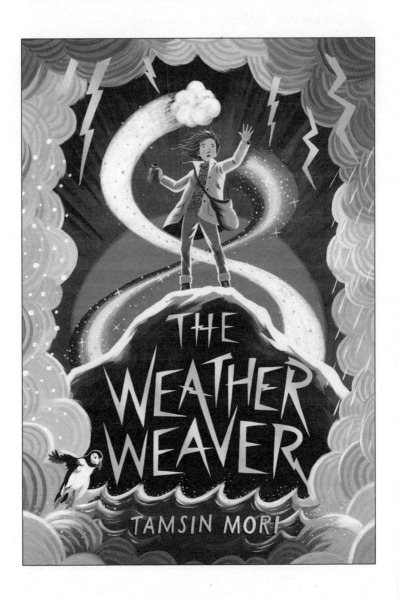

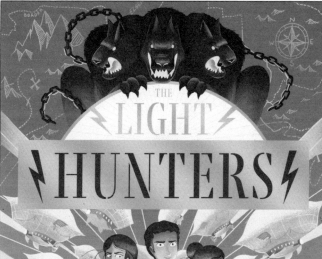

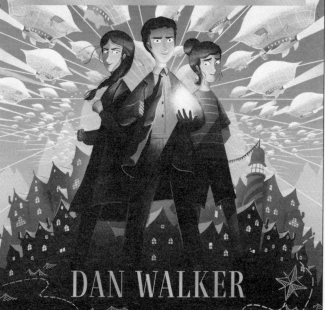